The Quest for Harmony

BOOK ONE OF THE
HARMONY SERIES

★ ★ ★

K. B. CONDI

THE QUEST FOR HARMONY

ISBN-13: 978-1-959677-45-1 (Paperback)
ISBN-13: 978-1-959677-44-4 (eBook)
ISBN-13: 978-1-959677-46-8 (Hardcover)

Published by Defiance Press & Publishing, LLC

Bulk orders of this book may be obtained by contacting Defiance Press & Publishing, LLC. www.defiancepress.com.

Public Relations Dept. – Defiance Press & Publishing, LLC
281-581-9300
pr@defiancepress.com

Defiance Press & Publishing, LLC
281-581-9300
info@defiancepress.com

"The hour is fast approaching, on which the Honor and Success...and the safety of our bleeding Country depend. Remember...that you are free men, fighting for the blessings of Liberty-that slavery will be your portion, and that of your posterity, if you do not acquit yourselves like men."

~ George Washington

"If it were to be asked, What is the most sacred duty and the greatest source of our security in a Republic? The answer would be, An inviolable respect for the Constitution and Laws-the first growing out of the last...A sacred respect for the constitutional law is the vital principle, the sustaining energy of a free government."

~ Alexander Hamilton

PROLOGUE

The year was 1797. On a warm spring night, twelve men gathered together in a field in a remote area of Virginia. All were men of prominence in the newly formed United States of America. Most did not know why they had been assembled that night, but the invitation had come from George Washington, and none would refuse a summons from that great man. All who had answered the call stood quietly, speaking in hushed tones, and looking at each other with curiosity and uncertainty.

It did not take long for nine of the men to learn that there were three men who did know the purpose of the meeting. Only Washington himself, along with Alexander Hamilton and Thomas Jefferson, knew what each of these twelve patriots would be asked to do that night. Washington, Hamilton, and Jefferson had each chosen three of the others who stood in the circle, and as they looked around, they studied those whom they had chosen. They hoped they had chosen well, for if they had not, the consequences were too dreadful to consider.

"Gentlemen," Washington announced at last.

Instantly, all turned to hear what he would say.

"Fellow patriots, you have been summoned here this night because the time is near at hand in which each of you will be invited to undertake a difficult task. It is a task that, if done well, will never be known to other men.

"It is an honorable task. Every task is honorable through which a man may serve his country, and this is such a task.

"Answering this invitation will require great sacrifice, and it is a sacrifice of which the world will never know. Lest there be any lack of understanding, I say again, there is extreme difficulty and no glory in what you will be asked to do tonight."

With that, Washington paused and looked around the circle, seeking any signs of weakness—anything that might give him doubt. Seeing none, he continued.

"What will be asked of you is a task and a burden on which the future of the United States of America will depend." He paused to allow the gasps and startled murmurs to quiet.

"I say without exaggeration that it is a task and a burden on which the entire future of all of humanity depends." He paused again to let the louder gasps and startled murmurs to quiet.

"It is the sole province of each man here," Washington continued, "to decide whether to accept this task. But let it be understood that your decision will bind not only you but also bind your posterity for many decades. Gentlemen, the secret that you will learn tonight will change you and your entire view of the universe. And it is a difficult thing to know.

"Anyone who stays will be bound by honor and conscience to keep the secret that will be revealed to you. The penalty for betraying your oath will be death. You have been chosen. But that does not mean you do not have a choice.

"Gentlemen, what you are being asked to do is difficult. It is *highly* difficult. With that understanding, any who wishes to leave may do so now, and rest assured, if you choose to leave, you do so with your honor intact."

All of the twelve men looked at each of the others in the

circle. Many looked apprehensive, but none left.

"Very well," Washington continued. "Gentleman, what you will learn, you will be asked to keep a secret from all except the eleven men around you. Before the secret is revealed to you, I must ask for your oath that you will reveal it to no one."

Washington went around the circle and looked to each man to give their oath. Each man did so.

Once all the oaths were given, Washington nodded . . . and every man disappeared.

CHAPTER 1

The United States of America was a nation under siege. At least, it felt that way. A deadly and highly contagious virus had escaped from a lab in China a few months before, and in March of 2020, it had hit the United States like a tidal wave. *Escaped*, thought Alecin Hamilton as she drove home. *That's a weird way to describe what a virus did.* It made it sound like the virus had the ability to execute some kind of nefarious plot. She imagined a virus sitting in a jail cell, rubbing its hands together while plotting, then—a la what's-his-face in *Shawshank Redemption*—crawling through sewage before finally emerging a free virus, ready to conquer the world.

Alecin was one of those people who was attractive without trying. Genetics had blessed her with beautiful porcelain skin, high cheekbones, and full lips, but her eyes—her eyes were what people immediately noticed when they looked at Alecin. They were perfectly shaped, framed with long lashes, and were a shimmering blue that brought to mind the clear waters of the Caribbean. Her brown hair was made interesting by the streaks of both blond and red that ran through it. She had it cut in a short pixie style, which highlighted her cheekbones and suited her 120-pound, 5'6" frame. But that's not why she had chosen it. She kept her hair short for the very practical reason that it took all of thirty seconds to style, and she didn't have to worry about constantly putting her hair up as was required when she was in uniform.

In uniform, Alecin wore minimal makeup in order to appear, in her mind, professional. In that khaki uniform of a United States Naval Officer—a uniform that hadn't flattered anyone in the entire history of the Navy—Alecin was attractive. But when she wasn't on duty—when she put on "going-out" makeup, as she thought of it—her blue eyes went from beautiful to extraordinary, and her lips and cheekbones went from there to hard to miss. Her body went from boring and shrouded in a nondescript khaki blur to spectacular in pretty much anything. When Alecin wasn't on duty, she went from attractive to stunning.

But on this April morning of 2020, her appearance was the very last thing on Alecin's mind. As she drove her completely sensible Honda Accord, Alecin thought only of getting home. Alecin rarely made choices that weren't sensible. Her idea of going wild was to choose the Accord in red rather than the black or white—which every other car seemed to be these days.

Many thought that her choice to buy a single-family home—even though she lived alone—in the Norfolk suburb of Wood-haven, rather than getting an apartment closer to her job at the Norfolk Naval Station, wasn't sensible at all. But to Alecin, it made *perfect* sense. After years of living in cramped dormitory rooms and even smaller ship staterooms, Alecin had determined that she was a person who preferred her living space to have . . . well, *space*. With her family money, she could easily afford a lovely three-bedroom house on a quiet street with a yard, which was, most importantly, to Alecin, outside of the city. So, when she was stationed in Norfolk, that's what she had done. Despite her wealth—or rather her family's wealth—

Alecin rarely splurged on the indulgent and, more often than not, went for the practical. But to Alecin, her home purchase was immensely practical; not only did it save her sanity, but her grandfather had always told her that real estate was an excellent investment.

As Alecin drummed her hands on the steering wheel, driving through the eerily empty streets, she laughed at the image in her mind of the escaping virus. What was happening in the world today seemed like the plot of a bad sci-fi movie. Only four months since the virus had been unleashed on the world, millions of people in almost every country had been infected. The virus had been sneaky, Alecin thought, imagining again the scheming virus, rubbing its hands together and laughing fiendishly. Some people got a little sick from it, some didn't get sick at all, and some got a lot sick from it. That made it hard to tell who had it, and right now, tests for the virus were few and far between. One infected person, not even knowing they were infected, could, in a day, spread the virus to many other people—some estimates said close to a hundred.

Hospitals worldwide were overflowing with patients with COVID-19, the deceptively innocuous name given to the virus. *Black Death*, Alecin thought. *Now* that's *the kind of name a virus capable of killing people by the thousands, possibly millions, should have.* Of course, the Black Death had killed almost everyone who became infected, and so far, COVID-19 seemed to have a death rate of only about ten percent, at most. So, maybe Light-Gray Death? Didn't quite roll off the tongue. *Whatever*, Alecin thought. She had other things to think about rather than the proper name of a virus.

Usually, Alecin ordered her groceries online—because she hated grocery shopping—but with everyone scared to venture out these days, the companies that delivered groceries couldn't keep up with the demand. That meant if she wanted food— and she *did*—she had to go to the grocery store in person. And hadn't that been an adventure? First, she'd had to wait in line, standing—outside, in the cold, wearing a mask (but not six feet apart)—to even get into the store so the store could ensure that everyone inside had enough room to stay six feet apart. The six-foot "distancing" and mask requirements were enforced with religious vigor—by store employees and customers alike.

Thinking of it, Alecin shook her head at how fear could so easily overcome logic. If there was any evidence that six feet apart did any good, the government hadn't shared it, and if there actually was any such evidence, she was pretty sure they would have. All of the evidence so far indicated the virus was airborne, and airborne viruses could travel much farther than six feet. And the mask everyone was paranoid about everyone else wearing? There was a mountain of evidence that the cloth and paper masks everyone wore did nothing to stop the microscopic virus. But people were scared. Standing six feet apart and wearing a mask comforted everyone, and if it was false comfort, no one seemed to care. So, Alecin had worn the uncomfortable and useless mask and said nothing as people kept their six feet of distance from her. She needed groceries more than she wanted to die on that particular hill.

After pulling her car into the garage of her single-story red-brick home, Alecin got out and briefly surveyed the fruits of her adventure. She was a once-a-week kind of shopper because she liked having fresh produce on hand, and she didn't want to put in the effort to plan her meals for more than a week at a time. But for this trip, Alecin had decided she should get enough for at least a month. Both because she didn't want the annoyance of going grocery shopping again any time soon and because with much of the country in lockdown mode—including areas that were home to some of the largest ports in the United States—the supply chains that stores relied upon to keep their shelves stocked was likely to break down, and Alecin wanted to make sure she had what she needed while it was still available. With a weary sigh, Alecin got busy taking the haul from her car into the kitchen.

As Alecin finished putting away the last of her groceries, her cat, Tonks, walked in. Tonks, a short-haired calico, eyed the groceries with the suspicion that befit her species. Like most of her generation, Alecin was a fan of the Harry Potter books and movies. Tonks was one of her favorite characters from that franchise, and her then-kitten had reminded her of Tonks—for some reason—and so Alecin had given her that name.

"Well, if you've come to help, you're too late," she scolded.

Tonks responded by jumping on the counter, suspicion apparently having been converted to curiosity. "Don't worry," Alecin said, picking Tonks up and cuddling her. "I got plenty of food for you too. Neither of us is going to starve."

In this world, there were dog people, there were cat people, and then there were people like Alecin who liked them both. She had been thinking of getting a dog since she had a yard, but Mrs. Miller had changed her mind on that point.

Mrs. Miller lived across the street. When Alecin had first moved in, Mrs. Miller had brought over a homemade apple pie, and Alecin had invited her in. Over apple pie, warmed and with whipped cream—in Alecin's opinion, the only proper way to eat an apple pie—they had gotten to know each other. Alecin learned Mrs. Miller's life story in the first ten minutes of knowing her. She learned that Mrs. Miller lived alone; her children were grown and gone, and her husband had passed away. Alecin got the feeling Mrs. Miller was lonely and decided then and there that she and Mrs. Miller were going to become good friends. One, because the woman could bake, and two, she liked her, and the thought of her being lonely made Alecin sad.

As they were talking, Alecin mentioned that she wanted to get a pet but couldn't decide between a dog and a cat. Mrs. Miller had told her that she had a severe allergy to dogs, and if Alecin got a dog, she didn't guess she would be able to see much of Alecin. But cats? Those Mrs. Miller adored. She didn't have any cats because she didn't want the full-time responsibility of caring for one. But if Alecin got a cat and needed her to watch it sometimes, she said she would be happy to do so. She knew how "Navy people"—as she put it—often had to travel. So, Alecin had gotten a cat.

Not that I can complain, Alecin thought, snuggling a purring Tonks. She loved Tonks. And Tonks didn't seem to mind the fact that Alecin was gone all day. Sometimes, Alecin got the feeling that Tonks actually *liked* it.

Alecin put Tonks down and finished putting away the last of her groceries. She was just considering what to make for lunch when her cell phone vibrated. Pulling it out of her back pocket, she saw it was her grandfather calling. Her grandfather, it seemed, was the only person who ever actually called her to talk anymore. She kept up with everyone else through texts and following them on Instagram.

After the usual exchange of pleasantries, her grandfather announced, "Alecin, I'd like you to come to visit me this coming Saturday, a week from now."

"But Grandpa," Alecin protested, "it's not safe right now—not until they get covid under control." She didn't want to be the one who gave her elderly grandfather covid. "How about we do a video chat?" Alecin suggested. "We can talk and still see each other."

"No," her grandfather said in a tone that made it clear that he would broker no discussion on the point. "It's important that I see you in person. *Very* important, or I would not insist. Trust me when I tell you my reasons far outweigh any risk."

Alecin was doubtful anything could be that important, but once he made up his mind, her grandfather could not be dissuaded. And one did not say no to Neil G. Hamilton.

"Okay, Grandpa. I'll be up early Saturday morning," she agreed begrudgingly.

"Very good. I'll see you then," her grandfather responded, sounding very pleased.

Alecin spent the next week alternating between being curious about what could be so important and working out an excuse not to go. In the end, though, curiosity won out. "Curiosity," Alecin told Tonks as she packed her bag for the trip, "as you should know, is a very dangerous thing."

The Saturday after her grandfather had called, Alecin found herself turning into the long driveway to her grandparent's house. Her grandmother had passed away three years before in a diving accident. Many people had thought that a woman her grandmother's age had had no business diving. Those people hadn't known Elizabeth Hamilton. Elizabeth had learned to dive when she was young and had fallen in love with the sea. Although Alecin's grandfather hadn't shared his wife's passion for diving, he did enjoy it and absolutely adored his wife, so he had often gone with her. Alecin thought it was fortunate that her grandfather hadn't been diving with his wife the day she died. She didn't think he would have been able to handle it. He was shattered enough when he received the news in his own home, with his son and daughter-in-law, Alecin's parents, by his side.

Alecin's grandmother had loved flowers and gardening almost as much as she had loved diving. As she always had, as she drove up to the house, Alecin admired the flowers, grasses, shrubs, and trees, all arranged to perfection over every inch of the vast space. What the garden offered in beauty, the house matched in grandness and dignity. The garden complimented the house and gave the stately and dignified house a sense of elegance and grace. Like many of the older homes in Virginia, the home was Colonial style, with red brick and white columns breaking up a white, wrap-around porch. Some people bought these kinds of old and traditional homes and painted the brick or covered it with siding or whatnot. Alecin did not understand these people. These old colonial homes brought some of the splendor and beauty of the past into the present. Why would anyone want to destroy that?

Alecin was grateful her grandparents hadn't "updated" the exterior of the old home. The original red brick remained, and when repairs were required, every effort was made to match that original brick. Although the original shutters hadn't survived the passing of time, her grandparents had had exact duplicates made and hung. Except for the security cameras tucked discreetly around the front entrance, Alecin imagined the house looked much the same as it had when it was first built hundreds of years before.

The house had been in Alecin's family for generations, on her grandmother's side. Her grandmother's only sibling, a brother, had died as a teenager, so the house had been left to Elizabeth. Alecin knew that someday the house might come to her, but she couldn't imagine living by herself in what was more a mansion than a house really. Maybe someday, when she married and had children of her own, she would change her mind. At least, she *hoped* so.

A cobblestone walkway led from the driveway to the front steps. The entrance boasted two magnificent carved mahogany doors with etched windows. But that entrance was for guests. Alecin was family. As she had all her life, Alecin walked to a side door—what had probably once been the servants' entrance—and into the mudroom. The mudroom was an essential room in Virginia to stop snow and/or mud-covered boots from tracking into the house. Not so long ago, the room had been filled with winter coats, and the stylish storage baskets had been near to overflowing with hats, gloves, and scarfs, each in its own specific basket, of course. But now the room was empty, save for her grandfather's spring jacket and one umbrella that stood alone in the umbrella stand.

Purposely not thinking of the emptiness of the room, Alecin walked through it into the expansive kitchen. While her grandparents had been faithful about preserving the outside of the house, the inside had had to be changed to accommodate twenty-first-century living. Not long before her grandmother's death, her grandparents had remodeled the kitchen—again. Over the years, they had slowly expanded the kitchen, each time taking a little more space from the adjacent dining room. Now the old dining room had been entirely absorbed by the new kitchen.

What once had been a sitting room had become the new dining room. Alecin loved that dining room. Her grandparents had always gathered the whole family together on holidays and other special occasions. The dining room table and chairs had been specially made—because her grandmother hadn't found anything she found "acceptable"—so the table was large enough to accommodate the whole family and filled the spacious once sitting room. As she passed by the door to the dining room, Alecin thought briefly of the many happy memories she had of sitting around that dining table with her family.

It was her grandfather who had pushed to update the kitchen. He loved cooking and being in the kitchen—baking bread or making his famous soup, for which, to this day, he still refused to reveal the recipe. Her grandfather always said, "If I tell you how to make it, then how am I going to get you to come to visit me?" Alecin was pretty sure that her family would still visit her grandfather even if he didn't have soup to offer. Nonetheless, her grandfather had assured everyone that the recipe would be included in his will and that no one would get it any sooner.

When Alecin walked into the newly remodeled, spacious kitchen, she saw Jim, her grandfather's . . . *everything*—butler, chef, housekeeper. Whatever was needed, Jim did it. Jim had taken a job with her family when he was twenty-two. It was just supposed to be a temporary summer job, but twenty-some-odd years later, he was still there. At this point, he was considered family. Jim was standing at the huge island that dominated the kitchen, cutting some vegetable that Alecin didn't recognize. At least, she *thought* it was a vegetable.

"Hi, Jim," Alecin greeted him. "It's good to see you. How's the family?"

"Well, hello, Alecin," Jim replied with a welcoming smile. "It's good to see you as well. My family is good, all things considered—no one is sick or anything. Judy is going a bit crazy being locked up in the house all day with three energetic kids. And if that wasn't bad enough, with the schools being closed, she has to try to keep them online all day. We had to borrow a computer just so everyone could attend 'school' "—he air quoted—"at the same time. But it's useless. The kids aren't learning anything. Every parent told them that virtual school wouldn't work, but they wouldn't listen," Jim vented, shaking his head.

"I thought your kids were in private school?" Paying tuition at a private school for Jim's kids was part of his salary. Her family believed in generously paying their employees who did their job well and were loyal.

"They *are*. But right now, that doesn't make a difference. The state made all the schools close, not just the public ones. I imagine that will change by fall. At least, I *hope* it will. I can't see parents willing to pay that much for their children to get a useless virtual education. I'm certainly not going to. Private schools will have to get back in session, or they might as well close their doors permanently."

"We can always hope that sanity will return by the fall."

"I have faith."

"Difficult to see; always in motion is the future," Alecin croaked, providing her best Yoda imitation.

Jim was well used to Alecin's habit of quoting movies and just smiled at her. "Anyway," he continued, "you're not here to talk to me. Your grandfather is in his study. He asked that lunch be served on the back patio forty-five minutes after you arrived."

"What's for lunch?" Alecin asked, trying and failing to sound unconcerned.

Jim smiled. "Don't worry, Alecin. I have the doctor's orders, and I'm making sure your grandfather follows them. All of his meals only contain doctor-approved foods."

Alecin returned Jim's smile. "Jim, what would we do without you?"

"You would end up cold, hungry, and helpless." Jim winked at her.

"Probably," she agreed, and Jim chuckled.

"Go on now. I've got work to do, and your grandfather is waiting for you."

"Okay. I'm going."

Just before Alecin reached the kitchen door, she heard Jim call her name, and she turned around.

"Now, I expect you to eat all the vegetables on your plate, Alecin, and not feed them to the dog when you think no one is looking."

"I never did that," Alecin said with mock indignation.

"Sure you didn't," Jim said, chuckling. He held his right hand up and used two fingers to point to his eyes and then at her.

The dignified Jim using such a silly gesture had Alecin laughing all the way to the study.

CHAPTER 2

When Alecin walked into the study, she found her grandfather sitting in an oversized brown leather armchair in the corner of the room, his feet resting on the matching ottoman. Her grandfather's study had always been Alecin's favorite room in the house. Maybe because she had been forbidden to go into it as a child, making it mysterious and inviting. Floor-to-ceiling bookshelves lined two entire walls of the masculine study—purely her grandfather's space. And every shelf was filled with books. Scout, her grandfather's yellow Labrador who never left his side, was sleeping on the ottoman. Scout had somehow managed to spread her entire girth over the ottoman and her grandfather's feet. Her grandfather's head was back, and his eyes were closed, as if he was sleeping. He still wore his reading glasses. A book lay sprawled across his lap. Alecin read the title: *101 of the Best New York Times Crossword Puzzles.*

It shocked and saddened Alecin more than she thought it would to see her brilliant and once-vibrant grandfather looking so frail. And just so miserable. It broke Alecin's heart. And it had every time Alecin had seen her grandfather in the year since he had gotten sick.

Until he had gotten sick, Neil had been one of those men who aged well. The lines and the gray hair he had boasted had given him an aura of distinction and wisdom. Her grandmother had said that her grandfather was the most handsome man she had ever known. He had always taken care of himself, believing that to have a fit mind, one needed a fit body. But now, Neil's age just highlighted the frailty that his illness had imparted. With the limitations on activity imposed by the illness—combined with the necessary medications—Neil had begun to put on weight. It was a sore subject, and everyone in the family had learned quite quickly not to bring it up.

"I'm not sleeping," her grandfather grumbled. "I'm thinking. I can feel you staring at me. Stop it."

"Well, hello to you too, Grandpa. It's so nice to see you as well."

"Sorry." Neil sat up and annoyed Scout by removing his feet from under her and putting them on the floor. "One of the most annoying things about being sick is people are constantly watching me and asking me how I am. It drives me crazy."

"I understand." Alecin waited for a beat. "So, how are you?"

"Oh, Alecin." Her grandfather laughed as she hoped he would. She had always loved the sound of his laughter.

He walked over to her, placing his hands on her shoulders. "Do you know I adore you?"

"I've heard rumors."

"The rumors are true. They're definitely true."

Alecin hugged him for a few minutes. He seemed to need it.

"Okay," he said at last, "let's get down to business."

"To defeat the Huns?"

"What?"

"Nothing. It's just from a song."

Accustomed to Alecin's habit of randomly quoting songs, movies, television shows, and anything else she ever came across, Neil went on. "Come on over here," he said, gesturing to a seating area. It held two chairs that faced an impressive fireplace in which a simmering fire burned. Between the chairs was a small table, which at this moment held teacups and a matching teapot.

Neil sat in one of the chairs and poured himself a cup of tea. Alecin took the other chair.

Scout trotted over and inspected the table. Apparently not seeing anything of interest to her, she lay down by the fire and resumed her nap.

"Would you like a cup of tea?" Neil asked.

"Sure."

Neil poured her a cup, and when Alecin took a small sip, she barely resisted spitting it out.

"What kind of tea is this? It's awful. It's like drinking boiled grass."

Neil chuckled. He hadn't expected her to like it. "It's green tea. The doctor said it was good for me. I'm still trying to get used to it."

"I hate to break it to you, but I've had green tea, and it tasted nothing like this."

"It's a combination of green tea and matcha. The doctor said matcha is good too. But it doesn't seem to help the taste."

Neil pushed a small container of honey with a little bee flying around on it over to Alecin. "Try putting some honey in it," he advised. "It helps."

Alecin didn't think anything could help this tea. Somewhere in the world, she thought, there had to be green and matcha tea better than this. She made a mental note to check into it. But for now, Alecin wanted to support her grandfather, so she added honey to the tea until she could sip it without gagging. It took *a lot* of honey.

Neil sat back in his chair and put his hands together in front of him, his fingers steepled. Alecin knew that this was his thinking pose and that the pleasantries were over.

"I've been debating how to tell you this, and I think it's just best if I start from the beginning," Neil said. "You know we are direct descendants of Alexander Hamilton, one of the Founding Fathers of this country." At Alecin's nod, he continued. "Yes, of course, you know." Everyone in the family had been taught about their heritage from the moment they learned to talk.

Neil took a long pause. "Have you ever wondered how we won the Revolutionary War? I mean, the colonies were outnumbered, outmanned, out-financed, and out-strategized. By any reasonable measure, we should have lost."

"But we won," Alecin pointed out, confused.

"Precisely. And have you ever wondered how fifty-five people, in just four months, could write and agree to a constitution governing an entire nation? And have that constitution be so successful that it has governed the most successful and prosperous nation ever? And governed it for nearly 250 years? Have you seen the Senate lately? It takes them months to write a law that's thousands of pages long, and it's so confusing, no one really knows what it means, and to get a majority to agree to it? If it's even possible, that takes months as well. And that's just one law. Not an entire constitution."

"Yes, well, it was an admirable accomplishment." *Where is he going with this?* Alecin wondered.

"Or maybe it was more than that."

Neil let the words hang in the air. He sipped his tea and watched her. Finally, he put his tea down and looked at her as if he was about to tell her something of vital importance. "Alecin, do you believe in extraterrestrials?"

"What the fuck?" Alecin exclaimed, fumbling her teacup, barely keeping it from falling and shattering on the floor.

Her grandfather looked at her with stern disapproval. In all her life, she had never heard the man utter a word of profanity. He always said that the use of profanity was a sign of an uncivilized and ignorant mind. There was an awful lot of profanity in the military, though. Sometimes Alecin thought that no one in the military could get through a sentence without inserting a cuss word. It seemed to be the preferred mode of communication. Alecin had long ago decided, "when in Rome," and began piercing her own language with profanity, at least around her military colleagues. But she had never sworn in her grandfather's presence in her life, and she had never imagined there would be anything that would ever cause her to do so.

"Sorry, Grandpa," Alecin stammered. "It was just that . . . that was the last thing I expected you to say. Ever. It caught me off guard. To say the least."

"Unacceptable," he chided. "I expect you to conduct yourself properly for the remainder of this conversation."

Alecin nodded like a child who had just been scolded.

Satisfied with Alecin's nod, Neil continued. "Alecin, what I'm about to tell you will change your life and the whole way you look at the world. And I need you to keep an open mind . . . and I need you to let me get through everything. I know that you'll have many questions, but I need you to let me get through everything before you ask them. And I need you to promise me that you will *never* repeat anything I'm about to tell you to anyone. No one. Ever. That's very important. What I tell you must stay absolutely between us. I ask that you not even speak of it outside of this room. Can you agree to all of that?"

Alecin was silent for a moment. She wasn't one to give her word lightly. She gingerly placed her teacup on the table. Scout had made quick work of the tea that had spilled out of the fumbled cup. *Must have been the honey*, she thought absently, *because not even dogs could like that tea*. She had no idea where this conversation could possibly be going, but there weren't many people in the world that she trusted and respected as much as she trusted and respected her grandfather. Finally, she took a deep breath. "Yes. I can do that."

Neil nodded, satisfied. In their family, when someone gave their word, they kept it. He knew he could trust Alecin to keep hers.

"But," Alecin continued, "I'm not so sure about Scout. She's always seemed a little squirrelly to me." Scout looked up at her name—or was it the word *squirrel*?

"She's kept all my secrets so far." Neil looked at Scout, as if considering. "No talking, or you sleep with the fishes," he ordered.

Scout barked, seemingly in agreement.

"There we go. She won't tell a soul." Neil then leaned back in his chair and assumed what Alecin had termed his *storytelling pose*. He loved telling stories.

"This story," he began, "concerns events involving Alexander Hamilton, George Washington, and Thomas Jefferson. I'll be telling you the story only from Alexander's perspective. Only his thoughts and impressions have been passed down through the generations to our family. So, everything will be from his point of view. Do you understand?"

Alecin nodded, and he continued.

"The story starts a few weeks before the *Declaration of Independence* was signed. On that day—and over the years, it has become unclear exactly what day this occurred—Alexander, Washington, and Jefferson were going about their business as they would on any ordinary day. Then, in the space of a breath, the day went from ordinary to extraordinary.

"Alexander was writing at his desk as he had done many times before, and then . . . he wasn't. In an instant, he found himself in a small room. The room was about the same size as his office, but it had plain white walls. The walls held no decoration whatsoever. There was no furniture in this room. His desk had disappeared. He no longer held the quill he'd had in his hand a moment before. He thought, *Surely I must have fallen asleep at my desk, and this is all just a dream.* Everything just felt so surreal to him. But at the same time, he thought it didn't feel like a dream.

"As he looked around, he realized that Washington and Jefferson were in the room with him. In his shock and confusion, he hadn't even noticed them at first. The three gentlemen exchanged questioning and confused looks. Alexander was about to ask what was going on when a door seemed to appear in one of the walls. In walked what appeared to be three men. Behind them, the door disappeared again and returned to being a seemingly solid wall.

"*How did they do that?* Alexander wondered. He thought maybe he had died and gone to Heaven, and these three men were angels. His brain was doing its best to try to make sense of the situation.

"The three persons were dressed as gentlemen of the day and appeared very similar-looking to each other. At first, Alexander thought maybe all angels just look alike. Looking at them more closely, though, Alexander decided they must be ordinary men despite the fact that they didn't *seem* like ordinary men.

"One of the strangers spoke to them. 'Gentlemen,' he began in a proper English accent, 'I apologize for interrupting your afternoons, but I hope you will come to understand that it was necessary. Now we'— he gestured to himself and the other two men—'all know who you are, so it seems only fair that we introduce *ourselves*. For your purposes, my name is Sam,'—Sam gestured to the person to his right—'this is Phillip,'—then to the person to his left—'and this is Mary.' At the confused expressions on the three faces of his guests, Sam said, 'Oh dear. Does that not work? Hmm, how about Jon? Is Jon acceptable to everyone? Yes, I can tell by your expressions that Jon is better. Jon it is.

" 'Now that we're all acquainted, gentlemen,' Sam continued, 'I'm sure that you must have many questions. I can assure you that all of your questions will be answered. But it would really be easier for you if you held your questions until after we have explained our purpose in bringing you here. Now, I'm going to show you something that I hope will make it easier for you to accept and believe the rest of what I will say. Do not be afraid. No harm will come to you.'

"Sam then waved his hand, and one wall disappeared. Alexander, Washington, and Jefferson suddenly found themselves looking down on the planet Earth. They could see the top and bottom of the planet . . . they could see each side . . . they could see how it curved to form a sphere. They could see the entire planet. It was amazing and beautiful.

" 'That is Earth, gentleman,' Sam said as if he were discussing nothing more unusual than the weather. 'Right now,' he continued in the same tone, 'we are all in space. We are a great distance above the Earth. To help you understand, you can think of it as if we are in a kind of ship, but instead of sailing on the water, this ship sails through space. It is a spaceship.'

"The three simply stood in awe of the splendor and majesty of Earth. Alexander thought it looked so much smaller than he'd ever imagined. He moved closer to where the wall had been. It appeared as if there was nothing between him and space. It seemed as if he could just walk out of the room and be in space. *What if I fell?* Alexander thought. Would I just fall all the way to the Earth?

" 'You need not worry about falling,' Sam assured them, as though Alexander had spoken out loud. Sam walked over and reached his hand into the apparent emptiness—yet, something shimmered . . . just for a moment. Then, a ball appeared in Sam's hand. Sam threw it at what appeared to be nothing. But the ball bounced off the nothingness and landed on the floor at Sam's feet. Then, the ball disappeared. 'It's a . . . well, how to explain it in terms you will understand. It's a force field, but you will not know what that means,' Sam said, apparently talking to himself now. He appeared to be thinking.

"Phillip then spoke for the first time: 'It's like a strong but invisible wall.'

" 'Yes,' Sam said. 'Thank you. It's like an invisible wall that we'—he waived his hand again—'can make visible again.' And the wall reappeared, looking exactly the same as it had before.

" 'This may take some time,' Sam began and then stopped

and appeared to be listening though no one said anything.

"Hamilton thought the strange men must be able to communicate without speaking. 'Quite right, Jon,' Sam said. 'I forget how frail and weak the human body is. I'm sure our guests *would* appreciate some chairs.' He no sooner said this before three chairs appeared in the room. 'Please sit,' he directed.

"Before they sat, Jefferson asked, 'Are you from the future?'

" 'No,' Sam said, looking at Jefferson in much the same way as an indulgent mother looks at her child. 'In fact,' Sam continued, 'we are not human at all. We have assumed this form for your comfort, and we thought it would make it easier for you to understand why we are here.' "

Neil then began to cough.

Alecin startled. She had become entranced by her grandfather's story. She jumped up, intending to do something. Then, she realized she had no idea what to do. So, she stood watching her grandfather cough, feeling stupid and helpless.

"I'm okay," Neil said after a few minutes. He took a small sip of his tea. "Sometimes, it just gets hard to talk for too long." His cell phone on the table vibrated. He picked it up and looked at it briefly. "Ah, Jim says that lunch is ready." He stood, then swayed.

Alecin quickly took his arm and attempted to carry as much of his weight as she could. She was terrified he would fall.

"Just a little dizzy is all. Nothing to worry about."

"Maybe you should sit back down," Alecin fretted. "I can just have Jim bring lunch in here."

"No," Neil declared firmly. "Come on. The break will do me good. The fresh air and food will do us *both* good. If it makes you feel better, you can hold my arm the whole way."

Alecin did just that.

CHAPTER 3

As Alecin and Neil settled into chairs on the patio, Alecin looked out, admiring, as she always did, the view. Her grandmother's garden continued into the backyard and, if possible, was even more magnificent. Alecin thought that her grandmother's garden could hold its own against any garden in the world. A few years ago, on a trip to Vancouver, Canada, Alecin had visited that city's famed Stanley Park. The park boasted a flower garden, reputed to be one of the most beautiful in the world. When Alecin saw it, she determined that her grandmother's was better or at least on par with it.

Alecin took a deep breath. The air was perfumed with every plant and flower. All Alecin's life, that same scent had wafted through the air from spring to fall. She had always loved it. With April nearly gone, the scent of the garden was a little muted. But it still sung.

Off to the right of the backyard was a pool house. It housed an indoor pool, spa, and changing facilities. Directly behind the house, behind a magnificent green lawn, was an intricate cast-iron fence. The reason for the fence lay just beyond it. A small river flowed through the property. Her grandmother had been terrified that one of her children would wander down to the river and drown. So, she had insisted on a fence as soon as her oldest child could walk. At the far end of the yard, there was a gate—a childproof one, of course—that allowed access to the river. Seeing it, Alecin thought again that the fence had probably saved her and her siblings' lives on numerous occasions. But Alecin had walked through that gate many times—under adult supervision—and spent countless enjoyable moments fishing with her grandfather and father in that river.

Like many homes in this part of Virginia, the patio was screened in. Every spring, residents were reminded that that area of the state and DC were once a swamp. The swamp had largely disappeared, but the bugs remained. From spring until the first frost of winter, mosquitoes were an ever-present nuisance.

Neil filled her glass and his with ice water from the pitcher that Jim had already placed on the table. Knowing her, Jim had placed a few lemon slices on a plate as well. Alecin added a few of these to her water. Then, she watched as her grandfather added a tablet and the contents of a small packet to his water and stirred them in. She had seen him do this countless times since he had gotten sick.

Neil had one of the most brilliant legal minds of this century. He had enjoyed a very successful career practicing law in various positions around DC, and about ten years ago, he had been appointed to serve as a judge on the Fourth Circuit Court of Appeals. He had been thrilled. And he had *excelled*. His legal opinions were so well written and so well argued that he was one of the most quoted judges in the federal court system. He had never said as much, but Alecin knew that his secret dream was to serve on the Supreme Court of the United States one day. And up until a year ago, it had seemed like he may just achieve it.

Then, one day, he was working at his desk when he suddenly had trouble breathing. An ambulance at the circuit court of appeals building would cause quite a stir and draw an awful lot of attention for something that Neil was sure was nothing. So rather than call 9-1-1, Neil had persuaded his clerk to drive him to the emergency room. The poor boy had been terrified the whole time. When they had arrived at the emergency room, Neil had walked in, gasping for breath with each step. He stopped the first person he saw wearing scrubs and asked her if she was a nurse. When she confirmed she was, he said, "I can't breathe," and then collapsed.

At the ER, doctors tested Neil for everything they could think of that would cause such a sudden inability to breathe. After spending hours in the ER, the doctors were no closer to an answer. Neil was admitted to the hospital. Since doctors had eliminated all the horses—the common causes of Neil's symptoms—they started looking for zebras—the not-so-common causes. Alecin's parents had gone to Richmond to be with Neil the moment they had gotten the call. Alecin's Dad told her how it had seemed that every kind of specialist was brought in on her grandfather's case at some point. They ran every test they could think of, and with each negative result, Neil had become increasingly frustrated. There had to be a reason for his symptoms; why could nobody find it? After two weeks, the doctors had run out of ideas, and helpless to do anything more, they had sent Neil home.

Eventually, after many more specialists and many more tests, Neil had finally received an answer, and it hadn't been a welcome one. Doctors had diagnosed him with Postural Orthostatic Tachycardia Syndrome, which everyone called POTS. Neil had learned that POTS affects the autonomic nervous system—the system controlling heart rate, blood pressure, basically, all those things the human body does on its own. With POTS, the body's normal fight or flight system is, as one doctor described it, "broken." Instead of being in the fight or flight mode for only brief periods and rarely, as healthy people are, people with POTS are in a constant state of fight or flight, and the human body was just *not* designed to stay in that state for very long.

The more the doctor explained the diagnosis, the worse it got. They said they didn't know what causes POTS, and without knowing the cause, they couldn't cure it. There was no pill and no treatment that would make POTS go away. The most the doctors could do was try to control some of the symptoms. But for the most part, the doctor had explained, people who suffered from POTS just had to get used to feeling "awful all the time."

"POTS isn't life-threatening," the doctor had told Neil, "but it is life-*altering*. You won't be able to do many of the things you did before for a long time—possibly ever again."

After the doctor had explained the diagnosis, Neil had said nothing. He had just asked Alecin's father to take him home. He couldn't even drive himself anymore at that point. He had said nothing the entire ride home. When he got home, he had walked into his study and shut the door. An hour later, he had walked out and handed Alecin's father an envelope. "Please see that this gets to the clerk of my court as soon as possible. It's my letter of resignation," he said simply. Unable to control the tears streaming down his face, Neil had walked upstairs to his bedroom and shut the door.

In her entire life, Alecin had only seen her grandfather cry twice. Once at her grandmother's funeral . . . and that day. Neil had known that he was giving up a job that he loved, was good at, and had worked for his entire life to achieve. And he was giving up his lifelong dream of being on the Supreme Court. Alecin couldn't imagine working so hard your whole life and doing everything right, only to have everything suddenly taken from you because your body betrayed you.

"Of all sad words of tongue or pen, the saddest are these: it might have been." This was a line from some poem that Alecin couldn't remember. But she thought it meant that no one has ever found happiness by brooding on what could have been instead of accepting what is. In the last year, that phrase had become Neil's motto. Whenever he felt anger or sadness or frustration because what could have been was taken, he would repeat his motto.

He was doing much better now, Alecin thought, watching him. Although the symptoms continued to plague him, they were somewhat muted now. People with POTS have about 15 percent less blood volume than they should have. The lack of blood volume was one of the reasons her grandfather often felt dizzy when he stood up. The highly advanced medical treatment for this? Saltwater. Basically. The doctor had told her grandfather to drink two liters of water containing electrolytes daily. And to either take salt pills or eat a tremendous amount of salt every day. Her grandfather had joked that POTS must be the only disease in the world where the doctor prescribes french fries as a treatment. The tablets he had added to his water turned it into the recommended salt water.

Jim arrived pushing a small cart with their lunch on it. Scout, who had been sitting quietly near Neil, came to attention. Scout never slept during meals. She remained on constant alert so that she could quickly gobble up any food that may accidentally be dropped.

Jim placed in front of Alecin a plate holding a fillet of tilapia—or was that Mahi Mahi? Alecin never could tell the difference. It was covered in some kind of fragrant sauce. A medley of vegetables accompanied it. Alecin recognized zucchini but had no idea what the other vegetables were. But she could see and smell the fresh herbs that flavored the medley and thought it couldn't be that bad. Alecin had already decided that she would eat everything on her plate because she wanted her grandfather to do the same. She was gratified to see that lunch actually looked appealing.

"Jim, you're amazing," she declared.

"Thank you, Alecin," Jim said, beaming. Then, he quietly rolled the cart away.

For the first few minutes, they ate in silence. Alecin assumed her grandfather needed to take a break from talking. And she couldn't think of what to say. Her mind reeled. She knew that POTS affected the brain. The disease would often cause insufficient blood flow to the brain, resulting in confusion and memory loss. Maybe that was what was happening. *Maybe I should take him to the emergency room*, she thought. Then, she quickly abandoned that idea. Neil Hamilton never did anything he didn't want to do, and she was pretty sure he would object to a trip to the emergency room. Besides, she thought as she studied him, he looked fine, all things considered. He didn't appear to be in any kind of distress. In fact, he seemed pretty content. And he was eating and drinking normally. He wouldn't do that if he wasn't okay, would he? And she had given her word that she wouldn't make any judgments and would hear him out until the end. Alecin decided she would keep her word. But she would watch him closely, and if there was any sign of trouble, all bets were off. Having resolved the situation in her mind, Alecin began to fill the silence with chatter about her job and Tonks and a vacation to Alaska she wanted to take when covid was over. Neil simply listened. He had always been good at listening. And Alecin's stories and ramblings had always amused him.

When they finished eating, Jim appeared, as if he had been watching and waiting. *It was just a little eerie*, Alecin thought. He once again pushed a cart. He quickly cleaned the table and seemed pleased that both had cleaned their plates. He then placed a small bowl of berries in front of each of them. Looking at the berries, Alecin silently wished for a bit of whipped cream. Berries were fine, but with whipped cream, they were terrific. To her surprise, Jim then pulled out a bowl of fresh whipped cream and placed a dollop in each of their bowls, and she was absolutely sure her dollop was a bit bigger. The whipped cream unreasonably thrilled her.

"This is whipped cream made from coconut milk," Jim announced.

Well, dammit, she thought.

CHAPTER 4

When Alecin and her grandfather entered the study after finishing their lunch, she saw that Jim had placed a fresh pot of tea and cups on the table. Sometimes, she wished that Jim *wasn't* so efficient. If the conversation continued as it had before lunch, it did *not* call for a cup of tea. It called for a shot of *bourbon.*

Alecin knew, however, that wishing for a shot of bourbon was a futile exercise. Her grandparents had never allowed a drop of alcohol in their home. Her grandfather had always said that the mind was too precious a thing to impair with alcohol.

Alecin's parents were a little more forgiving when it came to this particular point. They were both foodies and swore there were just some flavors that one could not fully appreciate without a glass of wine to accompany them. For her part, Alecin tried to avoid drinking, except for when social situations called for it. And that seemed to happen a lot in the military. But she never had more than one drink on any occasion and had never been drunk—except for that one night on shore leave in Australia that she would prefer to forget about altogether. That was enough of being drunk for a lifetime, in her opinion. Still, she thought she could do with a shot of something right about now.

"All right," Neil said, settling into his chair as Scout resumed her place by the fire. "Where *were* we?"

"The Founding Fathers were on a spaceship and Sam had just said that he wasn't human." *Whoa*, Alecin thought. That was a sentence she'd never thought she would utter—and certainly not seriously.

"Ah, yes," Neil said. "Now is when the story gets *really* interesting."

Alecin thought the story had already been really interesting—unbelievably so—but she said nothing.

Neil continued. "So, after saying he wasn't human, Sam told The Three—as I call them:

" 'However large and expansive you think the universe is, it is much bigger. There are billions of stars in just this galaxy, and this is not the only galaxy. There are hundreds of planets that we know of, and probably many that have yet to be discovered. The planet from which we come is outside of your galaxy, many light-years from here.'

"At this point, Sam stopped and again appeared to listen in silence. Sam then continued: 'I apologize. It is so easy to forget. Jon has reminded me that you do not yet know what a light-year is. Thus, let's just say our planet is very, very far away. In your language, our planet is called Kalec, and we are Kalecians.

" 'Even though there are many planets, the number of planets that have life is only a small fraction. And the number of planets with sentient life is smaller even than that. That is why Earth and humanity are important and why we have come.

" 'We are beings who believe that all sentient life should be respected, even cherished. We believe that intelligent beings are capable of—and should live in—peace and harmony with each other and the universe, and should respect the choices of others. We believe that all sentient beings should have freedom and liberty—a right to exercise free will. To choose their own destiny according to their own desires and beliefs. We believe that the attainment of knowledge is the greatest pursuit in life. There are many in the universe who share our beliefs.

" 'But, it is essential for you to understand that not all beings in the universe agree with us. There are some beings that have advanced in technology but not in wisdom. They have gained the ability to travel the universe, but they do not do so to expand their knowledge and to live in harmony with others. They created ships to travel through space only so they could find new beings to conquer and dominate and new planets to exploit.

" 'When they find a new planet, they strip that planet's resources until there is nothing left. They force the beings of that planet, whether sentient or not, to do work for them. They make them slaves. If they cannot use them as slaves, they use them as food. If neither of those options works, then they simply slaughter every sentient being on the planet so they can take the resources of the planet without resistance.

" 'In your language, the best word I find to describe these beings is *evil*, but that word does not fully encapsulate how *disharmonious* they are. The very word itself is vile, and it makes me ill to say it, but this is what we call the planets like this: the Disharmonious.

" 'Fortunately, the number of beings and planets like this is small. Since they only destroy planets, their number never grows. Unfortunately, however, their power does.'

"Sam stopped and appeared to listen. After a moment, he continued. 'Quite right, Phillip. I prefer not to think of that, but it is true. I misspoke when I said their number never grows. Sometimes, when they find planets suitable to their species, some of their species will occupy the planet, taking it over, and the planet will become one of the Disharmonious. In this way, their number does grow. But fortunately, their growth is very slow.

" 'The Disharmonious do not desire to destroy each other. But they do desire to destroy all beings who live in harmony and peace with the universe. To destroy the Harmonious. We are the Harmonious.

" 'The Disharmonious have very powerful weapons. We do not. We have used our technology to expand our knowledge and to spread harmony throughout the universe. We did not focus on the development of weapons. Only recently have some of the Harmonious realized that we might need weapons to defend ourselves. We have begun to develop weapons against the Disharmonious, but we are behind them in many ways.

" 'What has kept the Disharmonious from attacking all Harmonious planets thus far has been our sheer number. We vastly outnumber them. Those who lead the Harmonious have determined that our best hope for living in peace and for avoiding war is to grow our number. For many earth years, we have searched the universe looking for possible species that could join us—that could be Harmonious. We have been observing humanity for several Earth years. We have determined that, at this time, humanity cannot join us. There is too much greed, selfishness, ignorance, hate, conflict, and desire for power in your species.

" 'But, we have also seen humanity show love, caring, intelligence, kindness, curiosity, respect for life, and a desire to grow and improve themselves. We have concluded that while humanity is not yet ready to join us, humanity possesses that potential.

" 'Unfortunately, we do not have time to wait for you to get there on your own. We have brought you here today because we have determined that you three humans possess the greatest potential to move humanity forward—toward Harmony—and we want to help you.

" 'We will not force you. One of our most cherished beliefs is the belief in free will—that all sentient beings have the right to choice. Thus, before we give you our help, we must ask you:

Will you allow us to help you to save humanity?'

"For quite a while, Alexander, Washington, and Jefferson sat silently, staring at Sam. Finally, Sam said, 'I realize this is a lot to process, but we are asking you to let us help you to save all of humanity. It seems like an easy decision.'

" 'What happens if we fail?' Washington asked. 'What happens if humanity does not get to the point where we can join the Harmonious in time?'

" 'Humanity will be destroyed,' Sam said matter-of-factly.

" 'By these Disharmonious?' continued Washington.

" 'Yes.' Sam said in the same tone.

" 'And they will destroy Earth and either make all humans slaves, eat us, or just kill us?'

" 'Yes.'

" 'I do not understand,' Jefferson interjected. 'According to you, humanity is not at the point where we can join the Harmonious. So, why haven't the Disharmonious just come and destroyed us already?'

" 'Earth was only relatively recently discovered. Fortunately, it was a Harmonious species that discovered you. If the Disharmonious had discovered you first, you would already be destroyed. Since we discovered Earth, the Harmonious have kept you safe from the Disharmonious.'

" 'How?'

"Sam then stopped and pondered. 'How should I explain this? Remember that invisible wall that I called a force field?'

"At their nods, he went on. 'When we discover a planet like yours, or one that is ready to join us, we place a force field around the planet. It's like an invisible wall around the Earth. This force field prevents the Disharmonious from coming to your planet. If humanity proves . . . disappointing, we will remove this force field. It will then just be a matter of time before you are destroyed by the Disharmonious.

" 'Of course,' Sam continued, 'other Harmonious planets are permitted to come to observe Earth and to learn of humans.

They are supposed to keep their ships out of sight of humans, but mistakes happen. Your species has, from time to time, seen a spaceship of the Harmonious and will most likely continue to do so. But no being from a Harmonious planet is permitted to or would harm a human.'

" 'How?' Jefferson asked.

" 'Sam looked confused, 'How do Harmonious beings visit you?'

" 'No. How will you help us? Will you or one of your species become a ruler over humanity?'

" 'Ah, distrust,' Sam said, shaking his head, 'it is an ugly thing. Perhaps someday, humanity will evolve beyond it. But apparently not yet.' Sam looked sadly at Jefferson, then continued.

" 'We have no wish to rule over you. We cannot and will not take away free will. Humanity must choose for itself its own destiny. We will not force any being to believe as we do. This requirement for Harmony is absolute. Harmony can never exist where free will does not.

" 'We offer only guidance. We have wisdom beyond any human understanding. Our offer is nothing more than to share some of our wisdom with you. You and the rest of your species will need to make your own decisions. If you choose your own destruction, we will not stop you.'

"Sam seemed to pause to let this point sink in.

" 'How can you speak our language? How can you speak English?' Alexander asked.

" 'We are not speaking English.' Sam explained. 'It simply appears to you that we are. This ship'—Sam gestured all around him—'translates what I—or Jon or Phillip—say instantaneously so that it appears to you that we are speaking English. Likewise, when you speak to us, the ship translates your words into our language, the language of the Kalec. If you accept our help, we also have devices that we can wear that will do the same thing on Earth. With these devices, when we come to Earth to offer guidance, you will be able to understand us. And, of course, when we visit Earth, we will appear as humans.'

" 'You are going to come to Earth?' Jefferson asked.

" 'Well, yes. That would be most efficient and effective. Though we may bring you back here from time to time as needed.'

" 'Who steers this ship when you are on Earth?'

" 'Sam gave Jefferson the same indulgent look as before. 'We are not alone. There are others. They will take care of the ship while we are gone. You need not worry.' Sam paused, seemingly to see if there were any more questions. When none were asked, he continued.

" 'Now, it is time for you to return to Earth. Have you made a decision?'

"The Three conferred quietly. Washington spoke for them: 'If we agree, can we change our minds later?'

" 'Of course,' Sam replied.

" 'Then we accept, with humble and sincere gratitude.'

" 'Splendid,' Sam said, slapping his hands together. Phillip and Jon nodded and smiled."

At this point, Neil paused, needing to catch his breath a moment.

"I did wonder how they could communicate," Alecin said to break the silence. "A universal translator like they have on *Star Trek* sounds as feasible as everything else." She hurried on. "You're kind of in for a penny, in for a pound with this, aren't you? You either believe it all, or you believe none of it."

"Essentially, yes. There may be small, irrelevant things that have changed over the last 250 years. But the basic story, yes. You believe it all, or you believe none of it."

Alecin was quiet, and Neil could tell she was thinking. He drank his tea and watched the fire until she was ready.

"You didn't finish telling me about The Three being returned to Earth," Alecin pointed out.

"Well, according to Alexander, the Kalecians returned The Three to Earth at the exact moment they had left. Obviously, some time had passed, and this part of the story is rather vague and confusing, which is understandable considering humanity's understanding of time and space at that point in history. It would be more than a hundred years before Einstein put forth his theory of relativity. Basically—and I paraphrase greatly—the Kalecians told them that time did not move in a straight line as humans assumed, but from a non-linear, non-subjective viewpoint—that it's more like a big ball of wibbly-wobbly timey-wimey stuff."

"*Doctor Who*?" Alecin was shocked. "I'm not sure if I'm more surprised that aliens abducted Alexander or that you know *Doctor Who* quotes."

"Well, I have had a lot of time on my hands lately during which it seemed I had only two choices: watching TV or staring into the abyss. TV seemed to be the better option. And I found there are a few shows out there that do have some redeeming qualities. Plus, I like that Tennant person," he said, winking at her.

"Me too. We can get matching 'I heart David Tennant' T-shirts." Alecin joked. "Although," she continued, "Matt Smith was also quite good as the Doctor."

"Spoiler alert!" her grandfather exclaimed. "I haven't gotten that far yet."

"Sorry. Anyway, so because time is wibbly-wobbly, the Kalecians could return any humans they took up to the exact same time they left? If the Kalecians could time travel, essentially, why didn't they just jump ahead a few hundred years and see how humanity turned out?"

"Alexander asked the Kalecians the same question, essentially, at some point while the Kalecians were helping them. From what I understand, manipulating time a few days to the past or future was simple. But anything more than that, and it got difficult and dangerous."

Neil then stopped talking altogether.

"Do you need another break?" Alecin asked.

"No. That's just the end of the story."

"How can it be the end? What kind of end is that? What happened after they accepted? What kind of help did the Kalecians provide? How long did they stay? Are they still here?"

"They're not still here. Let's get that straight. As to what happened after The Three accepted the Kalecians' help, I only know what Alexander has passed down to his line. We do know that after The Three accepted their help, the Kalecians provided guidance to The Three through the Revolutionary War and the writing and adoption of the *Constitution* . . . everything until the end of Washington's second presidency, and maybe a little after. As you know, at the end of his presidency, many people wanted Washington to continue to lead the country, run for a third term, or become king. Washington refused. He felt that turning over power was the best thing for the country. Once there was a peaceful transition of power, once Washington conceded his power to the next elected president, they left. It was about 1797 when they left."

"Why did they leave?"

"They believed that the establishment of this country and its *Constitution* had sufficiently set humanity on the path to Harmony."

"So, that's why they helped us win the Revolutionary War and write the *Constitution*."

"Yes."

"And that's why they chose Alexander, Washington, and Jefferson. Because they wanted this country to exist, and they believed they could help them."

"Yes."

"But why Jefferson and Alexander? They hated each other. Alexander once told Jefferson that even with over a million words in the human language, he could not string enough words together to properly express how much he wanted to hit Jefferson with a chair. Wouldn't that kind of hostility have convinced the Kalecians that humanity wasn't ready? That we could never live in Harmony?"

"No. You see, the fact that Alexander and Jefferson disagreed but could still work together toward the good of humanity showed the Kalecians that there was hope for us. Understand that in Kalecian society, there was no conflict."

"None at all? How is that possible? Didn't they ever disagree?"

"Of course they disagreed, sometimes. But the Kalecians understood that there is always one truth. Truth is not subjective. If two Kalecians disagreed, they both understood that one was wrong, and one was correct. Then, they would communicate until they discovered who was right, until they determined the truth.

"Humanity isn't there. Yet. But we do have our own way that we have developed as a way of resolving conflict, without resorting to violence. Each side presents its point of view, and a neutral arbitrator decides the truth. Like a plaintiff and prosecution presenting their case to a judge. Alexander, Jefferson, and Washington were the perfect three to illustrate humanity's solution to conflict. Jefferson would present one point of view, Alexander the other, and Washington would listen to both impartially and decide the truth.

"That is why it was so important that the *Constitution*—or rather its amendments in the *Bill of Rights*—include protection for speech and the press. If people are prevented from presenting their side . . . if differing points of view are suppressed, then the conflict can never be resolved. It will just continue to exist until one side resorts to violence in order to prevail."

Alecin sat back in her chair. She hadn't realized that she had been literally on the edge of her seat. She didn't know what to say. Finally, she said, "that's a fascinating and creative story, Grandpa."

"It's not just a story, Alecin. It's all true."

"Come on, Grandpa. Stop messing with me."

Neil just smiled. "Perhaps I can convince you," he said enigmatically. He then went over to one of his bookshelves and picked up an elaborately decorated container? Box? Alecin wasn't quite sure what to call it.

Whatever it was, it was a little larger than two shoe boxes stacked on top of each other, but it wasn't rectangular in shape. It was slightly wider in the middle than at the top and bottom. It was different shades of blue and green, with gold detail in an intricate and complicated design. It was beautiful, but it seemed to have no real purpose. There was no way to open it. It did not look to have a lid or hinges. Her grandfather had told her once that he had brought it back as a souvenir from one of his trips with her grandmother, and Alecin had always thought it as no more than a pretty souvenir. It had sat on that same shelf for as long as she could remember.

Neil brought it over and set it on the table. Smiling at Alecin, he waved his hand over it. A top portion of it disappeared.

Alecin quickly jumped up in shock and instinctively put the chair between her and the obviously dangerous thing.

Scout stood at the commotion and did her best to look like she could take on an intruder.

"How did you do that? Do you do magic tricks now?"

"It's no trick," Neil assured her. He waved his hand over the thing again, and the top reappeared. He did this a few more times, the same thing happening each time. "This box is Kalecian."

So, it is *a box,* thought Alecin, purposely ignoring the implications of what her grandfather had said.

"They left it for Alexander Hamilton."

"I'm going to pass out," Alecin mumbled shakily.

"Sit down, Alecin," Neil ordered sternly. "Deep breaths," he said more gently once she sat. "It'll be okay."

Alecin took deep breaths. Neil waited patiently, sipping his tea.

A few minutes later, Alecin asked, "Why?"

"Why what?"

"Why did they leave the box? There had to be a reason."

"That's my girl," Neil said, beaming like a proud parent. "There is a reason indeed, and *that reason*, my dear, is where you come in."

CHAPTER 5

Quelling her curiosity—which she thought showed heroic self-discipline—Alecin insisted her grandfather take a break and lay on the couch in the study for at least thirty minutes. Initially, she had paced the study, but her grandfather had kicked her out, telling her that her thoughts were being too loud. So, she had decided to go to the kitchen to see what Jim was up to. But he wasn't there.

I have to do something, Alecin thought. If she didn't keep busy, she would go crazy. Patience had never been one of her virtues. She put together a small snack plate with whole-wheat crackers, cheese, and some fruit. By the time she was finished, the thirty minutes were up.

When she walked back into the study, her grandfather was still lying on the couch, his eyes closed. But he heard her come in.

"Time up already?" he asked.

"Do you need more time?"

"No. I've kept this to myself for thirty years. It feels good to finally be able to tell someone, and I want to do it." He noticed the plate she was carrying. "What do you have there?"

"I thought you might be hungry."

"How very thoughtful."

Alecin walked to the seating area and put the plate on the table. But instead of returning to his chair, Neil went to his desk. He moved stuff around for a few minutes and then shouted, "Aha!"

He came over to the table, holding two Oreo cookies. They had always been a favorite of his, and of hers. "One for each of us. But if you tell Jim, I'll deny everything and call you a dirty liar."

"Tell Jim *what*?" Alecin asked, assuming a look of complete innocence. "I never saw any cookies."

"None at all," Neil said, flashing her a grin. "Now stand up. I want you to do something for me."

Alecin stood, thinking he needed a blanket or pillow or something. Instead, he stood her in front of the box, took her right hand, palm down, and placed it on his hand, also palm down. Then, he guided her hand over the box, making the same motion as he had before. Nothing happened. He then switched so that her hand was on the bottom and made the motion again. Again, nothing happened.

"The box is now yours," he declared.

"What do you mean it's *mine*?"

"I mean, it will now only open for you. See." He waved his hand over the box and nothing happened. "Now you try it."

Alecin was doubtful, but also more than a little curious. She waved her hand over the box. The top disappeared as it had before.

"Holy crap on a cracker!"

"I don't know what that means, but I agree with the sentiment," Neil said, chuckling.

She waved her hand again, and the top reappeared. She did it several more times, and probably would have continued doing it if her grandfather hadn't stepped in.

He grabbed her hands. "This is not a magic trick." His tone and face were solemn. "This is Kalecian. Do you understand?"

Alecin was quiet for a few moments, contemplating. Could she really accept that the box in front of her came from another world?

"There are more things in heaven and earth, Horatio," Alecin said quietly to herself, looking at the box.

"Now, *that* quote I recognize. And the English bard was right. There are many, many things in this world that we do not understand, or even know about."

"I know *that*. I *accept* that. But I'm still trying to wrap my head around *this*. I mean, you just told me that three of the Founding Fathers of this country, including my many-times-great-grandfather, were abducted by aliens and that aliens helped form the United States of America. It's a heckuva lot to process."

"It is. I know. I felt the same way when I heard the story."

"You still haven't told me why they left the box and what it has to do with me."

"And I intend to do that right now. Sit down, will you?" When she complied, he continued.

"So, as I explained before, The Three received guidance from the Kalecians. But they weren't the only ones who knew of their existence. Before they left, the Kalecians had each of the original Three choose three other people. The Three and the other nine that had been chosen were taken to the Kalecians' ship and told of the Harmonious and the Disharmonious, and of the possible futures for humanity. After having everything explained to them, they were asked to take upon themselves and their posterity the responsibility of keeping the secret of the existence of the Kalecians.

"But that wasn't all that was asked of them. The Kalecians told them that there were other worlds to which they needed to attend. They were going to leave humanity to work toward Harmony on its own. They believed that the existence of this country and the *Constitution* on which it is based pointed humanity in the right direction. The Kalecians explained that that is why they had decided to step in when they did. Based on what they had observed, they believed that the people of what was then the thirteen colonies had the capacity to establish a country founded on the principles in the *Constitution*—principles that all Harmonious societies share. They were confident that the new United States of America would become a leader in the world and a model for the people of all nations.

"They didn't just abandon humanity, however. The Kalecians left a device, a sort of telephone, that could be used to contact them if it was determined that in humanity's quest for Harmony, their help was once again needed."

"Is that box the *telephone*?" Alecin said, panicking. "Oh my goodness, did I just call them?"

"No. Of course not. They weren't going to just hand one person the *telephone* and tell him to use their best judgment and good luck. That would have been a disaster."

"Okay. So, what *did* they do?"

"They didn't want one person to have this *telephone*, so they divided it into many parts and hid the parts in locations around the Earth. Around the United States, more specifically. As it was at the time, of course."

"So, all these parts are just sitting in different places all around the original states?"

"Not just sitting. Hidden. Well hidden. The Kalecians didn't want someone coming upon a part accidentally."

"Okay, but how are we supposed to call them if no one knows where the parts to this *telephone* are hidden? And it seems more like a bat signal than a telephone to me. You know, instead of Gotham telling Batman, 'Hey, we need your help; criminals are doing bad things,' by shining a big bat in the sky, Earth is telling the Kalecians, 'Hey, we need your help; humanity is doing bad things.' "

Neil chuckled. Alecin could always bring humor to the most

intense situation. "So, not a telephone, but calling it a *bat* signal doesn't seem right either. What do you think we should call it?"

"How about Kalecian Signaling Machine—no device. Kalecian Signaling Device," Alecin stated firmly. "We don't know if it's necessarily a machine. We don't want to impose any unnecessary preconceptions. It's a KSD. Definitely."

"That's a very nice suggestion. But as it happens, it already has a name. I was just saying *telephone* to help you understand. It is called an Appello . . . and now I've completely lost my train of thought."

Neil thought for a moment. "Ah yes," he continued. "In response to your question on how the Appello can be used if no one on Earth knows where the parts to it are? Because the Kalecians also left clues to the hiding places for the parts. Difficult clues. They wanted to ensure that whoever was called to retrieve the parts and assemble the Appello had a deep conviction of the need for it, as well as intelligence, morality, compassion, respect for life . . . all those qualities that Harmonious beings value."

"How many parts to the Appello are there?"

"I don't know. No one knows."

"But there's a part of the Appello in the box?"

"No."

"So, there are clues to where all the parts are in the box?"

"No."

"So, there's a clue to where *one* of the parts is in the box?"

"No."

"So, you already know the clues?"

"No."

"I'm so confused."

"Then let me explain and stop interrupting," he said with mild impatience.

Then, he continued more gently. "In addition to keeping the existence of the Kalecians secret, each of the original twelve—The Three and the nine they had chosen—was asked to com-mit themselves and their posterity to be a sort of guardian of humanity. They were asked to take upon themselves, and their posterity, the responsibility to determine if and when the Kalecians' help was needed again. These twelve are called Guardians. I don't know who gave them that name, but that's the name told to me. It makes sense because we are the guardians of humanity. I am a Guardian. Guardianship was passed to me by my father."

"I figured out you were a Guardian. I just didn't know you got it from great-grandpa."

"I figured, but I felt like I should still state it clearly."

"So, is this like an 'into every generation one is born thing?'"

"What?"

"*Buffy the Vampire Slayer.* It's a TV show. Never mind. Don't ever watch it; you'd hate it. You would think it was silly."

"If it's silly, then why did *you* watch it?"

"I was eleven, and the dark angel guy was really cute."

"Well, when I start judging television shows based on the attractiveness level of the actors, I'll check it out."

"So, never."

"Exactly. Now, if you don't mind," Neil said, mildly exasperated, "could we get back to this fate of humanity stuff?"

"Sorry. So, who were the original Guardians, the first twelve?"

"I don't know. Nobody knows. They were instructed by the Kalecians that future generations of Guardians should not know the identity of the other Guardians . . . *or* of the original guardians."

"So, the fate of humanity depends upon you and eleven other Guardians?"

"Yes."

"But what would happen if an idiot or a dishonest person became a Guardian? We would have to trust an idiot to decide the fate of all of humanity?"

"Well, the Kalecians took steps to ensure that wouldn't happen."

"*What* steps?"

Neil took a deep breath. He was unsure how Alecin would react to what he was about to say. "The Kalecians offered all those who had agreed to be a Guardian a gift. We all have free will," he continued, "and are responsible for our own choices, of course. The Kalecians value free will immensely and would never do anything to deprive sentient beings of their free will. Genetics do not determine destiny. Nothing in anyone's DNA deprives them of free will. I know you know this, but I just want to emphasize that point because it's essential.

"Now, all that being said, it's also a fact that there are many traits which are affected by genetics . . . by what's in a person's DNA. The Kalecians understood this. And . . . well, they had the ability to modify human DNA."

"To modify human DNA?" Alecin asked incredulously. "How could they possibly modify human DNA?"

"I don't know how. I don't *want* to know how. Maybe someday. But today, humans are not ready to have that kind of knowledge."

"How did the first Guardians even know what DNA was? DNA wasn't discovered until 1953."

"They didn't. I don't know how the Kalecians explained it to them. That part hasn't been passed down. But I very much doubt that they taught the Guardians about DNA. Anyway, the gift they offered was to modify the DNA of each Guardian's genetic line so that certain traits would be, let's say, *amplified.*"

"*Which* certain traits?"

"Intelligence, integrity, judgment, sympathy, dedication . . . all the traits that the Kalecians believed would best ensure that all future Guardians would fulfill their duty well. They hoped, or rather, they had faith, that with these modifications and with each Guardian entrusted to choose well to whom they passed Guardianship, that every Guardian would have both the ability and the desire to do what was needed."

Alecin got up and began to pace. It helped her think. "So, you, me, and everyone in our family that has Alexander's DNA—we all have this modified DNA, so we all have more intelligence, judgment, and all that other stuff?"

"Yes."

"Because Alexander's line—our DNA—was altered . . . modified by the Kalecians, and we inherited those modifications."

"Yes."

"Is that why so many members of our family have been so successful at whatever they chose to do? Is that why our family has been able to accumulate all this wealth all these years?"

Neil smiled. "Being a Guardian is a grave responsibility . . ." He paused and leaned forward, smiling. "But that doesn't mean it doesn't have its perks."

Not knowing how to respond, Alecin resumed pacing.

Seeing that Alecin needed a little time, Neil picked up his tea, took a sip, and promptly grimaced. "It tastes awful cold," he mumbled.

It tasted awful hot, too, Alecin thought but kept her silence.

"I'm going to ask Jim to bring us a fresh pot," Neil said, picking up his phone. Out of the corner of his eye, he saw Alecin pout. Whatever happened in life, come hell or high water, he would always be an indulgent grandfather. "Or, how about instead, I ask Jim to bring us a pot of his famous hot chocolate?"

Alecin had always thought that Jim made the best hot chocolate in the world, and she thought a pot of it sounded like a wonderful idea.

"Whipped cream or marshmallows?" Neil asked as he typed the request into his phone.

"Whipped cream, of course. And the real stuff. Not the coconut stuff. Jim's hot chocolate deserves the real stuff." Alecin paused, realizing how she must sound. "For me, but for you, the coconut stuff is great."

"What's life without a little indulgence every now and then? I told Jim to bring enough of the real stuff for both of us. I told him that you're really upset and that I thought us having some old-fashioned hot chocolate would make you feel better. That way, he won't make a fuss about it not being part of my diet. When he comes in, look like you've been crying or something."

"Grandpa," Alecin scolded, "I am not going to help you deceive Jim. What happened to us having all this integrity?"

"I didn't say it made us *perfect*." After a moment, Neil sighed loudly. "I risk life and limb for you by asking Jim to bring you some of his hot chocolate, with real whipped cream, and you can't do me this *one* little favor." His voice trailed off, and he looked mischievously at Alecin.

"You are incorrigible."

"I am what I am, and I'm too old to change."

Alecin shook her head. "Fine, I'll do it. Are you sure you're not really a Jewish mother? Cause you are really great at guilt trips."

Neil shrugged his shoulders. "It's easy to make people feel guilty when you're sick," he said nonchalantly. "They already feel guilty that you're sick, and they aren't."

Alecin wasn't quite sure how to respond to that, so she decided to change the subject. "Okay, so Alexander accepted the gift from the Kalecians, but did the others accept it?"

"Well, technically, I've only been told what Alexander did. But so much of being a Guardian depends on that box. And that box reads that DNA modification. No one could be a Guardian without that DNA modification. Plus, it was such a tremendous gift. They would have been fools not to accept it. And not accepting it threatened all of humanity because it increased the likelihood that there would be, in your words, an idiot as a Guardian. If any of the first twelve wasn't willing to do whatever it took for the sake of humanity, then he had no business being a Guardian at all. Therefore, the conclusion that all of the first Guardians accepted the gift is only logical."

"Okay, Spock." Seeing her grandfather's puzzled expression, Alecin explained: "*Star Trek*. Spock is a Vulcan. They're super logical. He's always saying that some course of action is only logical." After pausing briefly, she continued. "You should watch *Star Trek* when you are down and need some TV. I think you would like it." Then, without pausing, she continued on again, "I want you to know that I am taking everything you say seriously—very seriously. I joke around because this is intense stuff, and it's all hard to process. Joking around helps me process."

Her grandfather smiled at her. "I know, sweetheart. It's okay. I never doubted you for a second."

"Okay. Good." *It is nice to be with someone who understands me so well,* Alecin thought.

"He's coming," Neil said when he heard Jim in the hall outside the door. "Quick. Start crying."

"You are absolutely incorrigible," Alecin muttered as she walked over to the window. On her way, she grabbed a handful of tissues out of the tissue box on the desk. She positioned herself so that Jim could not see her face but could see the tissues. She hoped she looked like she was upset and looking out the window contemplatively. When Jim came in, neither he nor her grandfather said anything, but Alecin could practically feel them exchanging worried glances. She inwardly grimaced. Then, she smelled that heavenly aroma that was Jim's hot chocolate. And all was forgiven.

As soon as Jim closed the door, Alecin hurried back to her chair. She filled her cup halfway with chocolate and halfway with whipped cream.

"Want some chocolate with your whipped cream?"

"Grandpa, that joke wasn't funny the first twenty times you told it, and it's still not funny. As I have explained, this is the proper way to drink hot chocolate. It is the only way to get the right chocolate-to-whipped-cream ratio in every sip." Alecin sipped her chocolate. "Yummy. Perfect ratio."

Neil sipped his hot chocolate, which had a small dollop of whipped cream in it. "Yummy. Perfect ratio," he said in a spot-on imitation of Alecin.

Alecin laughed. And her grandfather laughed. It had been a long time since Alecin had heard him really laugh, and she was outrageously delighted by the sound.

"Okay," Alecin said when the laughter had died down. "I've been properly refreshed. Back to business. So, my next question is, if none of the current Guardians know who the others are, how do they communicate? They must communicate. They have to know when all twelve of them have decided it's time to send up the bat signal. All of them have to agree, right? They all have to decide that it's time."

"Yes. It must be unanimous."

"Why twelve? Why not twenty or fifteen?"

"I don't know. But I don't think it's the number twelve that's important. There is a number that appears much more often than any other number in universal mathematical equations—when physicists try to explain the universe with math—the number three. Three seems to be a number that has some special significance in the universe, and to the Kalecians. There were three Kalecians that came to help humanity. They chose three humans to put their plan into action. To form the Guardians, they had each of the original three choose another three. Three seemed to be their guide. And using three as their guide, the result is twelve Guardians.

"And isn't it interesting," he continued, "that the Kalecians determined that twelve Guardians were sufficient to judge humanity *and* determined the twelve must reach a unanimous decision to take action and that our federal juries here in the United States consist of twelve jurors who judge a person's guilt and they must reach a unanimous decision to find a person guilty?"

"That *is* interesting," Alecin replied. "Which do you think came first?"

"You mean do I think the relatively primitive beings—us—copied the supremely advanced beings—the Kalecians—or that the supremely advanced beings copied the primitive beings?

That *is* a puzzler."

"Well, when you put it like *that*," Alecin said with a small pout. "But you still haven't explained how the Guardians communicate with each other. It seems like it would be easier and make a lot more sense if they all knew each other."

"It would *not*," Neil said firmly. "But that explanation will have to wait until tomorrow. I'm suddenly very tired, and I would like to go to my bed and lie down."

Alecin jumped up. "Do you need some help getting up there?"

"No. I think I'll be all right. And if I'm not, Scout will let you know." He looked at Scout, who had jumped up at the sound of her name. "Won't you, girl?" Turning back to Alecin, he said, "It's unlikely that I'll come downstairs again. Will you stay here tonight?"

Alecin never understood why he insisted on asking her. Of course, she would stay. Where else was she going to go? But she just nodded.

"Good. I'll have Jim get your room ready. Try to relax tonight. I've put a lot on your shoulders today." He turned to Scout. "Come on, girl. You have to babysit me." Scout seemed eager to accept the job.

When Neil was nearly at the door, Alecin called to him. He turned and looked at her. "Are you telling me all this because you're going to pass being a Guardian on to me?"

"Yes," he said simply and walked out.

"I was afraid that was what you were going to say," Alecin said quietly.

CHAPTER 6

Long after her grandfather had left, Alecin remained in the study, staring at the slowly dying fire and lost in her thoughts. When Jim touched her shoulder, she screamed and jumped.

"Sorry. I didn't mean to scare you," Jim said hurriedly.

"It's okay. I was just, um, thinking."

"Are you sure? Cause you don't seem confident about that."

"I was just thinking," Alecin said more firmly. "I have a lot on my mind right now."

"Are you okay?" Jim asked with more concern than Alecin thought the situation called for. Then, she remembered her grandfather's earlier subterfuge.

"Yes. I'm fine."

"I just came in to tell you that dinner is ready. Your grandfather is taking his upstairs."

"I'm not really hungry right now. Too much hot chocolate," she said with forced cheeriness. She certainly didn't want Jim worrying over her all weekend. "Can you just put it in the oven for me or something, and I'll eat it later?"

"No problem. After I store your dinner, I'll prepare your usual room. Then, I'll be leaving for the evening."

"I brought an overnight bag with me. You don't need to do anything in my room."

"Always prepared." Jim smiled.

"Just like the Boy Scouts." She paused, "Do they even have Boy Scouts anymore? I know they got infected with wokeness and abandoned everything that made them a successful organization for decades. Didn't they file for bankruptcy or something? Every single time: go woke, go broke."

"Go woke, go broke?"

"Yeah, I just thought of it. Kind of catchy, isn't it?

Jim just looked at her patiently.

"Sorry. I'm rambling. Have a good night. Say hi to your family for me."

"I will," Jim promised and left.

Alecin pondered what to do next. She really wasn't that hungry. Maybe she should go for a walk? A walk had always been good when she needed to clear her head. She looked outside. It looked cold and dreary and about to rain. She was in no mood to be cold and wet walking around outside. She decided she would take advantage of the indoor pool. Swimming always relaxed her, and she could use the exercise after all that chocolate. Definitely swimming, she decided. Happy to have a plan about what to do next, she walked out of the study.

Early the following day, Alecin again sat with her grandfather at the patio table. She'd had a restless night and desperately wanted coffee. She chatted with her grandfather, wondering what was taking Jim so long. After what seemed like forever, Jim finally rolled out the cart to serve breakfast. When Alecin saw the coffee pot on the cart, she could have wept with joy. She had feared that the life-giving elixir would be yet another one of those things that had been eliminated from her grandfather's house.

But there, the good news stopped. Breakfast was oatmeal. Ordinarily, Alecin didn't mind oatmeal; she even liked it. But she enjoyed her oatmeal swimming in butter and brown sugar. The oatmeal in front of her didn't seem to have either of those things. Jim had served a bowl of fresh berries with the oatmeal. Her grandfather seemed to be enjoying the berries in the oatmeal. Alecin decided to try it.

She decided it wasn't that bad with the berries, but it was far from *good*. As Alecin contemplated how much of the oatmeal she would need to eat to be supportive, she suddenly remembered that she had brought food! In all the mental chaos of yesterday, she had forgotten. When packing, she hadn't been sure what her grandfather wanted to talk to her about but had figured that urgent and important news probably wasn't good.

Alecin thought her diet was pretty healthy overall, but when she was upset or stressed, she wanted fat and sugar. When packing her bag, she had thought there probably wouldn't be any junk food in her grandfather's house. So, planning ahead, she had stopped on her way and purchased some of her favorite comfort foods, just in case. And that included donuts! Alecin promised herself that if she ate five bites of oatmeal, she could have the powdered donuts in her room that were now calling her name.

After breakfast, Alecin told her grandfather she needed fifteen minutes of personal time before they resumed their talk. She used that time to run upstairs and scarf down about eight mini powdered donuts. She didn't think that she had ever tasted powdered donuts that were so good in all her life.

Feeling satisfied and just a little guilty, Alecin checked to make sure that there was no powdered sugar on her face, her clothes, or her hands. How did that stuff get everywhere anyway? Then, she took a deep breath and closed her eyes. "You can do this," she told herself. "You can do this." One more deep breath, and then Alecin left to continue her education in becoming a Guardian of humanity.

Arriving at the study, Alecin saw that Neil was again seated in his chair, watching a simmering fire. Her grandfather loved to sit by a fire. He would light one on all but the hottest days of summer. Scout lay at his feet, like always. On the table were a teapot and teacups. She just knew the pot was filled with that horrid tea.

But this morning, she was prepared. She had brought a filled water bottle. Support could only go so far, she had decided. She wasn't drinking that tea again. Instead, she would use her water bottle as an avoidance mechanism. She walked over, put her bottle on the table, and sat.

"I know you must have a million questions," Neil began, "and I intend to tell you everything you need to know to be a Guardian. But I want you to ask any questions you have along the way. It's vitally important that you understand exactly what you are committing to do if you agree to become a Guardian."

"*If* I agree?"

"Of course, if you agree," Neil said with more heat than he'd intended. He began again, trying to sound more comforting. "What I mean to say is, you don't have to do anything you don't want to do. I'm not going to force you to become a Guardian. It will be your choice."

"I know, I know," Alecin said warily. "I'm just feeling overwhelmed."

"Understandable. Do you want to continue?"

Alecin thought about the question. She didn't want to answer automatically. She wanted to mean it. "I do," she said finally.

"One more thing before we get into the Guardian stuff. I want you to understand that if you do decide to become a Guardian, I will be happy and proud. If you decide *not* to become a Guardian, I will be happy and proud. I will love you and be proud of you no matter what you decide. This is a decision that will affect the rest of your life. I don't want you to make this kind of decision based on what you think *I* want. I want you to be happy. Always."

"Oh, Grandpa," Alecin cried. "Now, if Jim came in, I really would be crying." Alecin grabbed tissues for real this time. After taking a few moments to pull herself together, Alecin looked at her grandfather. "Thank you," she said sincerely. And that was that.

"Okay," Neil began again. "When we left off, I was explaining how Guardians communicate with each other. Understand that the first Guardians were more than two hundred years ago. At that time, communication options were extremely limited. One, you could talk to someone in person. That wouldn't work for Guardians who weren't supposed to know each other. Or two, you could send a telegram. But that wouldn't work either because telegrams had to be sent through operators. That meant that an entirely new system had to be put in place in order for the Guardians to communicate effectively.

"Now, I want you to consider some facts. The Kalecians first made contact around June 1776. At that time, Benjamin Franklin was the postmaster general for the colonies. The Kalecians left in 1797 or 1798; it's unclear. But it *is* clear and very well established that between 1776 and 1790, while the Kalecians were advising and assisting humanity, Franklin put into place the foundations of the US postal system—foundations that were so intelligently designed that over two hundred years later, they remain the foundations of our modern postal system."

"Hold on, are you saying that the whole US postal system was established because the Kalecians needed a way for Guardians to communicate?"

"I'm simply stating the facts. Draw your own conclusions."

"Well, what do *you* think?"

"I think the whole US postal system was established because

the Kalecians needed a way for Guardians to communicate."

"But it was Franklin who developed and implemented the foundations of the postal system. He wasn't one of The Three, and he couldn't have been a Guardian then because you said the Guardians weren't called until near the end of the Kalecian's time here."

"Alecin," Neil gently chastised, "you're thinking too narrowly. You're ascribing to the Kalecians the same limitations as humans. They don't have those limitations. They could beam . . ." He stopped and looked at Alecin. "FYI, I have seen *Star Trek* before, thank you very much. Had you taken a breath yesterday, I would have told you that I watched it all the time when I was a kid." He shot a pointed look at Alecin, then continued. "I still fail to understand why you called me Spock, but I take it as a compliment. But, back to the discussion at hand, the Kalecians could beam anyone anywhere. The Kalecians could beam any *thing* anywhere. They could have created notes, schematics, designs . . . whatever Franklin needed to establish a postal system that would serve their purposes. They could have made these documents appear to be in his own handwriting, and then beamed them among his other papers. He would have thought that the documents were of his own doing. They could have modified or corrected his designs in subtle ways that he wouldn't have even noticed."

Alecin thought about that. "I can see it," she decided. "The Kalecians most definitely could have influenced Franklin to go in the direction they wanted him to go. That doesn't mean that they *did*, though."

"It does not. It would never hold up in court." Neil winked at Alecin.

"So, was Franklin a Guardian?"

"No, he died in 1790."

"Good point."

"Now, my dear, it seems to be a good time for a break. Go amuse yourself for about a half-hour."

"Actually, I was thinking Scout could use a walk."

At her name and the word walk, Scout jumped up and barked excitedly.

"Someone likes that idea. And I also think it's a good one. Her leash is—"

"Grandpa," Alecin interrupted, "the leashes have been in the same place for the last thirty years. I know where they are."

She kissed her grandfather's cheek and called for Scout. A nice walk along the river with a happy dog was just what she needed.

A little over a half-hour later, Scout and Alecin walked back into the study.

"How did the walk go?" Neil asked.

"It was more of a stop-every-few-minutes-and-sniff-at-everything than a walk—at least for Scout—but it was nice to get outside. I stopped by the kitchen and got her some water. Oh, I also ran into Jim in the kitchen. He said to tell you that lunch will be served at about noon."

"All right," Neil said. "Let's see how much we can get through until then, shall we?"

"Well, to start, I have a question. You said last night that you intend to pass being a Guardian on to me."

"I intend to ask you to be a Guardian," Neil clarified. "It's your choice whether or not you accept."

"Okay. But while I was walking, I couldn't help but wonder, why *me*? Why not someone else? Why not Dad, for example?"

"To be honest, I had intended to pass it to your father. I was going to recommend he pass it to you so that it would come to you eventually. Sometimes, though, the best-laid plans of mice and men get foiled again. For many reasons, the passage must be done in person. That's why I was so insistent that you came here. Your parents have made it clear that they're going to stay in Ecuador for as long as they're needed."

Earlier that year, in January, her parents—both doctors—had left for what was supposed to be a six-month stint in Ecuador with Doctors without Borders. But, like with so many other things, covid had changed their plans. Now Alecin had no idea when she would see them again. She knew they wouldn't leave as long as people needed them there.

"I'm a realist," Neil continued, "and it's unrealistic to think that I'll not get covid. Everyone will get it, at some point. I just don't know whether it will be sooner or later. With my health as it is, there's a chance that I wouldn't survive it."

"Grandpa!" Alecin was shocked. "You can't think that way. *Lots* of people survive covid."

"Those people are usually young and healthy. I'm neither. I'm not saying it will happen or even that it's likely to happen, but it *is* a *possibility*. And the fate of humanity is too important. I don't want to risk it."

"But if it's just a matter of geography, what about Beth or Luke?" she asked, referring to her brother and sister. "Is it because they're married and I'm not?"

"Goodness no. I was married and had your father when my dad passed it to me."

"Well, how about Shauna or Becky or Trenton or Scott?"

At the mention of Scott, Neil raised his eyebrows.

"Okay. I get why not Scott," Alecin said.

The Kalecians' gift, it was clear, was no guarantee of outcome. Reaffirming that genes don't determine destiny, her cousin Scott had decided to completely ignore his enhanced innate intelligence and judgment and had become a left-wing activist vegan living in Los Angeles. The last time Alecin had seen him, she made a comment about how men could not give birth, and he had lost his mind. She had avoided him since.

"Your aunt, uncle, and any of your cousins—well, except Scott—would make excellent choices. But Alecin, I've always known this was your path. You're free to take another one, but gosh darn, I'm going to give you the option of walking this one."

Alecin smiled. Gosh darn was about as harsh an expletive as her grandfather used. It indicated that he meant business.

"That helps. Thanks," Alecin said. "Next question: Why all the secrecy? Why is it so important that the identities of the Guardians stay hidden?"

"Two reasons, really: fear and greed. There are some out there—they are on the fringe but could be dangerous enough. They may have heard part of the story. And what they heard made them think that what Guardians would be calling for if they contacted the Kalecians was an alien invasion and take-over. They believe the *guidance* The Three received is code for some sort of mind control. Driven by this irrational fear, they will stop at nothing to prevent the Guardians from being able to call the Kalecians. Again, these folks are on the fringe. Conspiracy nuts, mostly.

"And then there's the other group, which is far more dangerous—as greed often is. They know enough of the story to know that the technology in each of the parts of the Appello is highly advanced. They want these parts because they think if they can get them, they'll be able to reverse-engineer the technology and make billions of dollars. And they think Guardians know where these parts are."

"But how does anyone but a Guardian know the story at all?" Alecin wondered.

"How does anyone learn a secret? Somebody told them."

"Who would do that?"

"It was probably unintentional. At least, I like to think it was. But whether intentionally or not, it only takes one Guardian being less than vigilant. The more of the story that gets out, the more risk every Guardian faces. You must understand, Alecin; there are people out there who would do whatever it takes to learn the identities of the Guardians because they would stop at nothing to find out where the parts of the Appello are hidden. And they have the resources and just enough knowledge to be dangerous. Luckily, I've never come across them, and I hope never to do so. But I know they are out there. That's why I take precautions. I'm vigilant.

"Before our meeting yesterday, I had a security team come in. They swept this room for any kind of bug and installed jammers or something; I'm not sure. But they assured me that no one would be able to hear anything we said in this room. I don't have any computers in here with audio or video capabilities, nor do I have any cell phones. I haven't allowed in anything that would allow anyone to listen. Jim must have thought I was just being a crazy old man, but bless his heart, he went along with it."

"Is that why you said I had to leave my cell phone in my car or in my room? Why I couldn't bring it in here?"

"Exactly."

"What about the cell phone you use to contact Jim? I've seen you use it in here."

"I very well couldn't just ring a bell for him, could I? It's not really a phone at all, actually. It can only be used for sending text messages. That's all. It has no audio capabilities at all. And its range is pretty much just this house."

"Where did you even get something like that?"

"That nice young man who swept for bugs—he told me where to find one. Apparently, they sell them on Amazon. Prime shipping and everything."

He looked her in the eye, and his tone became very somber. "Understand this," he said. "I will say again; there are some out there that will stop at nothing to uncover the identity of the Guardians and to find those parts. Theft, kidnapping, murder . . . nothing is beyond them. They see Guardians as nothing more than obstacles standing between them and billions of dollars. They care nothing for the fate of humanity. They care only for themselves. That is why *you* must be vigilant. If anyone discovers you're a Guardian, not only will your life be in danger, but the lives of everyone you love will be in danger."

"So, I can never tell anyone? Grandma never knew? Dad?"

"No one. I have never uttered a word about this since the day my father passed it to me. It wasn't worth the risk. And you shouldn't either. Ever. Trust no one." Neil let the silence hang in the air. "No. One. Ever."

"Okay. Well, at least I have you to talk to about this stuff, right?"

"No. After today, we will never speak of this again. The risk is just too great."

"Whoa. This is intense. The fate of humanity—yeah, I knew I'd be responsible for that, but it seems kinda surreal, you know? But Mom and Dad, you, Beth, Luke . . . that hits close to home. I mean, if I screw up, they could die. How do you deal with something like that?"

"I remind myself what's at stake. Why I'm doing it. And again, I am vigilant. Always. I never let my guard down. Even if it means Jim will think I've gone a little crazy," he said, smiling.

CHAPTER 7

H er grandfather had wanted to take a nap. He tired so easily these days. This gave Alecin a welcome chance to get in a swim and clear her head. Alecin saw through the windows of the pool house that it was raining outside. A big thunderstorm, it looked like. Alecin had always loved thunderstorms.

After her swim, Alecin moved from the pool to the hot tub. Sitting in the warm water with the jets going, watching the thunderstorm, Alecin thought about the tremendous gift that her family had been given. Not just the extra oomph in her DNA but the chance to really do something to make a difference. So many people live their lives never knowing if they made a difference. But if she became a Guardian, she would be safeguarding the fate of all of humanity. What more of a difference could she make than that? Even if no one ever knew, she would make a difference. She would have a purpose. Didn't that outweigh the danger? Didn't that outweigh all of the negatives?

Alecin thought of her grandmother. She remembered gardening with her one time and not being very happy about it.

At one point, her grandmother had had enough of her bad attitude and had gotten two large glasses of cold lemonade, then sat with Alecin in the rocking chairs on the big wraparound porch. Her grandmother told her that she enjoyed caring for her garden because "when you care and nurture a plant or a flower and let it reach its full potential, it becomes something beautiful, and the world could always use just a little more beauty."

"But, Grandma," Alecin had complained, "I don't like getting all that dirt on me."

"Alecin, dear," her grandmother had replied in her no-nonsense tone that was well known to every member of her family, "a little dirt never hurt anyone."

Being a Guardian of humanity? That certainly was doing something to bring more beauty to the world. And if it was dangerous, well, a little dirt never hurt anyone. Well, she *could* get hurt, obviously. But Alecin thought her grandmother's point was that there was always a cost to bringing beauty into the world, but that didn't mean it wasn't worth it. Wasn't protecting humanity worth the danger? For her, Alecin concluded, it certainly was.

Before she went downstairs after her swim, Alecin once again invaded her stash of goodies. She was ready to take on the fate of humanity, but first, she needed chocolate. She found a milk chocolate Godiva bunny that she had left over from Easter, which she had stuffed in her overnight bag. Ruthlessly, she ate the bunny's ears and then his head. She even bit off his little bunny tail. *What,* she wondered as she savored bunny tail, *did the world do before chocolate?*

Having gotten her chocolate fix, Alecin saved the bunny from further decimation by wrapping it back in its gold foil. She then grabbed her water bottle—her only defense against that horrid tea—and went downstairs to continue her crash course in everything she didn't know that she would need to know to save the world. Possibly. Someday. But hopefully not.

Walking into the study, Alecin found her grandfather much as she had this morning. Sitting in his chair, Scout at his feet, a low fire in the fireplace, and a pot of that horrid tea on the table. Seeing it, Alecin was extremely grateful she had remembered her water bottle.

"Did you have a nice swim?" her grandfather asked as she sat down.

"I did. I hung out in the spa and watched the thunderstorm for a while. I've always loved a good thunderstorm."

"I know. Your brother and sister were always scared of the lightning and thunder, but you were fascinated. During thunderstorms, it was all we could do to stop you from running outside and possibly getting struck by lightning."

"I remember that. It wasn't that I wanted to be out in the lightning. I just loved to feel the rain on my face." She paused, thinking back. "Anyway," she said, returning to the present, "I realized something while I was sitting there."

"What's that?"

"That being a Guardian means being able to make a difference in the world in the most meaningful way possible. It means having a purpose—knowing that my life means something. Some people search their whole lives for that. I know I've been searching for it. It seems cowardly to reject it now that I've finally found it. Having a purpose like that? It's worth the danger. It's worth the risk."

"Your many-great-grandfather would be so proud of you." He beamed. "I know *I* am. I just knew you were the one."

"And really, it's only dangerous if I screw up, right? So, I just need to not screw up."

"And you won't. I have faith in you."

"I know. And that helps more than you know."

"I hope so." He paused. "Now, let's get on with it. Where were we?"

"You were telling me to be vigilant, or everyone will die."

"I don't think I said it quite like that. But yes, I agree; that was the gist. Now, what's left to go over? What questions do you have?"

"You still haven't told me how Guardians communicate with each other, how we know when there's been a vote, what we do if the vote is unanimous—"

"I didn't realize we had such a long list remaining," her grandfather interrupted. "Let's take your first question first. How do Guardians communicate? Now, we discussed how the Kalecians established the US postal system, or at least it was established while the Kalecians were here guiding humanity, remember?"

"Yes. And then I think you went off on a tangent about Ben Franklin."

"And what an interesting tangent it was," he proclaimed. "But back to the topic at hand. So, all they had was the postal system. That's all they had to use."

"Why didn't the Kalecians just leave them something? Surely they had communication systems more advanced on Kalec than the US postal system."

"Yes. But you forget, as your many-times-great-grandfather himself once said: 'The passions of man will not conform to the dictates of reason and justice without constraint.'"

Sometimes, Alecin thought, her grandfather just seemed to throw out random historical quotes the way she threw out random movie quotes. They didn't seem to have anything to do with the conversation. She tried to think of what her grandfather could be trying to say.

"Soooo giving Guardians Kalecian technology would present too tempting a target for the passions of man? The constraint on greed is using the mail system to communicate instead of a highly advanced and possibly extremely monetarily valuable system? An envelope doesn't tempt the greedy?"

"Exactly." He beamed at her. "Developing a mail system was a much better option than just handing twelve people Kalecian technology in 1797 and hoping their fellow man wouldn't be greedy."

"Okay. So, how do Guardians use the mail system to communicate?"

"They don't."

"But you just said . . ."

"I said the original twelve Guardians used the mail system, and they did. Every Guardian of every generation used the mail system until something better came along. With the speed and security of email advancing as it has, using old-fashioned mail became more dangerous. So, about twenty years ago, a message was sent out, and all Guardians were asked if they consented to switch from regular mail to email. And everyone agreed. So, the switch was made."

"So, Guardians use email?"

"Yes."

"Good. Today that's a lot better than the US postal system. Okay. Now, how do they use email? Who communicates with whom?"

"The way it works is the same way it worked when they used regular mail. Every Guardian connects with two other Guardians, and that's it. Every Guardian has one Guardian that sends emails to her, and she has one Guardian to whom she sends emails. Guardians don't know the identity of those to whom they're sending emails or from whom they're receiving them. But that forms a loop so that all the Guardians can communicate with each other. But this way, if any Guardian was ever compromised, that could only possibly lead to one, maybe two other Guardians. No Guardian would ever know more than that."

"Has that ever happened? That a Guardian has been compromised by one of these two groups trying to determine the identity of Guardians?"

"Not to my knowledge. The system has worked well at keeping the identity of Guardians concealed. It may seem like overkill, but with the fate of humanity at stake, *nothing* is overkill. The Kalecians tried to anticipate and account for every contingency so that humankind would have the best chance of saving itself by being able to reach out to them when help was needed.

"So, for two hundred-plus years, each Guardian would have two addresses: one for the Guardian who communicated with him and another for the Guardian with whom he communicated. Those used to be actual addresses, though I would guess that all Guardians used post office boxes rather than their home addresses. Now they're email addresses. Email addresses that do not contain any information that would allow someone to determine the identity of the owner."

"Why would a Guardian need the address of the one communicating with her? Doesn't she just *get* mail from him?"

"Well, it was expected that people would move about. And that addresses may change when Guardianship changes. So, there had to be a way to let the Guardian who communicates with you know about the change. The one and only thing ever sent to the Guardian who emails you is basically a change of address."

"And to the Guardian with whom you communicate, what do you send?"

"Everything else."

"What if the emails are hacked?"

"Emails are to be encrypted, of course, but when the fate of humanity is at stake, belt and suspenders are used, Alecin. Always use a belt and suspenders. Mail wasn't written in plain English, and neither are emails. We use a cipher."

"What kind of cipher?"

"It's a simple but effective one. Rather than using words, you communicate using the line and word position, then the letter, using a known document. Like, if the code was 777, you would go to the seventh line of the known or referenced document, then to the seventh word, and then the seventh letter in that word."

"Does every Guardian use the same reference document?"

"The sender and receiver do, of course. That's the only way

to translate the message. But it's not always the same one for every message or even for every Guardian. It changes."

"So, which reference documents do Guardians use?"

"The known documents used to code Guardian communications are the *Constitution*—with the *Bill of Rights* included but not any of the other amendments—the *Declaration of Independence*, and the *Federalist Papers*."

"With so many possible documents, how does the receiver know which known document to use to decipher the message?"

"Well, if it's the *Constitution*, the subject line of the email will contain the letter C but not the letters D or F. If it's the *Declaration of Independence*, the subject line will contain the letter D but not the letters C or F, and so on."

"But there are numerous essays that make up *The Federalist Papers*."

"For *The Federalist Papers*, the one used depends on how many Fs are in the subject line. For Federalist One, there's one F. For Federalist Two, there are two F's. I recommend you don't try to use above Federalist Five. It gets challenging to work more than five Fs into a relatively normal-sounding subject line.

"Also, except for changes of address, of course, it's important that every Guardian get every message. So, the Guardian who originates the message will sign it "One." The next Guardian will sign it "Two," and so on. When the Guardian who originated the message gets it returned, because of the loop, it should be signed "Twelve." Then, that Guardian knows that all the other Guardians received the message."

"Okay. So, I'll need to have copies of all these documents?"

"Don't you already?" Neil teased.

"Of course," Alecin said in her obviously lying voice.

"Well, you can get them. These days they're on the internet, of course, but the cipher is tuned to the originals, so you'll need actual copies of the originals."

"Sure, sure, I'll just order those off Amazon," Alecin said sarcastically.

"Or," Neil said, drawing out the 'r,' "you could just look in that box I showed you."

"What?" Alecin exclaimed. "Really?" She ran over and grabbed the box from the shelf where it had been returned after the last time her grandfather had pulled it out.

She put the box on the table and looked at Neil expectantly.

"What are you looking at *me* for? It's *your* box."

"Oh yeah," Alecin said, eyes lighting up.

Taking a deep breath, she waved her hand over the box. Part of her believed that the box might find her unworthy and not open. Though her grandfather had never said that would happen, she wondered. But the box opened, or rather, the top of it disappeared.

Alecin lifted two envelopes from the box. One said, "send," and the other said, "receive." She put those aside for now. Then, she pulled out a stack of papers. These papers appeared to be original copies of the *Constitution*, the *Declaration of Independence*, and *The Federalist Papers*. She couldn't believe she was holding a copy of the *Declaration of Independence* that had been written in Jefferson's own hand. She said as much to her grandfather.

"Well . . . not so much, actually," he said.

"What? How can that be? I'm no expert, but these look like pretty original copies to me."

"Well, they are. It's just that . . . well, the Kalecians took all the originals and just *reproduced* copies for all the Guardians. The copies were exactly like the originals in every way. If you took this *Constitution* to an expert, they would say it's the original. But don't do that," he added in a cautionary tone. "These documents, as amazing as they are, only come out of the box when you are composing or reading a Guardian message."

"Of course. But how are these in such good condition? I saw *National Treasure*. They have a whole room controlling temperature and humidity, and some other stuff I don't remember, to keep the *Declaration* in good condition. This is just a box."

"I've noticed their condition too. The original Guardians didn't think much about document preservation. I mean, they had the *Declaration of Independence* in a glass box with the sun bearing down on it every day for years. The original Guardians didn't think to ask about preserving the documents either, so the secret of the documents' 'preservation' "—he air quoted the word—"hasn't been passed down. I think either the box keeps them in good condition, or the Kalecians did something when they made the copies to keep them in good condition. I tend to think it's the box. I always feel like if I keep the documents out of the box too long, they'll just disintegrate into a pile of dust. I don't know if that will happen. I've never tested it, of course. But I try not to keep them out too long."

"Okay, I get it." With no small measure of regret, Alecin returned the documents to their place in the box. As she put them away, she asked, "Grandpa, it doesn't seem like these papers should fit in this box, but when I put them in, they fit just fine."

"It's bigger on the inside."

"Whoa! Another *Doctor Who* reference? I have to write this down. This is a momentous occasion."

"What?" Neil asked, confused.

"It's bigger on the inside. That's from *Doctor Who*. I thought you said you had watched it."

"I have, but I still have no idea what you're talking about."

"But how," Alecin stammered. "It's like in every episode. The police call box . . . the Tardis . . . it's bigger on the inside."

"Gotcha," Neil said, laughing. Alecin attempted to glare but couldn't hide a smile.

"It's like the Tardis," he continued, "or that carpet bag out of which Mary Poppins pulls a lamp and mirror and everything else. I don't know. I agree that it doesn't look like they should fit. But they do. I've tried to fill the box a couple of times, just as an experiment. But everything just always seems to fit, with room to spare. I've decided just to accept what is."

"That's really cool," Alecin said as she put the two envelopes back in and closed the box. "So, those envelopes inside the box? The 'send' one is the address of the Guardian to whom I send everything, and the 'receive' one is the address of the Guardian from whom I get emails, I'm guessing?"

"Yes."

"Okay. So, the big question. What if the time comes? What if a Guardian thinks it's time to call the Kalecians? What happens?"

"If a Guardian decides that humanity has lost its way so much that it needs the Kalecians to help, that Guardian sends—just to the Guardian to whom he usually sends emails—an email that says: 'It is time.' Encrypted and in a cipher, of course. That Guardian will then send on a message that says, 'It is time. It is time.' if they agree that the time has come, or if they don't agree, the message says, 'It is time. It is not time.' If you ever need to send that message, do not accidentally leave out the 'not.' That's an extremely important 'not.' "

"If a Guardian decides that the time hasn't come, does the message end there because it has to be unanimous, so there's no point in completing the loop and getting everyone's vote?"

"No. Anytime a vote is initiated, all twelve have to vote. Eventually—hopefully after not too long—the Guardian who initiated the vote will get an email that has all twelve votes. Then, that Guardian will send out an email with the vote compilation that basically says, 'Four for *it is time* and eight for *it is not time*,' or whatever the vote is. Then, in most cases, unless the vote is unanimous, nothing further happens."

"I guess that makes sense. I'm sure all the Guardians want to know where the other Guardians stand."

"That, and notice how I said in *most* cases?"

"I *did* notice that, yes."

"Remember how I said that Guardians will never meet and never know each other?"

"Yes. I remember that quite clearly. Something about the fate of all of humanity depending on it."

"That's only mostly true. The Kalecians didn't want to risk that one idiot—in your words—could bind all of humanity to destruction. So, if eleven vote that it's time, and one votes it is not, then any of the Guardians who voted that it's time can challenge the Guardian who voted it was not time. If that happens, arrangements are made, through the established email system, for just those two Guardians to meet in order to discuss the situation and their votes."

"How much time do they get to discuss it?"

"Until they agree. Remember how I explained that Kalecians have no conflict because they understand there is one truth, and if Kalecians disagree, then they both believe that one knows the truth and the other is mistaken about the truth. So, they talk or communicate however they do, until they agree on what the truth is. Kalecians thought that two Guardians of humanity should be able to talk it out and reach an agreement. If they agree that it's time, then things move forward. If they agree that it's not time, then the challenging Guardian lets the other Guardians know what happened, and nothing more occurs."

"What happens if more than one Guardian challenges an 'it's-not-time vote'?"

"Then, it's whoever challenged first. That's why when you issue a challenge, you must indicate in your email the date and time that you issued your challenge. So that everyone will know who first issued the challenge."

"So, I think I know the answer, but have the Guardians ever called the Kalecians before? Has there ever been a unanimous vote?"

"No."

"But it seems like humanity has taken a lot of wrong turns since the Kalecians left. What about during the Civil War? I mean, that war seemed like it would split the country and destroy the model for humanity that the Kalecians had wanted."

"There were some who believed it was time. That's what has

been passed down to me. But others felt it was too soon. They thought that this was something humanity would have to work out for itself. And they had faith that it would."

"What about during World War II? I mean, concentration camps? That was the ultimate evil human beings could inflict upon each other—trying to wipe out an entire race . . . and in such a cruel way."

"Again, there were some. But the United States was united against a common enemy during that war. As horrible as it was, it was probably actually a good thing for the future of the United States to have it united against tyranny like it was. I mean, there's a reason the Americans who fought in that war are called the greatest generation. But . . ." He paused. "That doesn't mean that we didn't help," he said cryptically.

"What do you mean by that?"

"Well, you know how when you're working somewhere, you may leave behind a pen or a paperclip or something?"

"Yes." She drew out the word, looking at him with suspicion. "What did you do?"

"Not me, personally. But the Guardian from our line—he did agree with the action taken, and the story was passed down to me . . . and now to *you.*"

"What story?"

"Well, the Kalecians accidentally left behind a few little things when they left. And what were The Three supposed to do when they discovered these little things that had been left behind? It's not like they could call them and say, 'hey, you forgot your pen.' So, each of The Three kept a few of the things the Kalecians had left behind. They didn't want them falling into the wrong hands, and they had no idea how to destroy these things."

"Do we have something that belonged to the Kalecians?"

"Yes, we do," he smiled.

"What? What do we have?"

"Open the box again, and I'll show you."

Alecin opened the box.

"Look in the upper right corner," Neil instructed. Alecin looked, and she saw two cubes. They looked like dice, but they were absolutely clear. Alecin picked one up and was surprised at how heavy it was. She looked through it. It played with the light as a diamond would, but it was even more impressive and beautiful.

"What are they?" Alecin asked, awestruck.

"I don't know."

"What do they do?"

"No idea."

"So, you just have these extraterrestrial cubes sitting in a box, and you have no idea what they do?"

"Well, technically, *you* have these extraterrestrial cubes sitting in a box, and *you* have no idea what they do."

He has me there, Alecin thought. She looked at the cubes a little longer, seeing if she could discern some purpose to them. She put one to her ear to see if it made any noise. It did not. She threw one up in the air. It just fell back down. Finally, she shrugged and gave up. She had no idea what they did. She put them back in the box and closed it. "But what do these cubes have to do with World War II?" Alecin wondered.

"Well, one of the other Guardians had something from the Kalecians that may or may not have ended up in the hands of Oppenheimer."

"The creator of the atomic bomb?"

"Yes. And that something may or may not have pointed Oppenheimer in the direction that led to the invention of the atomic bomb."

"Why would a Guardian do that? I thought the Kalecians were all about peace."

" 'Peace or war will not always be left to our option,' " Neil said, quoting Alexander Hamilton. "Even those who desire peace 'cannot count upon the moderation, or hope to extinguish the ambition of others.' It's naive to think that war isn't sometimes necessary for peace, Alecin, and you're not naive. World War

II was a just and necessary war. It had to be fought. You and I both know that. But with the bomb, it didn't have to cost as many lives. The Guardian acted for the same reason the United States decided to use the atomic bomb. World War II had cost humanity nearly fifty million lives. The bomb brought an end to the war, it restored peace, and it saved millions of lives."

"You're right. Alexander was right. I spoke without thinking. I apologize."

"Never speak without thinking," Neil chastised. "It's better for people to think you are a fool than to open your mouth and prove them right." That was one of her grandfather's favorite quotes. He had said it countless times while she was growing up, thankfully not always directed at her. She wasn't even sure who had originally said it. To her, the quote belonged to her grandfather, and it always would.

"So," Alecin said after a pause that would have been awkward with anyone else, "how do I become a Guardian?"

"Before we get to that," Neil said, "there's another thing you need to know." He hesitated. He would have preferred that this topic wouldn't be necessary, but it was. "There may come a time," he began, "when you will need to send or receive a different kind of email. The Guardians have devised a warning system to alert other Guardians if and when there's a threat. If you receive an email with 'Yellow' in the subject line and nothing else, it means to be aware because someone is looking for you, but they don't yet know who you are. You need to be even more vigilant. If you receive an email with 'Red' in the subject line and nothing else, it means drop everything and run. Someone has found you and is coming to do you harm. Take these emails very seriously, Alecin. Guardians do not send them without good reason." He paused to let her think about what he had said. "I have never received either of those kinds of emails," he continued, "and I hope you never do. But you should be aware of them.

"Now, the first thing I need you to do so that you can become a Guardian is to set up an encrypted email account. I can help you do that. You will use this account for Guardian communications only. You will never tell anyone this email address or your password. You should change your password every sixty days. If you need to write your password down, you can do that, but the paper with the password on it has to be kept in the box. On the encrypted laptop I use, a thumbprint is also required to access my Guardian email. That young security man told me that they have newer models that require a thumbprint *and* a retinal scan. I recommend that you get one of those. You should keep your Guardian computer in your box. No matter what, no one can open that box but you."

"What if they threw it really hard against the wall?"

"Go ahead," Neil challenged, "try it."

Alecin picked up the box and hurled it against the wall. It simply bounced off the wall and landed intact on the floor. She tried again, throwing it harder this time, but the same thing happened.

"Put it in the fire," Neil challenged.

She did. It sat in the middle of the fire, completely untouched. It was like it was just sitting on the table.

"So, it's indestructible?" she asked.

"Well, it wouldn't do much good if it wasn't, would it?"

"What if somebody cut off my hand and tried to use it to open the box?"

"Alecin!"

"It's a valid question!"

"I don't know. Thankfully I've never had that happen, but I would guess that wouldn't work. I mean, your severed hand is going to read differently than your live hand would, wouldn't it?"

"What if I get attacked by a shark, and he eats my right hand?"

"Alecin, really."

"What have you always taught me as a lawyer? Think of every contingency and be prepared. This is something that could happen."

"I guess you're right. But maybe you just shouldn't be swimming with sharks. Try using your left hand."

She did. The box opened just fine.

"It's not like the box is reading your handprint. It's reading your *DNA*. As long as you have one remaining body part that you can wave over the box, then you can open it."

"Okay. That's good to know." She paused. "So, here's another something I've been wondering. What if a Guardian dies before calling a new one to take their place?"

"That's never happened, thankfully, but it could. If the person from whom the Guardianship was passed is still alive, Guardianship simply reverts back to him, and he lets the other Guardians know. Then, he will need to choose a new Guardian. If there's no living Guardian anywhere in that line, then it's more complicated. If a Guardian falls off the map, if he does not forward an email that should have been forwarded on for more than one week, then Plan Thirty-Three kicks in."

"Plan Thirty-Three?"

"That's what the original Guardians decided to call it. Trying to draw on the power of three, I guess."

"So, what's Plan Thirty-Three?"

"It's a little complicated, so it's written down. It's in an envelope in your box. If that ever happens, just pull out the envelope and follow the instructions."

"Can another Guardian open my box?"

"No. Remember how I said the box reads your DNA? Each box . . . serves, shall we say, one line. So, in order for a person to own a box, they have to be of the line which that box serves."

"Wow. That little box is really smart. The Kalecians really have thought of everything."

"Well, they are advanced beings. And we can learn something from them. Belt and suspenders, Alecin. Fate of humanity on the line. Nothing can be left to chance."

"Belt and suspenders, Grandpa. I know."

Alecin took a deep breath. She seemed to be doing a lot of that this weekend. "Now for the question I've been most scared to ask," she began, "and the part that most scares me and that I sincerely hope never comes. What happens if the Twelve decide that humanity has reached its darkest moment and it *is* time to call the Kalecians?"

"Ah, yes. The *raison d'être* for the Guardians. Okay. Now, *this* isn't written down in the box, so pay close attention. A vote is taken, as I told you earlier. After the last vote is received and it is unanimous, the longest-serving guardian will set a time and date for a few days later. Everyone has to acknowledge receipt of this message within twenty-four hours after it is first sent. If not, a new day and time must be set. On that designated day and at that time, every Guardian is required to open their box. At the very bottom of every Guardian's box, there is a gold envelope."

"I didn't see that."

"It kind of blends in with the bottom of the box since the bottom is also gold. But it's there, I promise. So, on that date and time, each Guardian retrieves their individual gold envelopes and opens them. That's the one and only time any Guardian is ever supposed to open that envelope. Unless there is a unanimous vote to make The Call, you must never touch that envelope. It's part of what you promise to do."

"Okay. I understand."

"That envelope contains instructions on what should be done next. Follow the instructions."

"That's it? No hint as to what these instructions will be?"

"Well, obviously, the instructions will instruct the Guardians on how to find the parts. But what those instructions are *specifically*? No one knows."

Neil paused and seemed to be thinking. Finally, he said, "I think I've told you everything you need to know. Do you have any more questions?"

"I don't think so." Alecin thought hard. "No, I think all of my questions have been answered."

"Okay then," Neil said solemnly. "Now repeat back everything I told you."

"You must be kidding!"

"I'm not. This is a vital and necessary step. I must be sure that you know and remember everything you need to know to be a Guardian. Consider it your Guardian test. You need to get 100 percent to pass. But you can take it as many times as you need to. Anything you don't remember, we'll keep going over until you *do* remember it."

At that moment, the phone on the table vibrated.

"Saved by the bell," Alecin muttered.

"Ah, you get a reprieve, it seems," Neil announced. "It's time for lunch. I think Jim made his amazing beef stew. Although these days it's more vegetable stew than beef stew."

"Somehow, Grandpa," Alecin said, "I couldn't care less about stew right now."

"Ah, you say that now," Neil smiled, "but wait until you try it. And then after lunch, I think I shall like another nap. Is that okay?"

"Take all the time you need. I'm working virtually now. I can do that here just as well as I can at home. And I checked with Mrs. Miller this morning. She and Tonks are getting along just fine. I can head home whenever."

"Splendid," Neil said with enthusiasm, "I was so worried we would run out of time."

"Nope, I'm here until we're done. Fate of humanity on the line, right?"

"Indeed," Neil replied. "Very much indeed."

CHAPTER 8

It took Alecin until the next evening—and the rest of that chocolate bunny—before she passed her Guardian test. And it was at the moment she passed the last part of her test that she became absolutely terrified.

She made up some excuse and ran up to her room. When she walked into her room, she thought, *What the hell am I doing?* She picked up a bag of Peanut Butter M&M's—the best of all M&M's, in her opinion—and began pacing her room, popping M&M's in her mouth every few seconds. She wasn't even thirty years old. How the hell could she be one of twelve people in the entire world who was responsible for the fate of all of humanity? Her grandfather must be crazy. She must be crazy. Her grandfather should just wait for her dad to come back. Or ask her uncle. Or her aunt. There had to be somebody more qualified than she was. She grabbed the door, intending to go down and tell her grandfather just that. Then, she stopped.

There was nobody she respected more than her grandfather. There was nobody whose judgment she trusted more. And he thought she could do it. He had selected *her*. Out of everyone he could have chosen, he had chosen *her*. He knew more about being a Guardian than she did. If he thought she could do it, who was she to argue with him? Besides, what were the chances that humanity would really go that far off the rails while she was Guardian? In almost 250 years, no Guardians had ever called the Kalecians. Why should her time as a Guardian be any different? Other than judging the fate of humanity, being a Guardian just sounded like having fun with some really amazing historical documents, doing ciphers and stuff.

Yes, it would be hard not to tell anyone. She had already lied to her friend Talia when she had canceled their plans they had had for this weekend. She had said that her grandfather was sick and needed her help, and that's why she was up there. Which technically wasn't a lie—her lawyer mind reasoned—her grandfather *was* actually sick, and she *was* helping him. She just wasn't helping him *because* he was sick. But lying for the sake of humanity—and to protect her friends and family—that seemed to fall on the moral side of the ledger.

I can do this, she told herself. She held a Top Secret Clearance. The military thought she could keep secrets. And she *could*. She had never let a classified document end up somewhere it wasn't supposed to be or be seen by somebody who wasn't supposed to see it. Did that mean she could be trusted with a secret on which the fate of humanity depended? Not necessarily. There were a lot of people she knew with Top Secret Clearance, but she wouldn't trust them any further than she could throw them.

Yet, her grandfather trusted *her*, she reminded herself. And she trusted herself. She stopped. *Didn't* she? Alecin thought for a moment, taking another handful of M&M's and popping them into her mouth. Trusting her not to eat peanut butter M&M's when they were right there? No, she couldn't be trusted with *that*. But this, she thought—this was something with which she *could* be trusted. She knew that. She truly believed that.

So, Alecin put down the M&M's, pulled on her metaphorical big-girl panties, and went downstairs to become a Guardian.

★ ★ ★

When she entered the study, it struck Alecin that her grand-father looked just like always, sitting in his chair in front of the fireplace, Scout at his feet. She wasn't sure what she expected, but she just thought he'd be different, somehow. Then, she looked more closely. He *did* look different. He looked at peace. He looked as if a tremendous burden had been lifted from his shoulders. Alecin felt warm and proud that she had done that for him.

"Okay, Grandpa," she said, walking to him. "I am ready." She took a deep breath. "What do I need to do? Promise my firstborn child? Make a blood oath? Pinky swear?"

"What's a pinky swear?"

"It's when you . . . never mind. Okay. So, what do I need to do?"

Neil came over and stood right in front of her. He placed his hands on her shoulders and looked her in the eyes. "Are you absolutely positive that this is something you want to do?"

"I am. And I don't just say that haphazardly. I have given this a tremendous amount of thought. I just had a minor panic at-tack upstairs. But I can do this. You chose well," she said with conviction.

"I know I did. Okay, That's it. You're a Guardian. Congratula-tions."

"That's it?!"

Neil smiled and dropped his hands. "No, it's not it. I was just messing with you. You still looked so tense. I wanted you to relax a bit."

"Thanks. I appreciate it," she said sarcastically. "Now, seri-ously, what do I need to do?"

"You need to take an oath. I have always taught you— and everyone in this family—that when you give your word, you *keep* it. This is part of the reason why. When you take the oath to become a Guardian, you give your word that you will perform the duties of a Guardian to the best of your ability. I know that you'll keep your word. You will have to. The penalty for betraying your oath is death."

"Death? Really?"

"Yes. But betrayal here is the same as in the *Constitution*. It requires you to work against the Guardians or aid the enemies of the Guardians. And it requires accusation by two Guardians. But yes, for any Guardian who betrays their oath, the penalty is death. A Guardian who betrays their oath threatens the death of all of humanity by their betrayal. Death is what they deserve."

"Well, when you explain it that way. Makes sense."

He paused. "Now, we will try to give this ceremony the importance it deserves, but necessarily there cannot be a lot of pomp and circumstance. It's just the two of us." He paused and called Scout over. "Now you sit there, Scout," he told her, pointing, "and try to look serious. You're our audience."

Scout sat and seemed to look as serious as she could manage.

"Okay," Neil took a deep breath. He had not expected the moment to feel so emotional and overwhelming to him. "Now," he said, clearing his throat, "it's kind of like the presidential oath. Though there are a few differences, obviously. The words to the oath are another one of those things that are written down and kept in your box."

"Got it."

"Okay. Now raise your right hand."

They both raised their right hands. Neil held out the box in his left hand. "Now, put your left hand on the box."

Alecin did so.

"We're ready to begin." Neil cleared his throat again. "I'll state the oath, and then you just repeat after me." Neil began. "I, state your name."

"I, Alecin Kristina Hamilton," Alecin repeated.

The oath continued. Alecin solemnly swore that she would "faithfully execute the duties of Guardian and that she would, to the best of her ability, preserve, protect, and defend the *Constitution of the United States*, the secret of the Kalecians, and the fate of humanity." And that she "took this obligation freely, without any mental reservation"—she hesitated slightly on that one—"or purpose of evasion."

Her grandfather hugged her. Scout barked. And it was done.

"This calls for a toast," Neil declared.

Alecin was almost as shocked as she had been when he told her The Three had been abducted by aliens. If her grandfather was offering her alcohol, then obviously, the Kalecians had returned and abducted her real grandfather, replacing him with this phony.

"I had Jim bring us a pot of his hot chocolate with whipped cream," he said, smiling at Alecin, "just for the occasion."

Alecin did a mental forehead swipe. No alien abduction. A toast with hot chocolate made so much more sense than alien abduction. She figured she just had aliens on her brain—which was understandable, given the circumstances.

After preparing their cups of chocolate, they held them up. "To my granddaughter Alecin. May her vision be clear, her judgment be true, and her duty be done."

They drank.

"Hold on. I have one for you too. Hold your cup back up." They lifted their cups again. Alecin looked at her grandfather. "To my grandfather: Thank you for all that I have been given this day."

"Hear, hear," Neil cheered, and they drank again.

Neil then looked at Scout. "Sorry, girl. No hot chocolate for you. But you should get something for being a good audience." He went and grabbed an Oreo from his secret stash. "Dogs can have Oreos, right?" he asked Alecin.

"How should I know? I have a cat. And *somebody* took my phone, so it's not like I can look it up."

"Oh well. You're living on the edge, Scout," he told her, tossing her the cookie. Scout didn't seem to mind living dangerously and ate the cookie happily.

"Well," Neil said, a bit forlorn. "That's it."

"It's late," Alecin said gently. She recognized that this was hard for him. "I should get on the road."

"Yes, yes. Well, you have your encrypted email address that you set up. As soon as you get home, you'll need to let the other Guardians know I have passed Guardianship to a new Guardian. You got the box?"

"Yes. It's in my bag."

"Well, here," he said, handing her a slip of paper. "Here's that copy of the oath. Put it in the box before you get on the road."

"I will," Alecin promised. "Don't worry, Grandpa. You've taught this Padawan well."

"I get that one!" he said excitedly, pointing at her. "*Star Wars*, right?"

"Got it in one," she smiled.

"So, I'll send you the contact information for those security people. Call them for everything you need."

"Thank you."

"Vigilance, Alecin," Neil reminded her.

"Belt and suspenders, Grandpa," she assured him. "Fate of humanity on the line."

"Okay." He nodded and looked around as if he had forgotten something. "I guess you're ready," he said, then sighed.

"If by ready you mean I feel like I've been thrown into the deep end when I can't even swim, and that the deep end has sharks, lots of man-eating ones, then yes. I'm ready."

"Alecin, you'll be fine," he assured her. "But I do really wish we could talk about this again. I want to know how everything is going for you. That you are, in fact, alright."

"Well, here, let's do this. Next time I see you, if things are going well, I'll quote *Star Trek*. And if it's going not so well, I'll quote *Star Wars*."

"Now, how am I supposed to remember the difference between *Star Trek* and *Star Wars*?"

"They are two totally different... never mind. How about this instead? If things aren't going so well, I'll say something about needing a sonic screwdriver, like the one from Doctor Who. And if I don't say anything about a sonic screwdriver, you will know that I'm okay."

"Okay. That sounds good. Thank you. You remember—"

"Grandpa," Alecin interrupted gently, "you're stalling."

"I know, I know. I was so worried about you being ready for this, I didn't even consider how hard it would be for me. A lot harder than I expected," he said, his voice breaking.

Alecin hugged him. "It'll be okay. I'll be ok. I promise."

"Okay. Well, you better just go before I think of something else."

"Goodbye, Grandpa. Thanks for everything. Really. It's a weekend I'll never forget."

Alecin looked back at him when she got to the door. He was seated in his chair, watching the fire, Scout at his feet. "Grandpa," she called out.

"Yes," he said, turning.

"One more thing. I love you lots."

He smiled. "I love you more."

Alecin walked out of the room. When she had shut the door behind her, she took a second to look at the door. It was hard to believe that only four short days ago, she had walked in believing that Earth was the only planet in the universe with sentient life, that there was no such thing as aliens, and that her life would never be extraordinary. Now she was the Guardian of an alien secret on which the fate of humanity relied. She felt overwhelmed.

"I'll make you proud, Grandpa," she said quietly to the door, tears streaming down her cheeks. "I promise."

CHAPTER 9

Four years later

For at least the tenth time that week, Alecin sat wondering how people could possibly be just so unbelievably stupid.

Six months before, she and one of her best friends, April, had decided to join forces and open their own law practice. They had decided to focus their practice on constitutional rights. They wanted to bring suit against the government when it violated people's constitutional rights; these kinds of cases were often called *1983 suits* based on the part of the US code that provided a cause of action for the violation of constitutional rights. Both she and April had a deep love and admiration for the *Constitution*, although only Alecin knew the true story of how that remarkable and extraordinary document had come to be. So, they had wanted to do what they could to protect it. It was their dream job. It was the reason they had gone to law school in the first place.

Except people are ruining my dream, Alecin thought angrily, *by just being so annoyingly stupid.* For the third time that day—

and she wasn't sure how many times since she and April had opened their doors—a potential client had called, claiming that his constitutional rights had been violated. Except they *hadn't* been. At all. Not even close.

Nearly everyone that called their office seemed to have a deeply flawed understanding of the *Constitution*. She understood that over the years, either dishonest or ignorant justices had "expanded" what the *Constitution* actually said—asserting that they weren't actually bound by the words in the *Constitution. You know*, Alecin thought bitterly, *those things that had actually survived the gauntlet of democracy*. Instead, "Liberal" justices had claimed that the *Constitution* was a "living" document that could change based on nothing more than five justices' opinion of society's "evolving standards of decency."

It was like they didn't even understand how democracy actually worked—or even basic biology if they thought documents could be alive. But even the most dishonest justices hadn't expanded the *Constitution* to say what it seemed the average American believed it said. The *Constitution*, Alecin fumed, did not say, "No one, whether government or a private citizen, shall ever do anything you do not like or say anything with which you disagree." If it did, Alecin continued her internal rant, no one in their right mind would ever have voted to be bound by it. That would be insane. No society could survive under such a constitution. But that didn't seem to stop a terrifyingly large number of Americans from apparently believing that the *Constitution* meant just that.

Alecin banged her head softly against her desk. She was just so frustrated with and disappointed in her fellow Americans. She pictured the scene from the movie *Liar Liar* where the criminal calls asking for legal advice, and Jim Carrey's character picks up the phone and screams, "STOP BREAKING THE LAW!" She imagined yelling at every potential client that called, claiming that the latest thing that angered or annoyed them was unconstitutional: THAT IS NOT UNCONSTITUTIONAL!

April walked into Alecin's office to see her law partner banging her head on her desk. April was slightly taller than Alecin and with a slimmer build. Her blond hair fell in waves to just below her shoulders. Alecin was jealous of the fact that April always seemed to have just the right amount of sun-kissed tan. April was from Georgia and had all the (what Alecin called) "Southernness" of her home state. Many opposing counsels had taken April's kind demeanor and Southern drawl to mean that April was easy prey. They had quickly learned their error. Alecin had seen April make opposing counsels crumble just by subjecting them to the penetrating glare of her gold-flecked green eyes.

At the moment, those eyes sparkled with amusement at Alecin's frustration. "*Another* one?" April asked.

"How," Alecin groaned, "is it possible for so many people to misunderstand their government so badly?"

"Because they stopped teaching civics in public schools?" April suggested in her overly helpful voice.

Alecin brought her head up and glared. Not at April. But at whatever imaginary person had decided that democracy didn't actually require its citizens to understand their own government. George Washington had once said, "A primary object should be the education of our youth in the science of government. In a republic, what species of knowledge can be equally important? And what duty more pressing than communicating it to those who are to be the future guardians of the liberties of the country?" *What moron*, Alecin thought, *was so arrogant as to believe they understood America's needs better than its first president and one of its Founding Fathers?*

"Someday," Alecin promised darkly, "I'm going to hack every television, tablet, and computer in America and make people watch School House Rock for twenty-four hours straight. And every other episode is going to be that one with the song about a bill sitting there on Capitol Hill."

"What does a bill sitting there on Capitol Hill have to do with the *Constitution*?" April asked.

"Nothing," Alecin answered. "It's just a really catchy song. Admit it. You're singing it in your head right now."

"Maybe," April said, smiling.

"So, Duckie, do you agree with me yet?" April asked, taking a seat in Alecin's visitor's chair. April had given Alecin the nickname Duckie in law school. One time, she and April had been studying for finals when April had commented that Alecin was like a duck; she may be paddling like hell under the water, but on the surface, she was always calm, cool, and collected. Secretly, Alecin liked the nickname, as long as April was the only one who ever used it.

Several months ago, April had lobbied to have their office manager, Jarrilyn, screen calls from potential clients. Alecin had resisted. She thought that without any legal background, Jarrilyn wouldn't be able to distinguish between calls that involved an actual constitutional violation and those that did not. *But while distinguishing between different shades of gray may be difficult*, Alecin thought, *telling the difference between black and white is not.*

"Yes. You win," Alecin conceded. "My faith in my fellow Americans was greatly misplaced. There are very few gray calls—where reasonable minds could mistake whether a constitutional violation existed—and so, so many black calls, where it is clear that there was no possible constitutional violation. Have Jarrilyn start screening all incoming calls from potential clients, but make sure she still sends all gray calls on to one of us. If she has any doubt, have her run it by one of us. I don't want to miss any potential clients."

"You got it," April said. "I just came in to let you know I was heading out. You got any plans this weekend?"

"It's the Sunday of the month for dinner with the family. Other than that, I was just going to try to catch up on some work."

"Alecin," April began, "and I say this with love"—April placed her right hand on her heart—"but you need to get a life. Why don't you let me fix you up? Evan has a lot of friends, and there are quite a few that I think you would really like. We could do it tomorrow night. We could go to the place next to the place, with the thing."

Alecin smiled. It may have surprised an outside observer to learn that Alecin knew precisely what place April was referring to, but Alecin and April knew each other so well that they could speak their own kind of code.

"This again?" Alecin asked warily. At least once a week, it seemed, April tried to fix her up with a friend of her husband, Evan, or even the guy she met getting coffee. Having been on the receiving end of many of April's match-making attempts, she knew that her friend wasn't any good at it. But what April lacked in ability, she made up for in enthusiasm. Alecin knew April did it because she was insanely happy with Evan, and she wanted Alecin to be just as happy. How could Alecin explain that be-tween trying to start a law practice and save the world, she just didn't have time for dating? But, Alecin considered further and decided that April *was* right. She needed to have a life outside of work and outside of being a Guardian. She needed to do better about being a well-adjusted person. Plus, she had dinner with her family on Sunday. If she could tell her family that she had gone on a double date with April the night before, that may cut short the let's-try-to-get-Alecin-married portion of the dinner.

"Okay," Alecin said, finally relenting over April's squeal of joy, "but I have some conditions. First, it has to be one of Evan's friends. Not some random guy you met at the dentist." Some-thing about April's smile.... "And not the dentist you met at the dentist." She saw April's quick pout. *Got it in one*, Alecin congratulated herself. "Second, no setting me up with anyone with whom you've already set me up. It didn't work then. It's not going to work now."

"No problem," April began.

"And," Alecin continued, "third, we go to the place next to the place with the thing. Now you got me hungry for their stuff."

"Agreed," April said, "but I have a condition of my own. No

doing the *thing*."

Alecin knew very well what the thing was. Alecin had an almost unreal—she had been told—talent for observation and deductive reasoning. To others, it seemed like she must be psychic or something because she knew things that they didn't think she could possibly know. Sometimes, though, she saw things that people didn't want her to see, and it made them angry—or at least uncomfortable. But Alecin looked at April with feigned innocence.

April gave Alecin "the look"—the very look that had brought many an opposing counsel to their knees. And Alecin crumbled.

"Fine," she agreed, "I promise not to do the thing."

April nodded with satisfaction. She knew that when Alecin gave her word, she kept it. It was something April loved about her—and strived to emulate.

"Okay," April said, clapping. "Seven o'clock tomorrow. At the place. Wear makeup," April instructed, "and no jeans." Then, she walked out, dancing and singing: "Going out with my bestie, cha, cha, cha, gonna be tasty, cha, cha, cha . . ."

Alecin laughed to herself. She was *not* as excited about her upcoming date as April apparently was, but she was happy that she had made her friend happy. Sighing, Alecin gathered up her things. She could finish up the rest of her work at home. Maybe she could find a good hacker when she got home? Start her plan for re-educating her fellow Americans. Cheered by the thought, she left her office, humming about a bill sitting there on Capitol Hill.

When she had been transferred to the Pentagon two years ago, Alecin had sold her house in Woodhaven—at quite a lovely profit, thank you, Grandpa—and had moved into her parent's old house in Springfield, Virginia. She had moved to the DC area soon after her grandfather's death.

Neil had received the covid vaccine when it first became available. He was at risk of dying from covid due to his health and age, and, given that at that time, the government was promising the vaccine was 99 percent effective, his doctors had strongly advised him to get "jabbed." He had had his doubts, and to this day, Alecin regretted that she hadn't tried harder to persuade him not to get the vaccine. To just wait. Just a few months later, the government realized that the covid vaccine really wasn't effective at all in preventing someone from getting covid.

When he got the first dose of the vaccine, it had made Neil very sick. But no one had been concerned. Many people got sick from the vaccine for the first couple of days. But after a couple of days, he was still sick. He went to his doctor and was diagnosed with COVID-19. His doctors assured him—and all of Alecin's family—that her grandfather could not possibly have gotten the virus from the vaccine. But her grandfather hadn't gotten covid until the day he got the vaccine. And then he just coincidentally got it on the exact same day he got the first dose of the vaccine? The odds were firmly against that. And the doctors' assurances rang hollow. The vaccine had never been tested on someone with POTS. They had no idea what the vaccine would do to someone with that illness.

Neil's body hadn't been able to fight off covid. A month after he had been diagnosed, he lay dying, alone, in his hospital room. The hospital had refused him visitors because he had covid. He had wanted to go home, but the hospital hadn't allowed that either—not because they were doing anything that could save his life. But just because he had covid.

Alecin's parents didn't play the money card very often. They strongly believed that wealth didn't and shouldn't give anyone special status. But they had played the money card then. They had given the hospital a choice: it could allow Neil to go home and receive a generous donation, or they could continue to refuse and be sued into oblivion. Neil had been discharged immediately.

Neil had died a few days later. The tender mercy in his passing had been that he had died in his own bed, with those who loved him around him.

Her parents lived in her grandparent's old house now. Her parent's old house may have been a little big for just her and Tonks, but it was close to Alecin's parents, and she wanted that. Plus, it had been her childhood home. *You never lose that sense of home in the house that you grew up in,* she thought, pulling up the drive. Every time she drove up, she felt like she was coming home. She needed that grounding.

In the two years since Alecin had left the military, the United States had grown ever more chaotic and farther away from the foundations and principles that had made it a model for all of humanity. There were many in the country that felt like the country was falling apart.

She felt it too, but she thought she felt it more keenly than others because she was a Guardian. She felt a duty to be constantly informed of . . . everything. She had become a news junkie. She watched and read everything she thought might help her determine the point where humanity had gone so far awry that The Call had to be made. Every day, she felt like that day was getting closer.

When she walked in her front door, Tonks was there to greet her, like always.

"Well, Tonks, it looks like it's just you, me, and trying to save the world again tonight." Alecin removed the takeout she had picked up on the way home from its bag, put it on a plate, and considered dinner done.

She put some kibble down for Tonks, who turned her nose up at it. "I wouldn't eat that stuff either," Alecin commiserated. "Come on," she told Tonks, "I'll share."

Tonks happily followed her into what Alecin's parents had called the TV room. Like almost every other night, she and Tonks ate dinner sitting in the TV room, with Alecin watching the various news programs she had recorded. Her many-times-great-grandfather had once said that the art of reading was to skip judiciously. Alecin discovered that the art of watching the news was the same. She skipped judiciously over the irrelevant fluff and banter and focused on the parts that mattered to her—all while taking copious notes on her laptop.

Two hours after she had started, Alecin finally completed her nightly news watching.

As always, Tonks had provided her love and support by repeatedly trying to lay on Alecin's keypad. When that hadn't worked, Tonks had sprawled out on the couch and gone to sleep. Yawning, Alecin now gathered up her dinner dishes and computer. She put her dishes in the kitchen sink and walked upstairs to what she considered her Guardian room.

The room had been her sister Beth's bedroom when Alecin was growing up. She had chosen it because it was the only bedroom other than the master with a fireplace, and she could burn any documents that she didn't feel comfortable just tossing in the trash. Alecin knew that she couldn't change much about the room, or her parents would flip out. But the door now required her thumbprint and a code to enter it. She had explained the heightened security to her parents by telling them she needed a secure space in which to keep confidential client materials. They had bought it.

After walking into the room, Alecin went to her desk, Tonks padding along beside her. It was the same desk that had been in her grandfather's study. The desk and chair were the only things Alecin had asked for when her grandfather had passed away. Somehow sitting at that desk helped her not miss him quite as much.

Sitting at Neil's old desk, she read over her notes on that evening's news and organized them with her previous notes. *It's getting close*, she thought. She wondered if every Guardian had felt that way when it had been their turn. Her grandfather hadn't said as much to her, but that didn't mean it wasn't possible. The thought comforted her anyway.

Her notes organized, Alecin reached for her box. She opened it and removed her encrypted Guardian laptop. The first few weeks she had been Guardian, she had checked the computer constantly for emails, terrified that she would miss something important. But she had nearly driven herself insane doing that. After a few months, she had compromised with herself, and now she checked it every evening before bed. It was often enough that she didn't feel like she would miss something important, but not so much that it made her crazy.

When her Guardian laptop had booted up, she opened her email. Her heart always beat a little faster when she saw there was a new email, and there was a new email tonight. Seeing that it was a long one, her heart beat even faster. If the message was this long, it meant something out of the ordinary had happened. *Maybe a Guardian had died before passing on Guardianship,* Alecin speculated absently.

From the subject line of the email, it looked like the *Constitution* was the reference document needed to decode this particular message. She pulled her *Constitution* out of her box and laid it flat on the desk. Then, since she preferred deciphering by hand, she pulled out her notebook and pen and began to decipher the message.

Deciphering the first two letters, she wrote down "it." *Well, that offers no clue what this message is about,* thought Alecin. Then, she deciphered the next two letters, "is." *Do not panic,* she ordered herself. *There are many ways that that sentence could end.* She deciphered the next letter, and her heart felt like it had just stopped. With her hand shaking, she wrote the letter "t," and then "i." *Holy crap!* Alecin jumped to her feet. *Someone had called for a vote!*

Do not panic! And breathe! Alecin ordered herself. She sat and took a sip of her water. Then, she looked at Tonks, who was sitting on the edge of the desk, cleaning herself judiciously. "We are talking about the fate of humanity here, Tonks. Try to show some decorum."

Tonks stopped and looked at her. Apparently deciding she had said nothing of consequence, Tonks returned to her bath.

"It's okay," Alecin said out loud to herself. "You always knew this day could come. Just take the next step, and keep taking steps until you've gotten through." She finished deciphering the entire message. With eight votes in, the vote had so far been unanimous. She sat back and looked at Tonks. Her thoughts raced. Then, she decided it was time for the next step.

"Well, Toto, it looks like we aren't in Kansas anymore," she told Tonks, who appeared to agree. It was now up to her to decide how she would vote. Alecin thought over the current situation the country was facing. For years now, the division in the country . . . the sense of "us versus them," had permeated everything.

Many had hoped that the division in the country would disappear with the "red wave," which had been expected in the mid-term elections of 2022. Before the election, numerous polls had shown Republicans leading in crucial races, which would have resulted in a Republican-controlled House and Senate. But, in nearly every critical race, the Democratic candidate had won and had, in each case, won by just over the number of votes needed. And the votes that put the Democratic candidate in office always came in toward the end of the vote counting. Cries of fraud from the Republicans had gone out across the country, followed by cries of injustice when they were unsuccessful at challenging any of the Democrats' questionable victories.

Now, with the upcoming 2024 election, an actual insurrection seemed possible. Just after the mid-term elections, President Joe Biden had died. Although he was fairly old and his health had been questioned repeatedly, the circumstances of his death had many in Democratic circles alleging it had been an assassination. A month after President Biden's death, former President Donald Trump was unquestionably assassinated.

No one knew who was behind the assassinations, but everyone had theories. Republicans accused Democrats of being behind Trump's assassination, arguing that it had been done as retribution for the perceived assassination of Biden. Democrats accused Republicans of being behind Trump's assassination as a way to cover up their assassination of Biden.

With the upcoming presidential election, tensions in the country were extremely high. Rumors and accusations that members of the Democrat party intended to take whatever actions were necessary in order to win the election, including illegally manipulating the vote, were rampant. After what they believed had been the fraudulent election results in the midterms, many Republican government leaders had announced publicly that they would consider the Republican nominee the President of the United States and only follow his orders, no matter what the votes said. Many military leaders had let known the same, although not publicly.

Firearm sales across the country had skyrocketed. A higher percentage of Americans now owned firearms than at any other time in the nation's history. Neither side trusted the other. Both sides intensely despised each other. Everyone was angry. And everyone was scared.

The stage was set for a civil war—but worse. In America's last civil war, The North and The South had been separated by geography, with a dividing line between them. Now, however, across the country, neighbors were enemies. Even within families, people had chosen sides.

If the Left began fighting the Right, there would be no geographic dividing line. It would be Americans fighting Americans—everywhere. If war did break out, the fighting would take place on the streets across the country. It would be urban warfare. Of course, a united US military could settle any conflict that broke out, but in the current environment, it seemed highly unlikely that the US military *would* be united.

Were they at the point . . . the point before the country reached the point of no return . . . the point where the Kalecians could help America avoid a civil war? The road to this point had undoubtedly been paved with idiocy, selfishness, and immorality. But worst of all was the prevalence in the government of those who had both a lust for power and a complete and utter disregard for the rights of others. Could humanity bring itself back from the brink? Would they even try?

The real problem, Alecin thought, was that no one no longer respected and cherished the ideals and principles enshrined in the *Declaration of Independence* and *Constitution.* Many didn't believe that every person had a right to pursue happiness anymore. Half of the country seemed intent on telling the other half how to live; damned be the country, damned be its institutions, and damned be the *Constitution.*

Could the Kalecians get Americans to once again value and respect the principles in the *Declaration of Independence* and *Constitution?* The republic was only a republic as long as we kept it. Didn't Benjamin Franklin say something like that? There were many in the country who weren't interested in keeping it. The FBI, DOJ, and IRS—once independent government agencies—had now taken sides. It seemed like everyone thought there was no neutral arbitrator anymore, and so there was no way to resolve conflict, except through violence.

The American Revolution had started over taxation without representation; the colonists had wanted a say in control over their own lives. Liberty. Freedom. Justice. They had always been the desire of every human soul. People who feel like they have no say will rebel; they will fight. And there were many in the country who felt like they no longer had a say. Had the country gone so far off course that it couldn't correct itself *by* itself?

Going over to the window, Alecin looked out into the night. She looked at the peaceful street with the pretty homes and the nicely manicured lawns lit by old-fashioned streetlights. How long would it remain peaceful? How many times over the last four years had she thought the country had gone astray? That the country was leading humanity astray? That it no longer served as the model for humanity of morality, liberty, and freedom, as the Kalecians and the Founders had hoped it would. A hundred? Two hundred? It seemed like it was almost every day.

It is time, she thought. She knew it. She had known it for a while. She had just been too afraid to do anything about it. She had been too afraid to take such a drastic step, to rock the boat. She thought back to the day she had taken the oath to be a Guardian. She thought about looking at the door after she left, and promising her grandfather she would make him proud.

"I'm going to do it, Grandpa," she declared out loud. "I'm going to make you proud, just like I promised."

Before she could change her mind, she opened her box again and pulled out her laptop. She pulled out her *Declaration of Independence* and stopped. She read the first line as she had hundreds of times before: "When in the course of human events . . ." This time, the phrase struck her as it never had before. *Sometimes, in the course of human events*, she thought, *it becomes necessary to upset the status quo—to rock the boat of humanity—in order to get humanity to a better place.* And now, the course of human events had led to humanity needing the Kalecians to once again help guide it. Humanity was still a species worth saving. And it was her duty to get over her fear and help save it.

Grabbing the *Declaration* to use as her reference document, she composed her message stating that she voted yes; it is time. Then she hit send. *That's nine down,* she thought. *Three to go.* "Fasten your seatbelt," Alecin told herself. "It's going to be a bumpy ride."

CHAPTER 10

E.T. kept touching her face with this hand. Looking at him, Alecin thought, *he must be one of the Kalecians.* Why hadn't he changed to human form? And why did he keep touching her face? "Stop it," she told him. But he didn't respond. Maybe the translator thing wasn't on. *I should try to find it,* she thought, looking around. But E.T. wouldn't stop touching her face, and she was getting really annoyed.

Alecin awoke to find herself at her desk, lying on her computer keyboard. She saw Tonks in front of her, staring at her and repeatedly pawing her face. For a second, she couldn't remember why she was in her Guardian room and not in her bed. Then, she remembered. She had not been able to pry herself away from the computer. She must have fallen asleep waiting to get the email on the final vote.

"What time is it?" she asked Tonks, sitting up and wiping her mouth. The clock on her computer said just after 3 a.m. "What's the matter with you, Tonks? Why did you wake me up?"

Tonks looked pointedly at the closed door.

"I guess you can't get to your litter box with the door closed, huh?"

Tonks answered with a plaintive meow. Alecin checked her email one more time. Nothing yet.

"I guess it's time both of us got out of here," said Alecin, closing down her computer and putting it into her box, which she proceeded to close as well. When Alecin opened the door, Tonks ran out like the room was on fire. "When you go to go . . ." Alecin muttered. She found her way to her room and to her bed. Not bothering to get undressed or under the covers, she lay on the bed and was back to sleep in thirty seconds.

Later that night, Alecin finally got home after what had been a disaster of a date. She had tried to get out of it, telling April she had to work. It was a lame excuse, she knew, but she couldn't think of one that made sense. If she had told April that one of her parents was sick, April would have just shown up at their door within the hour, a pot of chicken soup in hand. And work or sick parents were the only two excuses Alecin could come up with.

April had adamantly refused to let her back out of the date, no matter how much Alecin had begged. Finally, April had threatened to spend the entire next week walking around the office singing that one song where somebody gets knocked down, then gets up again, then gets knocked down, and then gets up again, and over and over and over again. . .for the whole damn song. In the face of such a terrifying threat, Alecin had relented.

She was sure that April was now probably sorry that she had made Alecin go. Alecin hadn't done the "thing," but she *had* been obviously *distracted*. April had had to kick her under the table more than once to bring Alecin back to the moment. The last couple of times, Alecin remembered, those kicks had been really hard. But she had probably deserved them. The guy April had set her up with, Tom, had been good-looking and had seemed very sweet. Alecin thought guiltily that he hadn't deserved to be subjected to such a horrible date. If she wasn't saving the world next weekend, she thought, maybe she would ask April to convince Tom to give her another chance.

As soon as she got home, Alecin nearly raced up to her Guardian room. Tonks protested loudly that she hadn't had her dinner, but Alecin promised to get it for her later. Annoyed, Tonks had refused to follow her upstairs.

Once in her Guardian room, Alecin immediately sat down at her desk and grabbed her box. After opening it, she took out her laptop. Taking a deep breath, she opened her email. There was a new email! Alecin's heart began to thunder out of her chest.

The email indicated that Federalist Two was the reference document, so she pulled that out and quickly deciphered the message. The message was simple: "All have voted. It is time. It is unanimous. The time and date will be August 15 at 2 p.m. EST."

Alecin sat back. Stunned. Amazed. Excited. Terrified. She would be a part of fulfilling the mission of the Guardians—the thing that all Guardians had prepared to do for over two hundred years. But what if she screwed it up?

Alecin's thoughts went back to a few months after her grandfather had passed Guardianship to her. She had gone to see him because once she was actually being a Guardian, she had begun to feel that she was not up to the task. Using their code—since talking about being a Guardian was off-limits—she had told him that she needed a sonic screwdriver because she had made a mistake. She had erred in deciphering a message, but she didn't tell him that. After she had told him, he had asked her to come over to his desk with him. He had pointed to a small drawer pull and told her to open it. She pulled out a small, very shallow drawer, the purpose of which she couldn't figure out. It was empty. But taped to the bottom of the drawer was a piece of paper. On it, it read:

A well-adjusted person is one who makes the same mistake twice without getting nervous.

—Alexander Hamilton

But lest some unlucky event should happen unfavorable to my reputation, I beg it may be remembered by every gentleman in the room that I this day declare with the utmost sincerity, I do not think myself equal to the command I am honored with.

—George Washington

"I put this here," he told Alecin, "so whenever I have those moments where I feel like a fool . . . where I don't feel up to the task before me, I can read this and remember some of the greatest men in history felt the same way from time to time. Everyone makes mistakes, and that's okay. Everyone feels that they are not up to the task before them sometimes. No one is immune to that feeling. But what separates the great ones from everyone else is that the great ones have the strength of character to acknowledge the feeling, and then get back to work."

Remembering that conversation, Alecin acknowledged her fear, and then got to work.

First, she composed and sent an email acknowledging the date and time. Her next step, though, required more thought. *August 15*, she thought. *That's Thursday.* That didn't leave her much time to prepare. She wasn't sure how long she would need to carry out whatever instructions were in that mysterious gold envelope her grandfather had told her she would find at the bottom of her Guardian box, but she wanted to give herself two full weeks, just in case.

To give herself that length of time, she would need some kind of excuse to tell her parents and April. A good excuse. A fake illness was out. They would all just try to take care of her. *A problem with having to lie to people you love and who love you,* Alecin thought, *was coming up with the right lie.* Lying to strangers was so much easier.

Briefly, she thought of just telling them to trust her; she had something she had to do. But neither her parents nor April would let that go. She knew that.

What she needed was to meet someone and start a whirlwind romance—a completely fake one, of course. *No*, she thought, reconsidering. No one would ever buy she'd do that. But a secret, long-term boyfriend where things had gotten serious, and they wanted to take a trip together? Both her family and April seemed obsessed with her love life. A fake but *serious* secret boyfriend just might work.

Alecin didn't often lie—just when her Guardian duties called for it. But when she did lie, she was thorough. The only thing she hated more than lying was the thought of getting *caught* in a lie. If she was going to have a fake romance, she would really need to sell it. She sat down and got to work figuring out how to do just that.

On August 15, 2024, at precisely 1:45 p.m. EST, Alecin was in a hotel room near the airport in Richmond, Virginia. She would have much preferred to be in her Guardian room at home, but her parents had bought the lie that Alecin was on her way to St. Thomas in the US Virgin Islands with Tyler, her serious heretofore-secret boyfriend. That being the case, she very well couldn't have stayed at home, with the chance that her parents could pop by at any time and figure out her deception.

Alecin sat cross-legged on the bed, her Guardian box on her lap and the gold envelope containing the instructions in her hand. On the dresser across the room was her bag for her imaginary vacation. It was full of clothing for every possible environment because she didn't know if she would have to go anywhere and, if she did, where she would have to go. Also on the dresser was the satchel that Alecin had bought the day before while she had claimed to be choosing new swimsuits and tropical attire for her pretend vacation. In her mind, a satchel was just what was needed for a quest, even if that quest turned out to be just one day long. She had gotten her name, "A. Hamilton," embroidered on the flap. *After all, how often does one go on a quest?* she had thought. She wanted to do it in style. She also had a matching backpack that fit her box inside it. There was no way she was ever letting her box out of her sight during her quest.

Alecin heard her phone vibrate, and she picked it up. It was a text from April, apologizing for interrupting her vacation but asking her a question about an ongoing case. Despite the importance of what she was doing and knowing she was where she needed to be and doing what she needed to be doing, Alecin still felt guilty about suddenly dumping all that work on April. She had promised April that if she and Evan ever wanted to take a second honeymoon, Alecin would take all the work for three weeks. But April had just been so happy to see what she took to be Alecin's excitement over a serious romance that she hadn't even complained about the work or the short notice. That selflessness was one of the reasons why April was one of Alecin's best friends.

Alecin checked the countdown timer she had set on her phone. One minute left. Her heart raced, and she felt like she was holding her breath, waiting for the time to come. Absently, she wondered if she was actually holding her breath. Then, her phone sounded. Time was up.

Alecin couldn't stop her hands from trembling as she opened the envelope. Slowly she pulled out the single card inside. Moving the box aside, she unfolded the card and read what it said:

Greetings Guardians,

The vote has been taken, and now the Appello must be assembled. The parts of the Appello are well hidden throughout the lands of the United States of America.

All Guardians should endeavor to go to a mountain of kings, where an enemy fell so that humanity may survive.

The first one to this place will be the Chosen One.

The Chosen One will finish the quest for all.

During their quest, the Chosen One will learn all that is needed to complete their quest.

Our hope, and the hope of all of humanity, goes with you.

May your quest be Harmonious.

Your friends,

The Kalecians

Alecin read through it a few times to be sure she hadn't missed anything. The Appello was the device—the bat signal, she reminded herself with a smile. So, every Guardian had to try to get to this mountain of kings place, and the first one there became the Chosen One. Seemed straightforward enough. And the Chosen One had to go on a quest to find all of the parts of the Appello and assemble it. And during this quest, the Kalecians would reveal to the Chosen One everything they needed to know to complete their quest.

Why didn't all the Guardians just join together on the quest? she wondered. Maybe it was because of the saying that if you didn't want anything to get done, assign the task to a committee. But here, didn't it seem like the more minds applied to the situation, the better? To take the one ring to Mordor, didn't they form a fellowship? *That fellowship broke down, though*, she reminded herself. In the end, it was just Frodo and Samwise who took the ring to Mordor. And if the Orcs had succeeded in killing everyone in the fellowship, there were others that could have taken the ring to Mordor, eventually. But if all the Guardians were in one place, and they were all destroyed, all hope for humanity would be lost. Not good. But with the Chosen One being the only Guardian on the quest, if they were destroyed, there were eleven other Guardians who could step up and finish the quest. That would certainly increase the odds that the quest would be completed. And everything depended on the quest being completed. So just one Guardian at a time had to do it all. Or at least try.

Speaking of the eleven other Guardians, Alecin's thoughts

continued, *I could just head home right now. I could tell every-one that Tyler and I had a fight, so I canceled our trip. If I don't go to this place at all, then I can't be the first Guardian to get there, and then there would be no chance I could be the Chosen One. Let some other Guardian become the Chosen One. I don't want to take on that kind of responsibility.*

But even as Alecin thought about just going home, she knew she could never do it. She had taken an oath. She had made a promise. She would honor both. So, putting those dishonorable thoughts aside, she settled down to try to figure out where this first place was.

She began where every member of her generation began when they were looking for something: the internet. She searched for "a mountain of kings." There was something about a movie. That didn't seem relevant. There was a Wikipedia entry about a piece of music. That was a strike too. She started to scroll through all the results for anything that could hint at a location. There was something about a state park in South Carolina called Kings Mountain. That was a place, and it was in South Carolina, a state that was part of the United States in 1797. But when she clicked on the link, she didn't see anything that could in any way be related to an enemy falling. Whose enemy was the clue referencing anyway? An enemy of humanity? An enemy of the Kalecians? An enemy of the Harmonious?

On the second page of search results, she saw a page en-titled "Kings Mountain Battle Facts and Summary." *This could be something,* she thought. She read the thumbnail: "The Battle of Kings Mountain was one of the few revolutionary war bat-tles . . . ." She got a tingle. *Right time period,* she thought. She clicked on the link and started reading. About halfway through the page, she read that Thomas Jefferson had once said that the Battle of Kings Mountain had turned the tide of the Revo-lutionary War.

It was essential that the Revolutionary War be won in order for humanity to have a chance at surviving. *More* tingle. This had to be it!

She still had to figure out where an enemy had fallen on this particular mountain of kings Alecin knew, but she decided she could do that on the plane. She scrolled back up to the navigation bar and clicked on "Visit." But that just took her to a bunch of links for stuff she didn't care about, like other battlefields and things. Impatient, she searched, "What's the closest airport to Kings Mountain Park?" The answer popped up right away. She grabbed her bags and headed to the airport to fly to Charlotte Douglas Airport in North Carolina.

Early the next morning, Alecin wandered the grounds of Kings Mountain National Park. By the time she had arrived in North Carolina the night before and rented a car, it was nearly 8 p.m., and the park had long been closed. After spending a frustrating night in the closest hotel she could find, she was finally there. At the park. At the place where she believed an enemy had fallen. At the place where the Kalecians had directed her to go.

Now I just have to find where an enemy fell, Alecin thought as she wandered. The problem was, an enemy had fallen all over the damn park. The whole place was a battleground. Or it *had* been. But now? It was just miles and miles of green grass and trees as far as the eye could see. *It's beautiful*, Alecin thought. *Okay*, very *beautiful*. But it's not like looking at the grass and trees told anyone where enemies had fallen centuries ago. No bodies littered the ground. No weapons either.

The clue said "*an* enemy," not "*the* enemy." How could she figure out where *a* particular enemy had fallen? "You know what a Revolutionary War Battlefield is in 2024?" she asked herself sarcastically. "It's just a freaking field! Or a field with lots of trees, in this case." The visitor's information had said the park was nearly seventy thousand acres! How could she possibly search the entire place?

Frustrated and annoyed, Alecin continued wandering the trails of the park, hoping for something to spark. But it had been almost three hours, and so far, nothing had. *Maybe I'm in the wrong place entirely*, she thought. She would give it another hour, she bargained with herself. If she didn't find anything in the next hour, she would head back to the hotel and do more research—figure out where she was really supposed to be. *If I really am in the wrong place, then some other Guardian has probably already found the right place*, she thought, with both a sense of disappointment and hope.

Alecin walked toward yet another monument. As she had expected, the Revolutionary War Battlefield Park had many, many monuments. Actually, this thing looked more like a large headstone than a monument. The headstone was a little bit off the trail and at an angle to it. She read the inscription: "To the memory of Col. Patrick Ferguson . . . killed . . . in action at Kings Mountain while in command of the British Troops." And there was the spark she had been waiting for! Finally! This place was definitely one where an enemy had fallen, and the commander of the British troops was an important enemy. *This could be it*, she thought excitedly.

Alecin took out her phone and did a quick search for Col. Patrick Ferguson. After a bit of scrolling, she found out he was the only British officer buried at Kings Mountain. And the spark became a flame. Then, she read that Col. Ferguson's death had had a significant effect on the morale of the British troops fighting the battle and that this loss of morale was part of what had allowed the Patriots to win their first significant victory in the Revolutionary War, which as Thomas Jefferson had observed, had turned the tide in the war.

"This," Alecin declared quietly to no one, "was undoubtedly an enemy that had fallen so that the tide would turn, the Revolutionary War would be won, the United States of America could be established, and humanity could survive."

This was the right enemy; she was sure of it, but was this the right *place*? She searched more and read that Ferguson was not buried at this headstone but in the Kings Mountain cemetery. She spent a few more minutes scrolling. She saw something that said that Col. Ferguson had been buried in an unmarked grave until the National Park Service had erected this headstone in 1920. So, in 1797, when the clue was hidden by the Kalecians, Col. Ferguson had been buried in this spot, in an unmarked grave. That would have made this place very difficult to find. And it was a significant place. Seemed like a good spot for the Kalecians to hide something.

It's rather depressing, Alecin thought as she studied the headstone. If Ferguson hadn't fallen, the Battle of Kings Mountain might not have been won by the Patriots. If the Battle of Kings Mountain had not been won, then the Revolutionary War may not have been won by the colonies. And then there would have been no United States of America; without the United States to be a model for all people, humanity would have been doomed. What had occurred in this place may have saved humanity. Yet, she had never even heard of Col. Ferguson until that day.

This place deserved more than a few words inscribed on an old headstone—an inscription that didn't even recognize that Ferguson's death at this place may very well have saved the United States of America. *When this is done,* Alecin vowed, *if the quest is successful, I am going to ensure that this place is marked with a monument befitting its importance to humanity.*

But back to the here and now, Alecin told herself, *and here and now, I have a job to do.* She looked all around to be sure no one was around. Thankfully, although it was an early Friday morning in mid-August, there were hardly any other people in the park. Still, she couldn't just start digging around the headstone, could she? She walked around the headstone, seeing if there was any indication of where she should dig. If she was going to dig up a headstone, she didn't want just to dig the whole thing up unnecessarily.

She continued to look for a perfect place until she realized she was just stalling. Digging up a monument in a National Park. Well, it just seemed wrong.

Fate of humanity on the line, Alecin reminded herself. Blowing out a breath, she pulled a folding shovel she had brought—just in case—from her satchel. At least she had thought to bring the right tool for the job. She unfolded the shovel, but before sinking the blade into the ground, she stopped. To open her box, she had only to wave her hand over it. The box could read her DNA. What if the Kalecians had the ability to have something that could read the modified DNA of every Guardian? What if the Kalecians had used that technology here?

Setting the shovel aside, she got down on her hands and knees. Slowly she began to move her hands just over the ground near the headstone. She only felt the soft grass brushing against her palms and nothing else, but she kept going. She moved her hands so close to the headstone that her fingertips felt its cement, which was cool from the evening chill. As she moved to the back of the headstone, though, she felt something. It felt like a pull of some kind. She moved her hands toward the pulling sensation. And suddenly, a small bit of ground disappeared. It just *disappeared*. It was what she was hoping would happen, but she still jerked back in surprise. Then, she leaned forward and looked into the pit she had just revealed.

The opening to the pit was small—about twice the size of her cell phone, she judged. It looked to be about six inches deep, but she couldn't be sure because it wasn't empty. Inside the pit, she could see a small envelope of gold on which sat a strange pair of glasses.

"I'm the first," she whispered in shock. "I'm the first," she whispered again, but with more conviction. "I'm the Chosen One," she whispered with even greater conviction. "I am the Chosen One," she repeated. She took a deep breath, feeling a little like she had just declared that she was Spartacus.

Now that she was the first, she could admit to herself that

she had secretly been hoping she *wouldn't* be the first. She had taken an oath to do her best, and she had done her best; no one could say that she hadn't tried her best. But that didn't stop her from thinking it wasn't too late. She could just close up the pit and walk away. No one knew she had arrived first. She could just pretend she had never found it.

But she *had*. She sighed. "I am the Chosen One," she whispered with resignation. She had taken an oath. She had made a promise. "I *have* to do this," she whispered resolutely. Taking another deep breath, she reached into the pit and took her first step as the Chosen One.

She pulled the glasses out first. They were strange-looking. The frames were made from some kind of material that she didn't recognize, and when she held them up, the lenses seemed to reflect light in a weird way. They kind of reminded her of the glasses in *National Treasure*, one of her favorite movies. Were these like those glasses? A tool to help her "see the treasured past"? And how weird was it that these glasses had been hidden over two hundred years ago in this pit, presumably to help her find stuff, and that movie had used hidden glasses to help Nicholas Cage find stuff? *Maybe not so weird*, she thought. After all, if altering a person's sight was the goal, it's not like there were that many options. Glasses were pretty much it.

She wondered, though, how these strange glasses would help her see anything. She put them on. Everything looked the same—maybe just a little blurry. Shrugging her shoulders, she put them in her satchel. She would have to figure those out later. She then took the golden envelope from the pit and put that in her satchel as well. She would read that later. Someone could come along at any second.

She noticed there were also numerous small white envelopes in the pit. She didn't count them, but she guessed there were eleven of them. She was extremely curious about what was in *them*. But they weren't for her, she reminded herself. With the fate of humanity on the line, she intended to follow the rules *exactly.*

Right now, she needed to find somewhere private where she could read the clue she was sure was in the gold envelope. Then figure out where she needed to go next. She waved her hand over the pit, and the grass appeared as before, looking completely undisturbed.

CHAPTER 11

As Alecin stood up, brushing her hands off on her jeans, she suddenly noticed a man standing on the nearby trail. He was watching her. *Now, how long has he been there?* she thought with annoyance. She hadn't heard him come up. *What had he seen? He didn't see me close the hole, did he? I was behind the headstone; how could he have? Dammit,* she chastised herself; why hadn't she been paying better attention? Fine Chosen One she was turning out to be.

The strange man was wearing jeans and a simple black T-shirt. He was just over six feet and lean, with a good build. She guessed that he was one of those guys who knew his way around a gym. He had dark brown hair, edging toward chestnut in the sun. His eyes were blue, but not like her eyes, Alecin thought. His eyes reminded her of the color of the ocean when it had pounded on Virginia's shore during a storm. He had finely chiseled features, and when he smiled at her, Alecin imagined he often had made girls swoon with that smile. But Alecin wasn't one to swoon. And in any event, she had no time for whomever this guy was. However gorgeous he may be.

"I was just leaving," Alecin stuttered as she walked toward the path, which happened to also be toward the man still staring at her.

"And I was just coming," he said easily, without moving. He was blocking the trail so that Alecin would have had to walk on the grass to get around him. Walking on the grass seemed foolish, so she was stuck. "I'm George Washington," he said.

"You're kidding," she blurted without thinking. *Holy crap!* she thought. *Is he a Guardian?*

"I get that a lot." He continued to smile at her. "Nope. Not kidding. My many-times-great-granddad was *the* George Washington, the first president of the United States."

"George Washington didn't have any kids."

"Okay. My many-times great *step-granddad* was *the* George Washington, if you want to get technical." He still kept smiling at her. "Anyway, the name has kind of carried on down through my family. My father was a George Washington, too."

"So, are you a junior?" *He was a Guardian! Why am I talking to him?* Alecin scolded herself. *Guardians aren't supposed to talk to each other. I should just walk around him and be on my way.*

"No, thank goodness. I can just imagine how the mocking would have been in school if I was George Washington the Fourth or something. My parents spared me from that humiliation by giving me a different middle name than any of the George Washingtons before me."

"Then it seems like it would be easier to just go by your middle name and avoid all the mockery." *Shut up*, she told herself. *Just stop talking and get on with what you need to do.*

"You would think so, but no. My parents were cruel. My middle name is Bartholomew, after my Mom's Dad."

"Ouch." What the hell was wrong with her? *Stop talking!* she commanded herself.

"Yeah, you can see why I stuck with George."

"Well, George, it was nice meeting you. But if you'll excuse me, as I said before, I was just leaving." *Good job*, Alecin told herself.

"It was nice meeting you too, Ms. . . . I'm sorry. I don't think I caught your name?"

"No, you didn't." She was leaving now. That was it. He didn't need to know her name.

George smiled again, unruffled. It was then that George noticed her embroidered satchel. "A. Hamilton," George read. He looked at Alecin, and recognition dawned. "As in Alexander Hamilton, I take it?"

"Yes," Alecin said matter-of-factly. *Why had I gotten that satchel embroidered?* She thought with frustration. *Dammit.* "He was *my* many-times-great-grandfather."

"I bet." George still hadn't moved from the trail. "I liked your musical."

"It wasn't my musical," Alecin corrected curtly.

"No, I guess it wasn't. I have a feeling, *Ms. Hamilton*, that you know why I'm here, and that you already got what I came for."

"I don't know what you're talking about," Alecin said stubbornly.

"Sure you do," George said, looking into her eyes. *Ms. Hamilton,* he thought, *would make an excellent poker player.* Usually, he was pretty good at reading people, but her? She was a closed book.

"There is," she began, then hesitated. "That is, there *may* be something here for you, too."

"Is there now?" He paused. "Well, Ms. Hamilton," he continued, "it's been a pleasure. I hope we'll meet again." He stepped aside and, with an exaggerated bow, said, "M'lady."

Now Alecin felt foolish. "Thank you," she muttered as she rushed by him. As she walked back to her car, she replayed the entire encounter in her mind. Who was this George Washington? Was he who she thought he was? It didn't matter; she had a job to do—a quest to complete. And she would probably never see Mr. George Washington again anyway. Just as she finished this thought, though, he appeared, walking nonchalantly beside her.

"Ms. Hamilton, how about you let me buy you a cup of coffee?"

"No. Thank you," she said in a voice she hoped sounded firm. "And my name is Alecin. Not Ms. Hamilton."

"Alecin," he repeated. "That's a pretty name. Come on, Alecin," he held up an envelope that looked just like the envelopes she had seen in the pit back at the headstone. "I'll show you mine if you show me yours," he sang.

Inwardly Alecin smiled, but her face remained unreadable. She didn't answer him. She needed to be sensible, and there was nothing sensible about having coffee with the charming Mr. Washington. But, darn it, she wanted to know what was in that envelope. And what could it hurt? She decided. They had already met. The proverbial cat was already out of the bag. By the time she had made her decision, they were back at her car.

"Tell you what, George. I was thinking about getting something to eat at that diner on Highway 29. Do you know which one I'm talking about?" George nodded. "How about you buy me lunch there instead?"

"I can do that," he agreed. "I'll meet you there."

Alecin nodded at him, then got into the very sensible sedan she had rented. She was shocked when she saw George get on a motorcycle. *What was he thinking?* she thought. *Those things are death machines. Why would anyone ride one?* Guess he wasn't actually as bright as he had initially seemed, she concluded. Why was she so disappointed by that?

About ten minutes later, Alecin pulled into a parking spot in front of the diner. George pulled his motorcycle into the spot next to her. Alecin got out of her car, then watched George get off his bike. He took off his helmet and smiled at her. And Alecin thought she just might swoon for the first time in her life.

Get ahold of yourself, Alecin, she demanded. *He's not even your type, and you certainly are not his. And besides, saving humanity, remember?*

George held the door open for her as they entered the diner, and Alecin smiled at him as she walked by him. *Now we are getting somewhere,* George thought. He was determined that he would be seeing much more of the lovely Ms. Hamilton.

"You know, you don't have to hold the door for me," she told him as they walked to a table.

"Ah, but I do. My momma raised a gentleman."

After they had sat down at a table by the window, Alecin busied herself studying the menu. When she looked up, she saw George simply looking at her, his menu untouched on the table. "Aren't you going to look at the menu?"

"Nope. In a diner like this, there's only one thing to order."

"What's that?"

"Cheeseburger and fries."

He made a good point, Alecin thought, and when the waitress returned, they each ordered a cheeseburger and fries. "What do you want to drink?" the waitress asked.

"I'll have a diet coke," Alecin said, "and some coffee creamer."

"So, you want coffee?"

"No, just the Diet Coke and creamer. Thank you."

"So, just the creamer? No coffee?" the waitress asked, thoroughly confused.

"Yes, thank you."

The waitress shook her head as she wrote down Alecin's order; then she looked at George as if daring him to order something weird too. "I'll just have a coke," he said hurriedly.

The waitress walked off, still shaking her head.

"Um, what was that all about? Why did you order coffee creamer if you aren't having coffee?"

"I like to put coffee creamer in my diet coke," Alecin said as if it were the most obvious thing in the world. "I prefer hazelnut-flavored creamer," she continued, "but I didn't think they would have any here."

George just stared at her. "Are you like Sally from *When Harry Marry Sally*? One of those super high-maintenance people?"

"I'm not high maintenance. I just want it the way I want it."

"That's exactly what Sally said."

"I know," she said, smiling. "But I promise not to fake an orgasm during lunch."

George blushed and looked around to see if anyone had heard her. Alecin had thrown that out there just to see what his reaction would be. *Precisely the right one*, she thought. *Score one for Mr. Washington.*

"Anyway, it's not that weird," Alecin said defensively. "People drink Coke floats all the time. Those are basically just coke and cream."

George thought about it. "You know what? You're absolutely right. I withdraw my earlier skepticism."

"Thank you."

"Okay, now that we're about to share a meal together, can I call you Ally?"

"Only if I can call you Georgie."

"So, definitely no Ally." He paused. "Okay, so tell me all about Alecin Hamilton."

"Well, what do you want to know?"

"Everything, but I'll settle for a thumbnail sketch. Like, where did you grow up, to start?"

"I grew up in Northern Virginia. My family has a house there—one that has been in our family for generations. My grandparents lived there while I was growing up. My parents bought a house just down the street. I could, and often did, ride my bike to my grandparents' house growing up."

"College?"

"UCLA, majored in philosophy. After college, I joined the Navy. I served for two years as a surface warfare officer. That's an officer serving on warships."

"Very cool. Why only two years?"

"The Navy has this program, the Law Education Program, where they send line officers, like surface or submarine warfare officers, to law school. You get to stay on active duty during law school, so you don't lose any time in rank or anything. I did that."

"Where was law school?"

"University of Chicago. That's where Sally picks Harry up at the beginning of that movie, by the way."

"I know. I'm impressed. That's one of the best law schools in the country."

"I'm very good at deductive reasoning; That's pretty much all the LSAT is. I got a perfect score," she said matter-of-factly.

"*Continue* to be impressed. After law school?"

"I served four years in the Judge Advocate General Corps. After four years, the military had changed too much. When I signed on—the position of the members of the military had been, 'I may not agree with what you say, but I will fight to the death for your right to say it.' By the time I got out, the military had changed its position to: 'If I don't agree with what you say, you should shut up, or I'll make you shut up.' That is and always has been the position of cowards. The military is full of a bunch of cowards now. I didn't want to be ordered around by cowards. 'If freedom of speech is taken away, then dumb and silent we may be led, like sheep to the slaughter.' "

George grinned. "My many-times-great-granddad."

"Yep. You know, I have always thought that your many-times-great-granddad was one the greatest men that ever lived."

"I've always thought so too." He smiled at her. "Your many-times-great-granddad was pretty great too."

"I've always thought so too." She waited for a beat. "Of course, they didn't make a musical about *your* many-times-great-grandad."

"*Yet.*"

"Yet?"

"I'm working on a Washington musical, and my Washington musical is going to kick Hamilton the musical's ass."

She laughed. "Anyway, I believe—as said in *Kindergarten Cop*—that 'men have penises and girls have vaginas.' I refuse to use peoples' preferred pronouns for the same reason I refuse to talk to the imaginary friends of schizophrenics. What people think does not and cannot alter reality. I will not abandon thousands of years of human language because of how someone 'felt,' "—she air quoted—"that day, and I didn't see why the entire world had to pretend to deny reality just to make some confused person feel better. It was getting to the point that I was being ordered to disregard reality and my own conscience in order to be perceived as 'tolerant'—more air quotes—"of someone else's confused perceptions of reality—perceptions that even ten years ago were rightly regarded as indications of mental illness. I was being told that my feelings weren't the right ones, so no one had to be tolerant of them, and what I was saying wasn't the right thing, so I had no right to speak at all.

"And then the straw that broke the camel's back? Wait, does that really work? Doesn't that apply when a small thing made a big thing happen because of the cumulative effect of all that had come before the straw? And this was not a little thing. It was the last straw? No, that's just another way of saying the same thing. Whatever. Then, they ordered me to put an experimental vaccine into my body. And I didn't even need it. I'm young and healthy. Statistically, I have a better chance of dying in a plane crash than of dying from covid. Making people take an experimental vaccine that they didn't need was nothing short of asinine. The vaccine had only recently been developed. No one knew what the long-term effects would be. It was an unnecessary risk. So, I got out.

"I worried though, and worry still, if all the people like me— those that aren't cowardly idiots—get out, if the military would even be able to defend America against her enemies. The military has turned from being a fighting force to being more worried about being woke than being ready for war. I worry about turning the military over to the woke. So far, they have run it into the ground. They kicked out good people over the stupid vaccine mandate. And for the last couple of years, they can barely recruit anyone. People join the military to fight for freedom and liberty. They don't want to join an organization that doesn't believe in doing that.

"Anyway, sorry," Alecin said when she realized she had gone off. "Guess I'm still bitter."

George had just been watching her, nodding along with her statements because, really, he agreed with everything she had said. "No problem. I asked, and I wanted to know. So, what do you do now?"

"Now, a friend and I have a law practice. We do constitutional law, going after the government when they violate people's rights. I love the *Constitution.* I want to do what I can to protect it."

"Okay. Based on what you said, that would mean you're"—he appeared to be doing math in his head—"thirty-three or thirty-four, depending on when your birthday is."

"It's in May, and I'm thirty-three."

"Wait . . ." George did the math in his head again. "That math doesn't work. Did you lie to me?" he teased.

"No. But I completed undergrad in three years, instead of the usual four."

"That's what it is," George snapped his fingers. "I'm thirty-three too. Weird, huh?"

The waitress brought out their food and drinks. George watched, fascinated—he couldn't help it—but said nothing as Alecin poured several coffee creamers into her diet coke and stirred.

"I can feel you staring at me," Alecin said without looking up from her stirring.

"Sorry," George said hurriedly and focused on his food.

After they ate in silence for a few minutes, Alecin said, "Your turn."

"My turn for *what*?"

"Give me the thumbnail on George H. Washington."

"Fair enough. So, I grew up in Tennessee, close to Nashville but not in the city. Same deal; my family has a house that we've had for generations. I grew up in it, though. My grandparents had decided they wanted to spend their retirement years traveling and not taking care of a house. They lived there, though, whenever they weren't traveling. Um. What else? I went to MIT."

"Very impressive," Alecin interjected.

"Thank you. I've never served in the military, but I work at Space X, and we do lots of projects with the military."

"So, you work with Elon Musk?"

"It's not like he is my immediate boss or anything. It's a big company."

"In which part of Space X do you work?"

"In the space launch program. I'm a rocket scientist, basically."

"That's amazing. Do you like it?"

"I love it. The only downside is, at least once a week, it seems, somebody will joke, 'Hey, it's not rocket science. Oh wait, it is.' It can get really annoying. I even put up a sign. You know those 'this-many-days-since-injury' signs. I put up a 'this-many-days-since-the-rocket-science-joke' sign. So far, our record is twenty-three days."

"How long have you had it up?"

"Two years."

Alecin laughed. "You're kidding."

"No. Apparently, rocket scientists don't know many jokes. Next step is to put out a rocket-science-joke jar, like a swear jar. Make everybody put five bucks in every time they make the joke."

"What would you do with the money?"

"Buy T-shirts for everyone that say, 'it's not like it's rocket science—oh wait, it is,' of course." He grinned.

Alecin laughed again. "I used to feel that way about people joking about 'that's why they call it The Windy City' every time it was windy in Chicago, and it was *always* windy in Chicago."

"That's why they call it The Windy City," George said, grinning. Alecin couldn't help herself. She laughed so hard that she started coughing.

George thought it had never been so gratifying to make a girl laugh.

When she had stopped laughing, Alecin took a sip of her diet coke/coffee creamer and decided it was time they got serious before she ended up giggling like a schoolgirl. "Okay, George," she began, "you didn't ask me to lunch to make me laugh. What do you want?"

"Technically, I asked you for coffee. Lunch was *your* idea."

Alecin just gave him a bland look. George cleared his throat and leaned across the table, moving his plate to the side and putting his hands together in front of him. He took a deep breath. "I want to help," George whispered quietly but with sincerity.

Alecin matched his position and tone. "With what?"

"You damn well know what."

Alecin sat back. She sipped her drink as she looked at him.

George got the feeling she was sizing him up, and it made him nervous for some reason.

After a few minutes, Alecin came to a conclusion. She decided to stop pretending she didn't know what he meant. But she was still a long way away from trusting him. She leaned back down. "How do I know you are who say you are? Or, for that matter, how do you know I am who I say I am?"

"We both know," George said, whispering even more quietly, "there are ways of finding out." George paused. "But not here."

"I agree, not here," Alecin whispered, "but where?" In the back of her mind, Alecin thought they probably looked like two young lovers, whispering sweet nothings at each other across the table.

"So, you'll give me a chance to prove I am who I say I am?"

Alecin hesitated. She looked into his eyes. He certainly *looked* sincere. But her grandfather had been clear that she was to trust no one, ever. *Sorry, Grandpa*, Alecin said to herself; she was going with her gut on this one.

"I'll give you a chance," she said at last. George seemed to breathe a sigh of relief. "So, where do we go?"

"There's a hotel down the street."

Alecin raised her eyebrows.

"No. I didn't mean that," George stammered, and Alecin could swear he actually blushed again. "My momma raised a gentleman. But we need somewhere private unless you have a better idea."

"I don't. I guess a hotel room works."

"As long as we take precautions. And yes, I know how that sounded as soon as I said it, but you know what I mean." George huffed out a frustrated breath. *Get it together*, he ordered himself.

Alecin smiled at how flustered he seemed. "I get what you mean."

"Okay. Good."

When the waitress came with the check, Alecin reached for it, but George was faster. "I got it," he said, taking out his wallet.

"At least let me pay for my half."

"No. I asked you. That means I pay. My momma raised a gentleman."

CHAPTER 12

When they arrived at the hotel, once again, Alecin got out of her car and waited for George. He pulled up on his bike and got off of it. And again, just like before, he took off his helmet and smiled at her. And this time, she did swoon. *What the hell is wrong with me?* she thought. *Get it together*, she ordered herself.

She held out her hand.

"What?" George asked, confused.

"Cell phone. Nothing that can be used as a listening device. Give me yours, and we'll lock them in my glove compartment."

"Them?"

She pulled her phone out of her pocket and waved it at him. He gave her his phone, and she locked them both in her glove compartment. Then, grabbing her backpack and satchel, she shut the door and made sure to lock it. George had a bag that he had grabbed as well. Together they walked into the hotel.

The clerk at the reception counter smiled at them. The smile looked tired, though, Alecin thought. She saw that the woman had been studying an MCAT book before they walked in. The clerk wore a purple button-down dress shirt and gray dress slacks with sensible gray flats. She was mixed race, with clear skin the color of Alecin's coffee after she "ruined" it with cream, as her father often put it. She was pretty, but her eyes were red like she'd recently been crying. She had long dark hair pulled back in a bun at the nape of her neck. Her name tag said "Jennifer."

"We'd like a room for the night," George said, suddenly having a Southern drawl that he hadn't possessed five minutes ago. "We don't have a reservation."

"We're pretty open this time of year," Jennifer answered with the same drawl, continuing to smile. "Why don't you let me see what I can do for you?"

As Jennifer walked over to the computer, George asked, pointing to the study book, "so what kind of doctor do you want to be?"

"Pediatrician," Jennifer and Alecin said together. Jennifer and George both stopped what they were doing and stared at Alecin.

"That's right," Jennifer said hesitantly. "How did you know that?"

Oh crap, Alecin thought. She had been distracted by the sudden appearance of George's accent and had spoken without thinking. "Well, um, the truth is, I don't like to really tell people, but . . . I'm a psychic."

"Really?" Jennifer asked in awe.

"Yes, and you, um, you have a very powerful aura."

"I do? Wow. What else can you tell me?"

"You're training for a marathon or some kind of sporting event that involves long-distance running."

"Biathlon," Jennifer confirmed. "That's amazing."

"Yes, well," George interjected, "my wife here, she finds it very hard to sleep at night if there is anyone in any of the neighboring rooms; all their psychic energy just keeps her up. So, if we could get a room at the end, with no one in any of the adjacent rooms, that would be great."

"Of course," Jennifer readily agreed. "I understand. Here," she said after a moment, "it's a room on the end, and all of the adjacent rooms are empty. It's like you knew we would have just what you needed," she added, beaming at Alecin.

"Perfect," Alecin said, trying not to squirm.

While Jennifer prepared their room keys, she asked, "is there anything else you can tell me?"

"Um, the spirits tell me you shouldn't worry about that fight with your boyfriend. He loves you, and you guys will make up."

"Really?" Jennifer's eyes brimmed with tears and hope.

"So the spirits say."

"Oh, I've never met a psychic before. That's just amazing." She handed them the room keys. "Just let me know if you need anything else. I can have someone help you with your luggage. Just give me a second."

"You know what?" George said. "That's okay. We left our luggage in the car. We just wanted to get checked in and go get something to eat. We'll bring our luggage in when we get back."

"Of course. Just let me know if you need anything else," she repeated.

"We will," George promised. Turning to Alecin, he said, "Come along, dear."

Jennifer waved at Alecin as she walked away, and Alecin smiled awkwardly at her.

As soon as the door shut on the elevator, George turned to Alecin. "Okay, I know you're not a psychic. So spill."

"How do you know I'm not a psychic?"

"Because there's no such thing."

"So, you'll believe in," Alecin stopped herself, "other things, but not psychics?"

"Yes," George said firmly.

"Fine, I'm not a psychic. I'm just really good at deductive reasoning, as I told you. But I thought the psychic explanation worked better for Jennifer."

"No way you knew all that stuff about her just through deductive reasoning."

Alecin sighed. Why could no one just ever take her word for it? "She used a picture as a bookmark in her MCAT study book. It was a picture of a kid who was obviously sick. Probably a brother because she didn't look old enough to be his mom. She probably kept it there to remind her what she was working for as she was studying, to become a pediatrician and help sick kids like her brother.

"Also, she was fit. She had the build and body tone of a runner. Her pants were loose because she had lost some weight recently, indicating that she had been training extra hard. Runners only train like that to prepare for an event. I deduced marathon as the most likely, but biathlon is close.

"As to the boyfriend, her shirt had a stain. Not a very noticeable one, but a stain. Her pants were frayed at the bottom, and her shoes were scuffed. You could see that when she was sitting on the stool when we came in. She obviously makes an effort to wear her best clothes to work. This tells me that she and her boyfriend don't have a lot of money right now. But she wore a heart necklace. Obviously a gift from her boyfriend, and it was real gold. It would have been hard for him to get that for her. You don't make an effort like that unless you love somebody. Her eyes were red like she had been crying. There is only one reason a woman her age cries at work—a man. Since I didn't see any indication of a wedding ring, it had to be a boyfriend."

They had arrived at their room by this point. It was a decent-sized room, with a king-size bed in the middle. The bed was covered in the kind of seriously ugly bedspread it seemed hotels like this always had. The walls were painted a neutral cream and decorated with large, framed pictures of different areas of Kings Mountain Park.

As they put their bags down, George let out a low whistle. "Let me just say, wow. You said you were good at deductive reasoning, but wow. You're like Sherlock Holmes. Or that guy on that old show about the really observant guy who pretends to be a psychic for the police. *Psyche!* That was it."

"I loved that show!" Alecin exclaimed. She paused. "So, does that make you my Gus?"

"You just want me to be your Gus so you can introduce me with weird names," George teased.

"Did you see that one episode where Shawn introduced Gus as John Jacob Jingleheimer Schmidt? And he said it used to be his name too, but whenever they would go out, people would always shout. Hilarious. That was my favorite fake name for Gus ever."

"I remember that. Like that old song." He paused. "What is that song about anyway?"

"Well, I assume it's about someone named John Jacob Jingleheimer Schmidt."

"No. I don't think so," George grinned. "So do me," he said.

"Excuse me?!" Alecin said, shocked.

"No, not like that," George stammered quickly. *Am I ever going to stop saying stupid things to her?* George wondered.

He was actually blushing again, Alecin thought.

"I mean, tell me something about me that you figured out from deductive reasoning."

"No."

"Why not?"

"Cause when I do people I know, sometimes I notice stuff that they would rather me not notice and they get mad."

"One thing," George begged. "Please. I promise I won't get mad."

"Okay, fine. You're angry that I got to the clue before you did—like, seriously pissed. But you don't want me to know that. You're not mad at me. You're not mad that I'm the Chosen One; you're just pissed that you're not. And it's not just pride; there's something else. There's another reason you wanted to be first, but you don't want me to know it. You are somewhat angry at yourself but angrier at something else. Something you think got in your way."

"Nope. Sorry. You're wrong on every count."

"Yeah, I don't think so. But I'll keep going. You have a house near here—within two or three hours, I'd say. But you didn't come from there this morning. You came from the airport this morning. Ah, I see. Your flight was late. I only beat you by what? Ten minutes. You think if your flight hadn't been late, you would have been first. Well, them's the breaks. Buck up, buttercup. There's no crying in baseball."

"One. Props on the movie reference. Two. Without acknowledging that anything you said is true, I will acknowledge your skills with a hearty *damn girl.* Three. I hope everybody saw what just happened there because I will not be doing that again. That is the last time I ever ask you to do that. To me."

"Fantastic. Now," she continued, "if you don't mind, I'd like to do what we came here to do. I'm kind of on a clock."

"Okay. But just tell me the truth. You looked me up or something on the way over."

"Yeah, 'cause you're what comes up when you google George Washington." Alecin rolled her eyes. "Clock's ticking."

"Right," George said, taking a black wand out of his bag.

"That looks like one of those things they use when you get special attention going through airport security."

"Well, it isn't. This is the latest thing in the detection of listening devices."

"And you just happen to be carrying it with you?"

"Well, considering what I had planned to do when I left my house today, I thought it might come in handy. I like to be prepared. And look, it *has* come in handy." He started to scan the room. "Now," he continued, "I know the chances of someone having bugged this room on the off chance we would come here are slim to none, but—"

"But," Alecin interrupted, "someone may have bugged this room for another reason and may just hear something they shouldn't. I agree. With what's at stake, you have to be vigilant."

"That's right. It's nice to be with someone with whom I don't have to explain everything. Although . . ."

"Although what?"

"Although, right now, I'm kind of wondering if you're sitting there thinking that it would be nice if you were with someone to whom you didn't have to explain everything. It's not very often that I'm not the smartest person in the room, Alecin. I'm not sure how I feel about that."

Alecin didn't feel very smart at the moment. Actually, she felt pretty stupid. Sitting there with nothing to do and not knowing what to say. "I'm just going to . . . go check that all the rooms near us really are empty." *Because I need something to do,* thought Alecin.

"Good call," George responded, distracted.

When Alecin got back, George appeared to be just finishing up. "There," he said. "All done. It's clean." He put the wand back in his bag and pulled out a small machine. He set it on the dresser and turned it on. It made a quiet noise, like static. "It's a particular kind of white noise machine," he explained. "It'll ensure that if anyone happens to try to listen, all they'll hear is white noise.

"Okay," he said, slapping his hands together. "Time to put our cards on the table." He took a box from his bag and set it on the foot of the bed. It was similar to Alecin's Guardian box. It had different coloring, but it was the exact same size and shape, and it had the same kind of intricate detailing. George stood at the foot of the bed with the box in front of him.

"I'll show you mine if you show me yours," he repeated his earlier taunt, grinning yet again.

Understanding, Alecin removed her Guardian box from her bag and stood next to George, her box on the foot of the bed in front of her.

"On three," said George. "One, two, three." On three, they both waved their hand over their respective boxes. And the tops disappeared. "So, we each have a box," George said, making the top of his box reappear.

"I guess we do. Hold on a second." Alecin removed the glasses and gold envelope from her satchel and put them in the box, then closed it.

"You mean, you've just been carrying those around? You didn't put them in your box right away?" George scolded.

"I was going to. But I didn't want to stop and do it in the middle of the park, where someone might see. I was going to wait until I was alone in my car. And then someone distracted me," she said, looking at him pointedly, "and wouldn't give me a moment alone."

"Well, from now on. All clues, and . . . anything else we find goes in a box immediately."

"We?"

"Yes, *we*, because I'm going to help you."

"*Are* you now?"

"Yes. Because unless you're an idiot, you will *let* me help you. And you are clearly not an idiot. Now, let me finish proving to you who I am so *we* can get on with the quest."

Alecin didn't like to be told what she should do and what would happen, but she decided storming out would be idiotic and foolish. Besides, he was right. The envelope and glasses should have gone into her box immediately. That was more important than risking someone coming in while she was putting them in there.

When George had opened his box before, Alecin had seen an envelope in it like the ones that had been in the pit at the park. "What did your envelope have in it?" she asked.

"No way. You still have to prove to me that you are who you say you are."

"You're right. We need more. Belt and suspenders, fate of humanity on the line."

"What?"

"Nothing. Just something my grandfather told me."

"So, what do you suggest we do now?"

"We'll ask each other questions that only a Guardian could answer."

"That works." George paused. "All right, Alecin, the battle of wits has begun. It ends when you decide and we both drink— and find out who is a Guardian, and who is dead."

Alecin laughed. "Well, that escalated quickly. Excellent reference."

"Thanks. Okay, I'll go first. What was the name of the planet from which the visitors came?"

Proper grammar, thought Alecin, sighing quietly. That almost made her heart pitter-patter as much as him taking off his helmet and smiling at her. Then, she thought, *Stop it! Time and place, Alecin, time and place.* "Kalec," she answered.

"Okay. Your turn."

"When did the Kalecians first come to earth?"

"Aha. Trick question. No one knows when they first came. The first time they made themselves known was when they abducted The Three in May or June 1776, just before the *Declaration of Independence* was signed."

"Right. Now—"

"Nope. My turn. Were The Three the original Guardians?"

"Now *that's* a trick question. The Three were the original Guardians, but," Alecin continued before George could interrupt, "they were *not* the only original Guardians. There were nine others."

"Who were they?"

"My turn."

"No, that was part of my question."

"You don't get to ask two-part questions. What gift did the Kalecians give the original Guardians and their line?"

"They modified their DNA. Which is why you and I are both geniuses."

"So, you're a genius now?"

"Actually, I am. I've been tested and everything. Certified genius," George pointed to himself, smiling. "My turn again. Who were the original Guardians?"

"Other than The Three and the Guardians in their line, no one knows. For their own safety and for the sake of humanity," Alecin said pointedly, "Guardians weren't supposed to know each other." She paused. "I shouldn't be here." She started gathering up her things.

"Wait a minute. Just wait a minute." George grabbed her arm. "Let me show you something first." He opened his box and took out the envelope from the park. He handed it to Alecin. "Open it."

Alecin stopped and looked at the envelope. She waged a quick war with herself, and her curiosity won. She took the envelope. Opening it, she saw just a white card. She pulled it out. In bold gold lettering, it read: "SUPPORT THE CHOSEN ONE."

"My job right now is to support you. To *help* you. You have to do this, Alecin." George moved to her and took her hand. "But you don't have to do it alone. I don't know about you, but there was nothing in the instructions I saw that said you had to do this quest alone. Let me help you."

He has a point, thought Alecin. There *was* nothing in the Kalecians' instructions that had said that the Chosen One couldn't have help from another Guardian. She looked down at the card in her hand. It seemed, actually, that she was supposed to have help. Fate of humanity, she reminded herself. Was she really so arrogant that she wouldn't accept help from another Guardian . . . from a *certified* genius . . . from someone that could obviously help her? No, Alecin thought. She was not.

"Okay," Alecin agreed at last. "George, you and I shall be the fellowship of the Appello," she pronounced.

George took her hand again and, in his best Aragon impression, said, "I promise, this fellowship will not fail so long as we stay true to each other."

"Are we just going to be quoting movies the whole time?"

George grinned. "It will be a plethora of movie quotes."

"Would you say that I have a plethora of pinatas?"

"*The Three Amigos.* But that's a party foul because it has nothing to do with what we were talking about."

"Sorry. I just think of that quote anytime someone says plethora. So, any idea how we should start?"

"Well, we need someplace private where we can set up and figure out the clue. You were right before. My house is just about three hours from here. I think we should work out of there, at least for figuring out the first clue."

"Hold up. I'd like to know how, if the location in the first instructions was just three hours from your house . . . why you didn't find it first?"

Embarrassed, George tried to explain. "Well, I didn't know it would be three hours from my house, did I?" he said defensively. "I was at my place in Texas, near work, when everyone opened the instructions. I thought it was better to be near an airport, so I could fly wherever I needed to go. And my house isn't anywhere near an airport."

Alecin thought about that, then said, "So, you chose, poorly."

George pointed at her. "*Indiana Jones.*"

"Yes."

George pumped his fist. "I knew it."

"But that brings up a question. How do you live three hours from here if you work in Texas?"

"I have a place near work—a condo. But my place in Tennessee—that's where my *home* is. I spend my summers in Tennessee mostly, working from home. And I go there a lot of weekends. I think you can live anywhere, but you only have one home." He paused. "Okay," he said, gathering up his things and shoving them back in his bag, "let's get out of here."

When they returned to the parking lot, George asked, "Why don't we just take my bike? It's faster, and then you can return your rental."

"Not going to happen. There is zero chance that I will ever get on that death machine. Ever."

"Are you kidding me? Your many-times-great-grandfather was a fearless badass. Are you telling me that his many-time-great-granddaughter is afraid of a motorcycle?"

"Motorcycles, spiders, and any baked good that claims to be vegan are all things I try to avoid. I'm just going to get in my nice safe car here that has doors and windows and airbags. I'll follow you."

"One question. What if the entire fate of humanity depended on you getting on this bike? Would you do it?"

"Maybe then. But it would seriously have to be a do-or-die situation."

"Well, then," George grinned. "We'll just have to see if we can make that happen."

"We don't have to make that happen between here and your place, though, right?"

"Don't worry. I swear on the soul of my father, Domingo Montoya, you will reach the house alive."

"That's just the pinnacle of all swears."

"One more thing. This quest we are about to go on: We'll never survive."

"Nonsense, you're only saying that because no one ever has before." Alecin shot him a grin before closing the door to her car.

This is going to be fun, George thought as he started his bike.

CHAPTER 13

Alecin gasped as George's house finally came into view after she had driven down what was either a short road or a long driveway. She couldn't tell. She didn't know what she had thought he meant when he said he had a cabin, but it wasn't this. The large wood-and-rock home was on a cliff, with an absolutely stunning view of the Smoky Mountains.

The front door was carved oak, with an etched window that showed a bald eagle in flight. Steps that appeared to be made from cut logs led to a porch that extended the entire length of the house. On one side of the porch were two Adirondack chairs, with a small table between them. At the other end of the porch was a swing that looked just big enough to hold two people, if they sat very close together. Next to it was a wooden storage table that Alecin noticed held blankets. Briefly, she wondered how many women George had snuggled up with on that swing, under one of those blankets, but she brutally suppressed the thought.

Alecin got out of her car, walked to the front steps, and just stood, admiring the house. George came up beside her. "What do you think?"

"I think it's breathtaking."

George beamed. "I bought the land sometime back, then had her built from the ground up. It was a labor of love."

"I can tell."

"Come on inside."

Alecin grabbed her satchel, backpack, and a small overnight bag out of her car. When she went to lock her car, George laughed. "Not that much need for that out here."

"It's a habit," she said, shrugging—proceeding to lock her door.

When Alecin walked in the front door, the house took her breath away again. Dominating the room was a massive rock fireplace. A stack of firewood sat neatly stacked next to the hearth. The ceiling above half of the room soared two stories. There were large wooden beams that extended across the ceiling. On the opposite wall from the fireplace was an impressive kitchen that ran nearly the depth of the house, and an equally long island. The kitchen had stainless steel appliances and either gray or white everything else. *It's a man's kitchen,* Alecin thought. Not a touch of fabric or color anywhere. There weren't even any curtains on the window over the sink.

To the right of the kitchen was a cove created by large bay windows, in which sat a small dining set. On the other side of the kitchen was a door. Alecin guessed that behind the door was a bathroom. Maybe a laundry room.

Over the fireplace, George had a large copy of John Trumbull's famous painting depicting Samuel Adams and Benjamin Franklin submitting a draft of the *Declaration of Independence* to the Second Continental Congress, in what looked to be an antique gold frame. The rest of the decor continued with the same theme. Reproductions of—or maybe real—Revolutionary War artifacts were scattered tastefully around the room, and art highlighting that part of history decorated the walls.

Alecin thought it was all just wonderful.

"Come on," George said after she had looked around the great room, "let me show you my pride and joy."

"This isn't it?"

"Well, this is some of it. But I want to show you the room where we can work." He led her up a staircase that was at the far end of the house. Made with those same wooden logs, it wound its way to the second level. The stairs stopped at a long balcony of sorts that overlooked the fireplace and great room. When you turned around, the balcony became a hallway with three different doors. George opened the first door. It led to a bedroom.

"This is the guest room. You can put your stuff down in here if you want."

The room contained a queen-size four-poster bed made from what looked to be oak logs. It had a white duvet, and when Alecin put her overnight bag down, she could feel its warmth and softness. On either side of the bed were small matching end tables. Silver pendant lights hung from the ceiling over each end table. Across from the bed was a simple dresser made of the same wood as the bed. The room was painted white and held no adornment of any kind. *Apparently*, Alecin thought, *George's instinct for design only covered architecture and didn't extend to interior design.*

"There's a bathroom through there," George said, pointing to the far-left corner of the room. "It's all yours. When I designed the house, I insisted this room have its own bathroom. I hate visiting places and not having my own bathroom."

"Me too," Alecin said. "I appreciate it." She looked in the bathroom. It wasn't something you would find in a high-end resort, Alecin thought, but it would do. It had a large walk-in shower, a toilet, and a sink. She didn't really need anything else.

"Do you want to see the master bedroom?" George asked. "I mean," he stammered when she looked at him, "you just seemed to like the rest of the house. I thought you would like to see all of it."

"I do, and I would love to."

They walked into the master bedroom, and Alecin thought it was a room that lived up to its name. Against one wall was a king-size bed with a padded gray headboard. There was a nightstand on either side, made from a glossy dark wood. Seeing her look at them, George said, "It's mahogany. Not local, I know. But I've always loved the look of it, so I decided to go for it in here since it was just these two tables." On the wall across from the bed was a large unadorned, rectangular mirror. "Watch this. TV on," he ordered the mirror, and the mirror turned to a television screen. It was tuned to the news.

"Art on," he ordered. The television screen disappeared, and a reproduction of Monet's Starry Night appeared in its place. "Starry Night, by Monet," a voice began. "Mute audio," George ordered, and the voice went silent. The painting then changed to "Bowl of Fruit" by Vincent Van Gogh. "It cycles through all the great paintings. I don't know much about art, but I decided this might be a good way to learn. Um, the bathroom is back here," he said, walking to the far-left corner.

Now, this was the kind of bathroom you *would* find at a fancy resort, Alecin thought when she looked into the bathroom. It had a huge walk-in shower with multiple jets. A large jet tub that Alecin guessed George could fit his entire six-foot frame into with both his knees and his toes in the water. An installed electric towel warmer warmed luxurious-looking white towels. A spacious counter held double sinks with antique mirrors above each. And everywhere was gorgeous Carrera marble.

"It's perfect," Alecin sighed in pure female admiration and envy.

"Thanks."

George couldn't explain how important it was to him that Alecin liked his house. "Through there"—George pointed to a door at the end of the bathroom—"is the walk-in closet. But we won't go in there. I'm pretty good at keeping the rest of the house clean, but my closet is another story. It's kinda embarrassing. But through here," George said, leading her back into the bedroom and to glass French doors, "is the deck." George opened one of the doors, and Alecin stepped out onto the deck. "This," George said, gesturing to the view, "is why I bought this land and decided to build a house."

"I can see why." The view that Alecin had seen from her car was nothing compared to this. The magnificence and splendor of mountains and untouched wilderness spread out before her. It was truly amazing. "Sometimes," Alecin said quietly, looking out. "Sometimes . . . since I became a Guardian . . . in my darkest moments, when I've been faced with the worst of humanity . . . I wonder if humanity is really worth saving. But when I see beauty like this, I know the Earth is worth saving. And there are still people . . . people like us and so many others . . . who can appreciate this kind of beauty . . . who have peace . . . who can live in harmony with the world around them. And then I know, humanity is worth saving at any cost."

George didn't know how to respond to that. Finally, he said lamely, "there's a door to out here in your room too."

Alecin smiled at him. "Well," Alecin gestured to the view, "let's get to work saving this."

"I have just the place," George said, his voice tinged with excitement.

George led her back in and to a door between the two bedrooms. There, he scanned his fingerprint. Then, he did a retinal scan. Then, he entered a code. And only then did he open the door. "This," George said proudly, walking into the room and holding his arms outstretched, "is my pride and joy. I call it, to myself anyway, my Guardian room. And I make sure no one gets in here but me. You're the first person I have ever let in here. The walls and windows are lined with the same material they use at the Pentagon, for SCIFs. That means . . . "

"Secret Compartmented Facilities. I know," Alecin said, looking around. "I used to work in one when I was at the Pentagon. We did a lot of work with classified material, and in the SCIF, secret or below material could just be left on our desks at night. Top Secret still had to go in a safe. But there wasn't a lot of that. And you could discuss classified material in the SCIF, which was nice, because then we could talk about what we were working on. The walls and windows, I was told, were lined with a material that made it impossible for people to listen in in any way. You have the same stuff here?"

"Yes," George said proudly. "But I still sweep it once a week for bugs. I talk to myself a lot when I'm working," he explained.

"Belt and suspenders. Fate of humanity on the line?"

"Exactly."

The room was sparse on furniture, like the rest of the house. *George certainly is one who believed in minimalism in his decorating,* Alecin thought. On either side of the window were two tall bookcases. Alecin could see an empty spot which she assumed was where George usually kept his box. The rest of the space was filled with books and pictures of people that Alecin guessed were George's family and friends. In one picture, George held a beautiful woman in each arm. Alecin looked at it and raised her eyebrows at him.

"My little sisters," he explained.

Alecin felt relief, and that annoyed her for reasons she didn't care to explore.

On one side of the room was a large, old-fashioned, carved wood desk. "This desk is gorgeous," Alecin admired, running her hand over it.

"It was my grandfather's," George said. "It was the only thing I took from my parent's house. They weren't happy, but I insisted. I've just always loved this desk. And it seemed to be a desk that . . . I don't know, lived up to the purpose of a Guardian."

Over the desk hung a copy of the painting by Emanuel Leutze of Washington crossing the Delaware. "I like to keep it there because I like feeling like Great-Grandpa is watching over me." He walked over to the painting. "You know, that guy," he said, pointing to a man sitting in the back of Washington's boat who had white hair and wore a black hat, "that was a Kalecian."

"No way," Alecin said, moving closer, as if she would be able to tell just by looking at the painting.

"No, I'm kidding. Come on, this painting was done like seventy-five years after Washington crossed the Delaware, and it's not like Leutz had a photograph to work from."

"Of course. Sorry. I knew that. Just got caught up, I guess," Alecin explained sheepishly.

"But one of them *was* with Washington on this campaign, advising and guiding him. I don't know which one, but one of the Kalecians was with him. At least," he grinned, "that's what's been passed down to me. And that is 100 percent true."

"What other stories about Washington have been passed down? Wait, don't tell me. We have other things to do. When all this is over, though, I want to hear them all."

"Same goes, for your Hamilton stories."

Alecin nodded and then focused on the desk once again. The desk was clear except for a computer. "It's encrypted," George explained, seeing her looking at it. He blew out a breath. "I don't know why I'm explaining that to you. I'm sure you have one like it."

Alecin smiled. "I do. What's with the brown paper bag next to the desk? It seems out of place."

"That's my burn bag," George explained. "I use it for—"

"—you put stuff in it that you don't want anyone to see so you can burn it." Alecin interrupted.

"That's right."

"They have them on ship. To collect all the classified material that can't be thrown out and has to be burned. Funny story. I don't usually get seasick, but once, I was on watch on the bridge, and it was extraordinarily rough seas. I got sick rather suddenly and ended up vomiting in the burn bag. The intel people were not happy with me," Alecin said, laughing as it came back to her. "They had to burn the bag with my vomit in it, which I'm sure didn't smell good. Don't worry, though; I won't vomit in your burn bag."

"If you do," George warned, "*you* are burning it."

"Fair enough," Alecin said, laughing again.

Across from the desk, two large maps hung on the wall. One was of the United States as it existed in 1797. And one was the United States as of 2024. Alecin nodded at them in appreciation. "Those should come in handy. Well," she said, turning to him, "let's get started."

Alecin woke early the next morning. It took her a second to remember where she was. After getting up, she walked to the door to the deck and stepped out. If possible, the view was even more glorious in the early morning sun. She could see clearly how the Great Smoky Mountains had earned their name. She saw George sitting on a couch, his feet up on some kind of ottoman, looking out and drinking coffee.

He turned when he heard her. "Good morning," he said.

She was wearing Avengers sleep pants and a blue sweatshirt that declared that David Tennant was her doctor.

George wasn't sure if he liked the outfit or the girl wearing it more. Her hair was tousled from sleep, and she didn't look like she had quite woken up all the way yet. He found that oddly alluring. *Definitely the girl more*, he decided. He cleared his throat. "Would you like some coffee?" he asked, fervently hoping he sounded casual.

"That sounds great, but I can go downstairs and get it."

"No need. I have a full coffee bar up here. I like sitting out here and drinking coffee—a lot. I think it's one of the greatest pleasures in life." As he talked, he walked over to what was, indeed, a full coffee bar. It was tucked up against the house in what appeared to be a little alcove.

"That's awesome," Alecin said with enthusiasm. "I must have missed this yesterday."

"No, you didn't," George explained. "When I'm not using it, the bar is covered behind a stainless-steel wall. So the bar isn't ruined by exposure to the elements. I just push this button here," George said, pointing to the side of the bar, "and the wall comes down or goes up."

George took out a coffee cup, intending to make her a cup of coffee, but then—remembering Alecin's unique way of drinking diet coke—stopped. "Maybe I should just let you make your own. I have a feeling you are, I'm just going to go with 'particular,' about your coffee." He put down the coffee cup and leaned against the wall with his own coffee, watching her. If she was that weird about how she drank her diet coke, he was curious about what she would do to coffee.

"Thanks," Alecin said, relieved. She had resigned herself to drinking coffee however George had prepared it for her, just to be polite. Now she could make it how she liked it. She took out some creamer and poured what George thought was a lot and what she thought was the perfect amount, into the cup. She then put the cup in the little microwave of the coffee bar.

"You heat up your creamer?"

"Yes. I use what I've discovered many people, including my dad, think of as a lot of creamer. If I add cold creamer to the hot coffee, I end up with warm coffee. And I like hot coffee. So, I warm up the creamer first."

"Makes sense. But why don't you just use less creamer?"

"Because I like *more* creamer," Alecin said simply.

She has me there, George thought. He couldn't argue with that logic.

"I like brewing each cup as I drink it, so I use a Keurig. I like straight coffee, but I have some different coffee flavors for, um . . . company. The K-cups are in that drawer there." George pointed.

Alecin thought she had a pretty good guess what *company* meant.

While Alecin reviewed her options, George said, "I didn't

know you liked hazelnut, or I would have had some. If we stay here much longer, I can go out and get some."

Alecin selected a K-cup labeled "Butter Toffee." "This will work fine," she said, placing it in the Keurig. When her coffee was ready, she and George walked back to the couch. Sitting there, drinking coffee, and listening as George pointed out different mountains and told stories about the area, Alecin thought he was exactly right. It was one of life's greatest pleasures. *When this is over*, Alecin promised herself, *I'm going to build a house just like this for myself.*

When they had finished their coffee, George took their cups and put them in the compact dishwasher he had at the coffee bar. *The man really had thought of everything*, Alecin thought.

As the wall lowered over the bar, George said, "Why don't we take a few to shower and get dressed? I'll meet you downstairs in twenty."

"That works," Alecin said, and walked to her room to begin another day of saving the world.

After her shower, Alecin considered her options. What is the appropriate attire for trying to figure out a clue to the location of part of an alien bat signal with some guy she met yesterday? *Finishing school didn't cover that one,* Alecin thought, still bitter that her mother had made her go through what she considered to be a complete waste of time. Jeans and one of her old law school T-shirts, Alecin decided. An ensemble that worked for nearly every occasion.

Once she was dressed, Alecin ran a little product through her hair. After she got out of the military, she had initially tried to grow her hair long, but she soon realized that she had neither the time nor the motivation to manage long hair, and had returned to short hair. It was longer than her former pixie cut, but it still took all of thirty seconds to do, and Alecin considered that perfect. She briefly thought of putting on makeup, but then, annoyed with herself, she rejected that idea. She had serious work to do, after all. She wasn't going out on a date.

When Alecin came downstairs, she found George already in the kitchen. His hair was still damp from his shower, and Alecin had to fight the urge to brush his hair back from his face. Alecin noticed that he had had the same idea about attire. He wore jeans and an old MIT T-shirt. Alecin thought it wasn't fair that he looked so rugged and attractive in a T-shirt and jeans while she looked boring and frumpy in her T-shirt and jeans.

There were several boxes of cereal on the little table in the alcove, as well as milk, bowls, and spoons. George was at the kitchen island, making toast.

"Good morning again," he said. George thought it wasn't fair that she looked so beautiful and sexy in a T-shirt and jeans while he looked boring and plain in his T-shirt and jeans. "I'm sorry. I wasn't expecting company. All I have is cold cereal. I can go get other stuff later. Do you want toast?"

"What kind of bread?"

"Brown. I think it's maybe wheat. To be honest, I hate grocery shopping. I have a woman, Irene, that comes in once a week and brings me all my groceries. I just eat whatever she buys."

"Brown is fine. Thanks."

Alecin sat and contemplated her cereal options. "Is Irene under the mistaken impression that you're five years old?"

"What do you mean?" George asked, puzzled.

"I mean, you have Apple Jacks, Frosted Flakes, and Froot Loops. Don't you have any . . . grown-up cereal?"

"Why would I want to eat that stuff?" George asked, genuinely confused. "If I wanted to eat twigs and bark, I'd just go gather some up outside. And it's not as if I eat cereal all the time. I wasn't really expecting I'd be back here so soon. This is my emergency food stash." He brought over a stack of toast and a couple of plates. "There's butter there. And you should try the strawberry jam. My mom made it. It's amazing."

Alecin buttered her toast and cut it into neat triangles. She then put a small amount of jam on one triangle and took a small bite. "You weren't kidding. That really is amazing."

"Yeah," George agreed proudly. "She's been making it since she was a kid. She and Grandma used to do it every summer." As he spoke, he spread butter and jam all over his toast and took a large bite. Looking at her neat little triangles, he raised his eyebrows.

"It's just how I was raised," she said defensively.

"I was raised that way too, but then I grew up and realized cutting your toast into triangles was stupid and a waste of time. I don't like doing anything that's a waste of time. This way is more efficient."

I'll need to think about that, Alecin thought, but for now, she'd keep to her way. She selected Apple Jacks. She poured some milk into her bowl and then added about a handful of cereal. She ate it and then added another handful. Then, she noticed George watching her.

"What in the name of all that is Southern are you doing?" he asked, thoroughly perplexed.

"What?" She had been raised in the South, but she had never heard that expression before.

"It's something my mom says," he explained, "it means—"

"I think I can figure it out from context," Alecin said, cutting him off. "If you add the cereal and then cover it with milk, the cereal gets soggy'" Alecin patiently explained. "It's gross. You only get a couple of good bites. This way, every bite is good. No soggies."

George thought for a second. "That is the most ingenious thing I have ever heard. Why have humans been doing it the other way all this time? It makes no sense." He got up and dumped his bowl of soggy frosted flakes into the sink. Then, he came back, filled his bowl with milk, and added a handful of frosted flakes. "That is so much better!" he exclaimed after a bite. Alecin grabbed another piece of toast. She covered it with butter and jam and bit into it. If he could change, so could she. They grinned at each other across the table.

An hour later, Alecin and George were in his Guardian room. "I think we, or really I, should send a message to the other Guardians. Let them know that the Chosen One has been Chosen."

"Why?"

"Well, when I was thinking about why it would be only one of us, and not all of us, that went on this quest, I thought that the reason was probably so that if something happened to me, or whoever became the chosen one, one of the other Guardians could step up, complete the quest. But no one will be able to step up if they don't know what's happening. And how can they support the one if they don't know what's happening? I was planning on sending the other Guardians daily updates—just a general idea of what was happening. Enough information so if something happened to both of us, one of them could continue the quest."

"That's a good point. Plus, if I weren't here with you, as a Guardian, I would really like to know what's happening."

"I'll get the message sent out, and you can keep working on figuring out the clue."

"Right. Maybe I'll have a burst of brilliance."

"We can only hope."

George turned to look at the clue for what seemed to be the millionth time. "What we've got here," he said quietly to himself, "is a failure to communicate."

CHAPTER 14

Alecin and George had worked late into the night the night before, but the only progress they had made was to write the clue in large letters on a piece of poster board and hang it on the wall with the maps. This morning, the only progress they had made so far was to write the first clue on another poster board and hang it next to the second clue. They were trying to figure out if there was a pattern to the clues. If there was, so far, they weren't seeing it.

Alecin read the clue yet again.

NORRIS CALLS JOHN

It still made no sense.

"Are you sure there is nothing else written on the card?" asked George.

"Unless you can think of another way to reveal possible secret writings, then, ya, I'm sure."

Since the clue was only three words, they both had thought there must be something else written on the card. Operating under this theory, the night before, they had tried to read the possible invisible writing. First, they had looked at both sides of the card with the glasses that were with the envelope. Then, they had looked at the envelope itself with the glasses. Then, they had carefully taken the envelope apart and examined every inch of it with the glasses. They each had tried holding the card for five, then ten, then, in desperation, thirty minutes, to see if their DNA could make something happen. They had held the card over a flame. They had held the *envelope* over a flame.

At nearly midnight, when they were both going crazy with frustration, they had tried putting lemon juice on the card and the envelope and blowing on both with a hair dryer, as they had done in National Treasure, to see the hidden writing on the *Declaration of Independence*. Nothing had worked, and they had given up on the idea of secret writing.

"Maybe we should try looking 'Norris' up on the internet again?"

"Why? So we can look at more fan sites for Chuck Norris?" George asked sarcastically.

"Well, it's not like we can search for 'calls' or 'John' on the internet," Alecin said with some heat.

"I know that. Maybe we can try searching for 'Norris calls John' again?"

"We did that already. We looked at twenty pages of search results. I don't think the internet has changed that much since last night."

George ran his hands through his hair. Alecin had learned that was what he did when he was frustrated. "We need a break," he declared. "We need to get away from this and come back to it with fresh eyes."

"Sounds good to me." She liked to be alone when she was thinking, and in her frustration, George was beginning to drive her crazy.

"I have a home gym downstairs," George began. "It's nothing fancy, but we can both get a workout in. We can clear our minds. Working out always helps me when I'm dealing with a difficult problem I can't solve."

"George, that is the best idea you've had all day."

George did not quite know if that was a compliment or an insult, so he chose to ignore it.

Ten minutes later, Alecin walked into George's home gym. Apparently, the door next to the kitchen that she had thought led to a bathroom actually led to a powder room, a laundry room, *and* a home gym. George had said it was nothing fancy, and as far as the equipment went, he was right. He had some free weights, a bench, a rowing machine, and an elliptical machine. But the view. The view is what took this home gym to the next level. One entire wall was a window that took advantage of George's fantastic view of the mountains. Alecin thought she had never worked out in a more beautiful place.

George was already on the rowing machine, and it looked like he was just starting his warm-up. "Okay if I use the elliptical?" she asked.

"Go ahead. I have it because my mom likes to use it when she comes to visit. But I always use the rower. I like to listen to music when I work out, and I hate headphones. Okay if I blast some music in here?"

"Perfect. I'm not a fan of headphones either."

"What kind of music do you like to work out to?"

"I'm open. I just hate that pulsing stuff they blast in gyms and call music."

"Got it. This is the South, so when in Rome . . . " He hit a button on a small remote control, and country music, which sounded like a workout remix, blasted into the room.

I could get used to this, Alecin thought, listening. It was pretty good.

They worked out in silence for about twenty minutes; then, George switched to free weights. Alecin stayed on the elliptical. She preferred the constant and steady rhythm of the machine.

In her head, she repeated, "Norris calls John," in rhythm with the elliptical. But after a while, she was getting annoyed. *What does that mean anyway?* she thought. It didn't even make sense. Nobody could call anybody in 1797. They didn't even have telephones. Then, she stopped. Maybe that was it.

"Stop the music a minute, George," she shouted at him over Dierks Bentley singing about calling 5-1-5-0.

George muted the music. "What have you got?" He knew that tone. She had thought of something.

"What if we're looking at this too twenty-first century? When we read 'call,' our mind goes to telephones . . . we think of somebody calling somebody else on the telephone. That's how the word is usually used in our time, but not in 1797. So, if in 2024, we use telephones to call someone, what did they use in 1797? If, in the late 1700s, Norris had wanted to call John, how could he do it?"

"Well, he could just call at him from across the room."

"Okay, but maybe Norris isn't a name at all. What if the clue is talking about an object calling John? What objects in 1797 were used to call someone?"

They were both silent for a minute. Then, it hit them. "A bell!" they shouted in unison.

"Let's go," George yelled, and they ran upstairs.

Back in his Guardian room, George grabbed his computer. "Okay, what should I search for?" he asked.

"Well, John is still way too common. Try searching 'Norris' and 'bell.'"

George quickly scrolled through the first four pages of results. "I'm not seeing anything," he said.

Alecin paced. What was she missing? She knew she was missing *something*. "Maybe the bell belonged to Norris. Try Norris's bell."

George started scrolling through the search results. "Nothing on the first page . . . nothing on the second page . . . wait, I think this may be it!" George said excitedly. Alecin ran and looked over his shoulder. George pointed at the computer screen.

"The Liberty Bell. It's the Liberty Bell," she said quietly. "It's the Liberty Bell!" she shouted. She grabbed her laptop. "Let's find out everything we can about the Liberty Bell."

After a few minutes, George said, "Okay, the Liberty Bell was ordered by Speaker of the Pennsylvania Assembly Isaac Norris—"

"—and it was hung in the Pennsylvania State House—" Alecin picked up.

"—which was later renamed Independence Hall—" George continued.

"—where both the *Declaration of Independence* and *Constitution* were signed," Alecin finished.

"During the Second Continental Congress, the bell was used to *call* members to a session, and the President of the Second Continental Congress was John Hancock!" Alecin said triumphantly.

"We need to go to Philadelphia!" they shouted together.

"Meet me at my car in ten minutes," Alecin said, packing up her things.

"Let's do twenty. I need a shower before I go anywhere," George said.

Alecin looked down at herself. She forgot that she had just been exercising. She could definitely use a shower too. "Okay. Twenty," she said. "And then we've got a bell to see."

Several hours later, Alecin and George were driving through the streets of Philadelphia in a Ford Mustang they had rented because George had steadfastly refused to rent a sedan and had agreed that Alecin could drive if they got the Mustang. It was kind of fun driving a Mustang, Alecin thought. But there was no way she was going to tell George that. George was in the passenger seat, trying to learn everything he could about the

Liberty Bell, just like they had been doing every spare minute since leaving his house.

"What time does the Liberty Bell visitor center close again?" Alecin asked.

"5 p.m. We have an hour to find the part and the clue, or we'll have to come back tomorrow."

"Let's hope it doesn't come to that."

"Agreed. Okay, this is it, coming up on the right. Just find a spot in the parking garage."

Alecin pulled into the garage and, given the hour and the fact that it was a weekday, had no problem finding a parking space near the elevator up to street level.

"A parking space right in front," Alecin said. "That's a good omen." She looked a George expectantly.

"What?"

"What movie?"

"That's from a movie?"

"Yep."

"Um, give me a minute." George thought for a moment. "I got nothing."

"My point then." Alecin grinned. "We should get going."

Once in the visitor's center, Alecin and George walked around the Liberty Bell, or at least as close as they could get to it without crossing the velvet ropes meant to keep people away. After a half hour passed, Alecin began to get anxious. Their hour was slipping away, and they still hadn't found what they were looking for.

"Do you think we should be looking in the bell tower over at Independence Hall?" Alecin asked.

"I don't know. I mean, the bell tower is where the calling would have taken place, right? Maybe we've been wrong to focus on the Bell."

"Well, by the time we walked over there, it would be closed. So, let's stay here and see what we can find."

"There may come a day," George said, adopting the voice of

Aragorn in *Lord of the Rings*, "that we will go to Independence Hall, but it is not this day."

It made Alecin laugh, as he had intended. Alecin looked around. She was thinking they would need to get closer to the Bell, and she was wondering if anyone would notice. In the visitor's center, there was a family reading about the history of the Bell, and their backs were to Alecin and George. There was also a man by himself, who didn't seem to be doing anything but walking around. *That's a bit weird*, Alecin thought. *He doesn't look like he belongs here.*

George came over and stood next to Alecin. He whispered under his breath, "Remember how we had to touch the ground at Kings Mountain?"

"Yeah," Alecin whispered suspiciously.

"I think you may have to touch the Bell."

"But I don't want to touch the Bell," Alecin whined. "I'm pretty sure that's illegal. There are security cameras everywhere. I can't complete the quest if I'm in jail."

"Hold on," George said, taking out his cell phone. He worked on it for about five minutes.

"There," George told her, "the security cameras are off."

"You can . . . do that?" Alecin was more than a little shocked.

"Hey, it's not like it's rocket science," George said, flashing her a grin. "But I can't do anything about the guard."

"He won't do anything. He has a new baby at home, and she's been keeping him up nights. He just wants to get home."

"How . . . but . . . *really*?"

Alecin rolled her eyes. "Circles under his eyes, baby spit up on his uniform, and he keeps checking his watch."

Alecin looked around. Everyone else had left. They had ten minutes until closing.

"It's now or never," George whispered.

"Where should I touch it?"

"I don't know. The crack?"

"But it didn't crack until the 1800s."

"Right. Good point," George said, then fell into thought. "Just . . . touch it *anywhere*. See what happens."

"Wait," Alecin said, suddenly inspired. She pulled the special glasses that had been in the pit with the first clue out of her satchel. She put them on and looked at the Bell.

The Bell had an inscription: "Proclaim Liberty Throughout All the Land Unto All the Inhabitants Thereof."

Was she crazy, or did the word *Liberty* shimmer when she read the inscription through the glasses? She handed the glasses to George.

He put them on and looked as well. Handing them back to her, he nodded and whispered the word: "*Liberty*."

Guess I'm not *crazy*, Alecin thought. The word was shimmering. And that meant George was probably right. She probably had to touch the word.

Alecin looked around. The family and the strange man had both left. Glancing at the guard, Alecin saw that his back was to her. She gulped. Now or never. She quickly but quietly stepped over the velvet rope.

Gingerly, she touched the word *Liberty* on the Bell. She felt something like a mild electrical shock. Turning to look at George, she mouthed, "How long?" He just shrugged his shoulders. *Well, he was no help*, Alecin thought. She counted to ten and pulled her hand away. As soon as she pulled her hand away, the metal of the entire Bell began to shimmer, like it was going to liquefy. *Oh crap*, Alecin thought, panicking. *I've melted the Liberty Bell!*

After a few moments, though, it stopped shimmering. Right below *Liberty*, a metal bar emerged from the Bell. Alecin stared at it.

The metal bar was about the length of a candy bar, but twice as thick. It looked to be made from the same metal as the Bell.

She stood staring at it, transfixed.

The security guard began to look over, and George quickly positioned himself between the guard and Alecin. He smiled and waved at the guard, who smiled awkwardly, then turned back around.

"Alecin!" George whispered—with force.

Right, she told herself. *Think later. Act now.* Quickly, she grabbed the metal bar, and once she had taken the bar, a small gold envelope emerged. She grabbed that, too. Then, she stepped back over the velvet ropes.

"Alecin, look!" George whispered in shock, pointing at the Bell. The crack had disappeared. The Bell had repaired itself.

"Oh shit!" Alecin exclaimed quietly. "We need to get out of here. They're definitely going to notice that."

Nodding, George grabbed her arm, and they walked quickly out the door. They didn't slow down until they got to the parking garage. They looked at each other, both a little shell-shocked.

"What the . . .?" George stammered.

"I have no idea. But I feel like somebody is going to notice the Liberty Bell being miraculously repaired. You sure the security cameras were off?"

"Yes." George took his phone out of his pocket. "That reminds me," he mumbled. He worked on his phone for a few minutes. "Back on. Let's go."

They were just about to their car when three men stepped out of the darkness.

Where did they come from? Alecin thought. Each of them held a gun pointed directly at them. *What's going on?* George and Alecin looked at each other in confusion.

The three men were all large, muscular, and dressed in black. They looked like somebody had ordered three "bad guys" off the internet. They fit the stereotype right down to their close-cropped haircuts. They made no effort to hide their faces, which George felt was a particularly not-good sign. One of them was the man that had been in the visitor's center earlier.

The man in the middle spoke. "I believe you have something we want." He was Caucasian with a nose that had been broken more than once and a scar that extended from the inner corner of his right eye to his chin. His eyes were dark and devoid of emotion.

He'll kill us and not give it a second thought, Alecin concluded.

"Just take it easy," George said with a calm that surprised Alecin. He put his hands up in a gesture of appeasement. "We don't want any trouble. She doesn't have anything. You can have my wallet. It's in my right jacket pocket. And my watch. It's a nice watch. Expensive."

"We don't want your money," Scarface—as Alecin had instantly dubbed him—snarled. "We want whatever you got from that bell up there."

George and Alecin exchanged looks of shock. How did anyone know they had taken something from the Bell? How was that even possible?

"Now!" Scarface demanded when neither Alecin nor George made a move to hand him anything.

Alecin looked at George, silently asking what she should do.

"We have no idea what you're talking about," George said, trying to sound as soothing and innocent as possible.

"We don't have time for games," Scarface snarled. (*Can this guy do anything but snarl?* Alecin wondered.) "Now give me what you got from the Bell, or the girl gets a bullet in the head." Scarface aimed his gun directly at Alecin's head.

"Okay, okay," Alecin stammered, trying to keep her fear out of her voice. She reached into her satchel and slowly pulled the Appello part out. "Here," she said, holding it out to him. "You don't know what . . . " she started to say.

Suddenly, a blinding white light shot out from one side of the bar. Instinctively, Alecin turned the bar to shine the light directly at the guys with guns. They all screamed and grabbed their eyes, dropping their weapons. Then, they all fell to the ground, still holding their eyes and still screaming.

I'll think about that later, Alecin thought and ran to the car. She hopped in the driver's seat and started the Mustang. As soon as George had shut the passenger door, Alecin peeled out of the garage as fast as she could. Once she'd forked over a few "Washingtons" at the pay station—a routine that felt comedically slow—she tore through the city streets as if speed limits and traffic signals were just suggestions.

"How did they know? How did they find us? Why did they want the part? How did the part do that? How did it know? How did it stop? Are they following us?" Alecin asked, streaming the questions together as if they were one long question.

"I don't know," George replied.

"For which one?"

"All of them. Look, slow down. They're not following us. I don't think they *could*. It looked like the Appello part blinded them—at least temporarily. And you're just risking our lives— and jail—by driving like a maniac this way."

"You're right. Sorry." Alecin slowed and began to drive normally again. But then, mild hysteria kicked in. "I've never had a gun pointed at me before. I've never had someone threaten to kill me. Why did they want to kill us?!"

"Alecin, it's okay. Pull in there," George instructed, pointing to a parking lot. He had heard the hysteria in Alecin's voice. Alecin pulled into the nearest parking lot and stopped the car.

"It's ok," George told her, his voice calm and soothing. "Deep breaths. Deep breaths." He demonstrated taking a deep breath.

Alecin took deep breaths. Then, she looked at George accusingly. "How are you so calm?"

"Because only one of us can freak out at a time, and right now seems to be your turn."

Somehow, that made Alecin feel better. "Okay, okay. I'm calm," she declared after several deep breaths. "Before we do anything else, we need to get that stuff in a box." Alecin pulled her box out of her backpack. She quickly put the envelope and the Appello part from the Bell inside.

"Just FYI. I'm going to start freaking out again, but it's going to focus more on the idea that they found us because somewhere along the line, I screwed up."

"Okay. But before you freak out again, can we talk about what just happened?"

"In here?"

"Ya. Just a minute." George took his wand out of his bag and began to sweep the car. "By the way, it was *Girls Just Want to Have Fun*."

"What?"

"Your parking space quote, it was from *Girls Just Want to Have Fun*."

"You looked it up, didn't you?"

"Of course. Why would I ever watch a movie from the 1980s about a dance contest? And we're good. We can talk now." George put the wand away.

"Well, here's what I know about what just happened: absolutely nothing. I mean, who were those guys? Any idea?"

"None. And how did they know we got something from the Bell? And how did the part do that? How did it know to do that? And how about some warning? It could have blinded *us*. Would it have been so hard to write 'this side toward enemy' on it?"

"Hmmm. I was thinking, the Bell and the ground at the mountain—it seemed like they could read Guardian DNA, right?"

"Yeah . . . "

"Well, what if the Appello part can read more than that? I mean, given the stakes, a self-protective method for the parts makes sense. The part was in my hand before the light of a thousand suns came blasting out. What if it read my increased heart rate and adrenalin and knew there was danger? So, it tried to protect itself?"

George considered. "That actually makes a lot of sense. Do you think all the parts will do that?"

"Makes sense that they would."

"Whatever happened, we should get moving. This time, I drive." George said insistingly.

"Okay," Alecin agreed. Once they were on their way, Alecin warned, "I'm going to start my next freak-out now."

"Just FYI, I'm going to go ahead and drive to the airport while you're doing your freakout. It doesn't mean I don't care," George said, grinning.

True to her word, Alecin began freaking out, focusing on everything she had done since becoming a Guardian and wondering where she had screwed up. As she did her freak out, George asked if she agreed they should go back to Tennessee because it wasn't safe to stay in Philadelphia. She nodded and continued. By the time they got to the airport, she had calmed down again. Once inside the airport, they became a happy, normal couple that had taken a sightseeing trip to Philadelphia and was just as shocked as everyone else by the news that the crack in the Liberty Bell had mysteriously been fixed.

CHAPTER 15

When Alecin walked into George's home, she thought she had never been happier to enter a house in her entire life. Their trip to Philadelphia had been strange and terrifying.

As she looked around, Alecin was taken aback when she noticed that there were new locks on the door and that security cameras had been installed in the less than one day they had been gone. "When did that happen?" she asked, gesturing to one of the new security cameras.

"I called a guy I know when we were waiting at the airport. I told him I didn't care what it took; it had to be done by the time we got here. After Philadelphia, I didn't want to take any chances."

"Do you think they know where you live?"

"I don't know what they know, so I'm going to assume they know everything. You probably didn't notice, but I also had my guy put in motion detectors around the perimeter points of entry. If someone tries to get through, it will let us know, and we'll have time to get into the Guardian room. Except for the fact that it's easy to find, it's pretty much a panic room. I also hired some private security. They'll also be notified if a perimeter alarm goes off. So, if someone does try to break in, we just need to hold them off until the cavalry arrives."

"That's a lot of security. Do you even know how to work the security system?"

"I *should*. I *designed* it."

"You *designed* it?" Alecin gaped.

"Yeah. I leased the design to my guy so he can use it, and in return, he installed the security system and is providing the private security guys."

"So, you just designed a security system in the airport?"

"Well, I had it mostly done already. I just *finished* it at the airport. And once my guy signed the contract my lawyer had sent over, he got to work installing everything. I figured better safe than sorry. Belt and suspenders, fate of humanity at stake, right?"

"Belt and suspenders, fate of humanity at stake," Alecin agreed, slightly dumbfounded. "You had your lawyer draft up and send a guy a contract for the lease of a security system that you had just designed, all while we were at the airport. Where was I?"

"You had gone off so you could call into your office in private."

"You know," Alecin said after a moment, "you're a pretty handy guy to have around, George Washington."

"Good, that means you'll keep me around," he said, donning his signature grin. "Now, bed, food, or upstairs to look in your box?"

"Box."

"I was *hoping* you'd say that."

In the Guardian room, George grabbed a couple of bottles of water out of the mini-fridge he had hidden in something that looked like a closet. *It probably started out as a closet*, Alecin thought.

"So, I was thinking," Alecin began, "we should just keep the

Appello parts in my box. Keep them all together."

"Agreed."

"Great. Let's see what the next clue is." Alecin opened her box and pulled out the gold envelope that had emerged from the Bell. After reading the clue, she handed it to George. He read the clue and then looked up at her, a huge grin on his face—one that could only be described as a Cheshire Cat grin.

"What?" Alecin demanded. "Why are you smiling like that?"

"Because . . ." George paused for effect. "I know exactly where we need to go."

"Where?" Alecin asked with equal measures of skepticism and excitement.

"We need to go to Mount Vernon," George declared with barely concealed excitement—and some pride.

"What?" Alecin grabbed the clue and read it again.

EAGLE, BELL, STARS

Mount Vernon certainly didn't jump out at her. "How could you possibly know that?" she demanded.

"Alecin, I've been raised on a steady diet of stories about George Washington since I could first hold a bottle. I've been to Mount Vernon I don't know how many times. I know it better than the guides that work there."

"But how does 'eagle, bell, stars' point to Mount Vernon."

"Here. It's easier if I show you." He grabbed his computer and typed for a few minutes. "See," he said, turning the screen to Alecin. Alecin saw a picture of a family crest with lots of red and white. There was an eagle at the top. Below the eagle was a bell and then three stars below that. "It's the Washington family crest," George informed her.

"It's the Washington family crest," Alecin repeated in amazement.

"That's what I said. We have the crest hanging up in our house, but I doubt the Kalecians cared about my house. Plus, it hadn't been built in 1797. But the Washington family crest is displayed prominently at Mount Vernon, and the Kalecians would have cared about Mount Vernon, and Mount Vernon did exist in 1797."

"We have to go to Mount Vernon," Alecin stated.

"We have to go to Mount Vernon," George repeated, still smiling.

"So, where in Mount Vernon is it?"

"*That* I don't know."

"But . . ." Alecin stammered. "Mount Vernon is huge. How are we supposed to find one tiny little—assuming the next part is approximately the same size as the last one—part in that gigantic estate?"

"I don't know," George replied defensively. "I said I knew it well. I didn't say I had every square inch of the whole estate memorized. It's a massive estate. And it's not like I once saw an Appello part sitting there and thought, 'Hey, look, that's part of some kind of alien calling device. I should just file that away for future reference.' "

"You don't have to be *snarky.*"

George looked about ready to snarl, but then he sighed. "You're right, you're right. I'm sorry. It's just been a long and difficult day. I'm tired and stressed about somebody trying to kill us. But it doesn't help anything if we start snapping at each other. Look, once we get there, I bet we will be able to figure it out. I have faith in us."

Alecin nodded. She had faith too. And it *would* probably speed up the process to look for the part with someone who knew Mount Vernon so well. She would need to learn all she could about Mount Vernon before they got there, though. She didn't want to feel like she was just along for the ride. She wanted to do her part.

George's face then turned somber. "Before we go anywhere, though, we need to talk about these guys from the parking garage. How did they know about the Appello?"

"They may not know about the Appello," Alecin pointed out, "or the Kalecians. Maybe they just knew enough to think that there was some potentially valuable advanced technology there that could be very profitable. And that we are the ones who would be able to find it."

"That's true," George agreed thoughtfully. "They never mentioned the Appello or any kind of device. But I think it's safer if we just assume they know everything."

"I agree, to a point. I don't think we should assume they know where the next part is. I mean, we are literally the only people on the planet who have ever seen this clue." She gestured with the clue. "How did they know to go to the Liberty Bell, though?" Alecin continued, then answered her own question. "They didn't. They followed us. They know who we are, and they're going to follow us until they get all the parts they can by any means necessary, aren't they?"

"Yes." Thinking back to Alecin's self-accusing tirade in Philadelphia, George continued. "I don't think it does us any good to try to figure out where we may have screwed up and beat ourselves up about it. For all we know, we didn't. Maybe one of the other Guardians did. Maybe someone in our lines did at some point in history. At this point, though, it's irrelevant. What's done is done, and we need to focus on moving forward."

"You're right. You're right. Guilt is *not* a productive emotion right now. Just going to shove that guilt to the bottom," she said, moving her hand as if she were trying to shove something down. "I'll deal with it later." She took a deep breath. "Okay. Done. Guilt is all gone."

"Great. Now, we need to figure out how to keep them from following us to the next place. Those guys are probably still tracking us, and they probably know our names. We're going to need some fake IDs and some cash. I know a guy who does fake IDs—pretty good ones, too—but I can't do it until morning."

"Just how many guys do you know?"

"I get around," he said, shrugging. "I'm a likable guy."

"Do I even want to know how you know a guy that makes fake IDs?"

"Um, no. Definitely not. Here," he said after a pause, pulling out his phone and looking around. "He'll need a photo of you for the ID, and we need a white background. Go stand over there." He pointed to an area of clean wall. She did as instructed.

"Okay, one more thing," he said after taking her picture. He walked over to her, took her hand, and then got down on one knee. "Will you marry me?"

Alecin jumped back as if he had given her a solid electrical shock. "What? How?" she stammered.

George laughed. "Just for the IDs, Alecin. The bad guys are looking for two single people. I think we have a better chance of them not being able to find us if we're a married couple."

Alecin took several deep breaths while George continued to laugh. "Okay, yeah, that makes sense. I'm glad you find me nearly having a heart attack so funny," she said.

George stopped laughing. "You know," he said with mock indignation, "you didn't need to freak out *that* much. I'm quite a catch."

"No matter how good a catch you are. Any guy that proposes after knowing someone for two days deserves to be thrown back."

"Fair enough," he laughed, but he was actually a little hurt that she had freaked out *so* much.

"Let's grab some dinner and head to bed. I had Irene bring some groceries in while we were in Philadelphia, so we should be able to scrounge up a decent meal."

Suddenly realizing how hungry she was, Alecin agreed and followed him downstairs.

Early the next morning, Alecin wandered downstairs and looked over breakfast options. She found what she needed to make an omelet, one of the few things she could make well. She had just gotten started when George walked downstairs.

He was slightly shocked to see her cooking but tried to hide it.

"What's all this?" he asked, trying to sound nonchalant.

Alecin looked up from her egg whipping and smiled at him. "I'm making omelets." On seeing George's look of mild terror, she added defensively, "I can make *omelets*. I make *good* omelets."

If George had learned one thing in his life, he had learned that when a woman cooked for you, you ate what she served you. So, he really hoped Alecin could actually make an omelet.

"Anything I can do to help?" he asked as he got his morning coffee.

"I saw some fruit in the fridge. Could you put together two small fruit bowls to go with our omelets?"

"I can do that," George said, going to the fridge.

When breakfast was ready, they sat in the breakfast nook. George took a cautious bite of his omelet. It actually tasted pretty good, he thought, relieved. Alecin had been watching him and was unreasonably pleased that he liked her omelet.

As they were finishing breakfast, the doorbell rang. Alecin looked at George with panic.

"Don't worry," he said, rising, "I invited him."

"But what about the perimeter alarms," she asked, still uneasy. "Why didn't they go off?"

"They *did*," George assured her, walking to the door. "I got an alert on my phone. I cleared him."

Alecin watched as he went to the door, prepared to run upstairs at the first sign of trouble. George hugged whoever was at the door. *He can't be that bad if George is hugging him*, she thought. *Maybe he's the ID guy.*

The two men walked over to where Alecin still sat. The stranger looked like George with just some slight differences. *Brother*, Alecin decided. *Probably not the ID guy.*

"Alecin Hamilton, Mark Washington. My brother."

"It's nice to meet you, Alecin," Mark said, smiling. "George has told me absolutely nothing about you."

"Hi. Ditto."

As Mark laughed, George explained, "Mark is going to help us get out of the house without anyone noticing. He's going to drive your car, and I hope that the bad guys will think that's me and follow him. And you're going to lie in the backseat while I drive his car. I'm hoping the bad guys won't follow us. Mark is going with me to see my ID guy too. He's a good guy, but it never hurts to bring back up." George smiled. He had explained his plan like it was a done deal, and Alecin wasn't happy.

"That's great," she said pleasantly. "George, can I talk to you for a second? Over there." She pointed to the fireplace.

"Go ahead," Mark told George, "I'm just going to fix something to eat." He walked into the kitchen and looked in the fridge.

As soon as Alecin and George were far enough away that she thought Mark wouldn't hear, she turned on George. "What the hell?" she whispered harshly. "*I* am the Chosen One. You're supposed to be helping *me*. And you go and set this all up behind my back. Without even discussing it with me first?!"

George was genuinely astounded. "What?!" he exclaimed. But Alecin just glared at him and said nothing. "Okay," he said, aiming for calm. "I didn't do anything behind your back, okay? I was thinking last night about how we were going to get to the airport without those douchebags following us, and I thought of Mark. People are always confusing us. I thought Mark could help us. I didn't talk to you about it because you were asleep. You have made it abundantly clear that your number-one rule is not to wake you unless the house is on fire or someone is in need of medical attention. Since neither of those situations applied, I didn't wake you. I thought, though, that you would want to head to DC as soon as possible, and Mark lives a few hours away. So, I called him last night, and he agreed to drive up this morning."

"What," Alecin said through clenched teeth, "does he know?"

"He doesn't know anything," George said, confused.

"So, he just agreed to drive up here in the middle of the night and help you thwart some bad guys without asking any questions?"

"Yes."

"Why?" Alecin asked incredulously. "Why would anyone do that?"

"He's my brother," George said as if that explained everything. "He knows I would do it for him." He paused. "Remember that time in Barcelona in twenty-sixteen?" he yelled to his brother.

"No idea what you're talking about," Mark yelled back, smiling knowingly.

"Still don't know what that was all about." George continued whispering to Alecin. "But he asked for my help, so I helped him. No questions asked. Because he's my brother."

"Really?" Alecin asked. *That's actually really sweet,* she thought.

"Yes. Really. And I was going to talk to you about him before he got here, but I got distracted by tasty omelets." He grinned.

"But," Alecin said, still not wholly placated, "you told me your plan as if it was a done deal. You didn't even ask me if *I* had any ideas."

"Do *you* have any ideas?"

"Well, no," Alecin conceded. "But you didn't even ask my opinion on your plan before you put it into action." Alecin was still determined that she was going to be angry about something.

"Okay," George said calmly. "What's your opinion?"

"I think it's a good plan," Alecin grumbled.

"So, you're mad at me because I came up with a good plan and put it into action as quickly as possible so that we could get to DC as soon as possible so we could find the next part as soon as possible? Safely?"

Well, when you put it that *way,* Alecin thought, feeling foolish.

"You're right. I'm sorry. I just felt like you were taking over, and I didn't like it. I like it better when we're partners."

George touched her arm and looked into her eyes. "Me too. So, are we good?"

"Yes," she grumbled. "Next time you get a good idea, though, at least give me a chance to say it's stupid. Okay?" Alecin smiled.

"Agreed. Anything else?"

"Can your fake name be Tyler?"

"Why?"

"No reason. I've just always liked that name."

"Okay. But I'm naming you Barbie." He stated and walked away.

"Wait," Alecin said, hurrying after him, "I don't like Barbie . . . ."

CHAPTER 16

Alecin, now Jessica Jones, and her husband, Tyler Jones, waited in line to get tickets to tour Mount Vernon. So far, George's plan had gone smoothly, and it seemed like it was working. They had seen no sign of the guys from the parking garage, and they had been looking. Constantly.

While they waited, Alecin looked down at her "wedding ring." George knew a guy—of course—so he got some inexpensive rings that looked expensive. It was weird, Alecin thought. She knew it was fake marriage, but still, the ring looked odd on her finger. She didn't think the first time she wore a wedding ring, it would be for a fake marriage. Of course, she didn't think she'd still be single at thirty-three either. Life, Alecin thought, was sometimes like those old choose-your-own-adventure books her Dad had given her from when he was a kid. Choose to take the shortcut across the valley and end up having to fight a tiger. Choose to go visit your grandfather one weekend, and end up at Mount Vernon with a fake wedding ring. You just never ended up where you'd thought you'd be.

As they walked away after getting their tickets, George whispered, "That was weird."

"What was?" Alecin asked.

"I've never had to pay before," George commented.

Alecin just shook her head. "Well, you didn't expect *Tyler Jones* to get special privileges, did you? So, where should we start?"

"Well, the visitors center is new. Not likely that we will find anything there. Let's start at the house."

After they had explored the entire grounds and every building and outbuilding they saw, they stopped together on the grounds in front of the mansion.

George was fuming. "George Washington," he said through clenched teeth, "was one of the greatest men to ever live. He was brilliant, and he was brave. He was a natural leader. He led this country to independence for the love of all that is Southern." Despite herself, Alecin couldn't help but smile at his choice of words. "He led this country through its infancy. Without him, they would be no United States!" He shouted. "And these idiots—these absolute morons—they judge him by their own stupid and ridiculous standards. Almost every single sign, almost everything that was said about him, ignored his greatest . . . ignored everything he did that was admirable and amazing . . . ignored who he actually was . . . and they just . . . they just criticized him and said horrible things about him because he didn't live up to their *social justice* standards." He spit out the words as if they were vile.

Alecin felt the same way. She had been enraged while they were looking around but had tried to ignore it and focus on the mission. Now, she thought George had more of a right to be angry, so she let him vent.

"I swear," George continued, "after this is done, I don't care what it costs or who we have to sue. My family is getting Mount Vernon back. We will *not* let him be remembered this way. He deserves so, so much more."

"Okay," Alecin said tentatively, looking at his face and touching his shoulder, "I agree with you, and go get 'em. You have my full support. But we have to get this done, right? Before you can do that."

"Yeah, okay. You're right." George took a deep breath, trying to calm down. "I'm going to take a page out of your book," he said, "and just shove that anger all the way down, and I'll just deal with it later." He moved his hand as if he were shoving something down in front of him. Then, he took a few deep breaths. "Okay, let's go find the thing."

"Great. Love the attitude, but where are we going to go? We've been through the whole estate. We've looked at everything. We didn't see anything. And you know how good I am at observing stuff. If there was something to see, I would have seen it. Maybe we're just in the wrong place."

George began to pace, softly singing to himself. "He was looking for a soul to steal. He was in a bind 'cause he was way behind, and he was willing to make a deal—"

"What are you doing?"

"Singing 'The Devil Went Down to Georgia.'" George said as if it was the most obvious thing in the world. "It helps me think. Now shush." He continued singing and pacing.

Maybe that *was* a good idea, Alecin thought. She started pacing and softly singing "Midnight Train to Georgia." George stopped and looked at her. "Just thought I should keep with the theme of people going to Georgia," she said. George shrugged, and they both went back to pacing, singing, and thinking.

"Johnny, rosin up your bow, and play your fiddle . . . I got it!" George exclaimed. "The house. We need to go back into the house."

"But we already went through the house."

"It's where the coat of arms is. It's where Washington would have spent most of his time. It's *gotta* be there."

"But," Alecin repeated more firmly, "we already went through the house."

"We didn't go through it with you wearing your weird glasses."

"That's right!" Alecin pointed at him. "We needed the glasses to see . . ." She stopped herself. "To see the other thing, so it makes sense we would have to use them for every clue. I mean, that would be really clever, right? 'Cause only the Chosen One would have them and—"

"Alecin," George interrupted. "Time and place. The thing on the thing."

"Right," said Alecin, looking around. "Um, I need to use the restroom, I think. Let's find a restroom."

"What? Why? I mean, I know why. But now?"

"I have to get something out of my backpack," Alecin said pointedly.

"Wait, you don't have the something in your satchel?"

"No. I forgot to put the thing in there, okay? Are we going to stand here all day discussing it?"

"No. You're right. I've been here a million times. I'll show you where the bathroom is."

Once Alecin had discreetly opened her box in the stall of the ladies' room and put the glasses in her satchel, she and George waited in line so they could go in with the next tour of the house.

As their tour began, Alecin pulled George back. "No, wait for the next one. The tour guide in the next one is tired, and her feet hurt. She just wants this next tour over with so she can go home. She'll be less likely to give us a hard time should we need to . . . do something unorthodox."

"How do you know?" George asked. Alecin gave him a bland stare. "Sorry, never mind. So, ready to have some fun storming the castle?"

"Yep. Think the glasses will work?"

"It would take a miracle," George grinned.

"Anything yet?" George asked fifteen minutes into the tour.

"Yeah," Alecin said sarcastically. "I saw it. I just thought we should finish the tour first."

"We're people of action. Sarcasm does not become us."

"Well spoken, sir," Alecin replied. She and George burst out laughing, and everyone on the tour turned to look at them.

"Sorry, sorry," they both said insincerely.

Then, Alecin gasped. She kicked George, harder than was necessary. At least, that's how George—stinging—felt. He looked at her, and she mouthed, "Key."

He pointed to the famous Key to the Bastille, which was hanging on the wall, enclosed in a glass box.

She nodded.

"Fuck," he mouthed, and she nodded again.

Fuck was definitely the only apt term here. How were they possibly supposed to get the Key to the Bastille? *Couldn't it have been just a lamp or something?* Alecin whined to herself.

The Key to the Bastille was given to George Washington by Marquis de Lafayette in 1790. Lafayette had been given the key during the French Revolution, and Lafayette had presented it to Washington as a gift. It was one of the most famous artifacts—if not *the* most famous artifact—at Mount Vernon. And it was *not* going to be easy to steal. And they hadn't really come up with a plan.

"Maybe we should just break the glass and take it?" George whispered.

"We can't just take it."

"Do you have any better ideas?"

"No, but in the history of bad ideas, that idea ranks just above parachute pants and New Coke."

"But sometimes a bad idea is the only idea you've got."

What the hell, George thought, proceeding to push Alecin down. "Oh, honey, are you okay?" he said loudly.

"Everything okay back there?" the tour guide asked.

"Yes. My wife gets a little dizzy sometimes. She just needs a minute. We'll catch up with the next tour."

The tour guide looked at them. George and Alecin watched her anxiously as the tour guide debated what to do. Finally, she mumbled a weary "fine," then turned and led the tour group away.

"No, that's fine. I don't need any help getting up," Alecin muttered, getting to her feet. George was busy on his phone and ignored her.

"Okay. I've disabled the security cameras and the motion sensors and everything else they have guarding this thing. Start coughing."

"What?"

"I need to break the glass, and I don't want anyone to hear," George explained. Alecin began coughing as loudly as possible. "Okay," George said, preparing to break the glass with his jacket-covered elbow. "Once I grab this, we will need to haul ass out of here, but not look like we're hauling ass, got it?" Alecin nodded.

"Forgive me, Grandpa." In one swift move, George broke the glass and grabbed the key. He could feel it hum in his hand, but he didn't have time to wait to see what would happen. He shoved the key into Alecin's satchel and grabbed her arm. He started moving to the exit as quickly as he could without looking like he was moving to the exit quickly.

They passed the next tour group, and the guide leading the group looked at him with surprise and suspicion. "My wife," George explained hurriedly, "is feeling very sick. We don't want her vomiting in the mansion, do we?" Alecin began making gagging noises, and everyone quickly cleared a path.

Once they got out of the mansion, George started to make a beeline toward their car, but Alecin pulled him into a deserted garden area where trees would hide them.

"What are you doing? We need to get out of here. Now. They

are going to come after us."

"Well, I don't know about you, but if they start searching people, I don't want the *thing* in my bag. We need to see if it will change form." So saying, Alecin put her hand in her satchel and grabbed the key. Holding her jacket to block anyone from seeing it, she pulled it out. As she held it, it moved and melted and transformed until it became a metal bar—identical to the metal bar of the previous Appello part. Alecin and George just watched in stunned amazement.

"But where's the other thing?" Alecin realized suddenly. "Oh crap," she panicked, "what if it was back there where the *thing* was?"

"What?" George asked, thoroughly confused.

"You know the thing that's usually with these kinds of things," she indicated the Appello part. "The clue!"

"Oh ya. You're right! I was just so focused on getting the thing that I didn't look for the other thing. Hold on." He pulled out his phone. "First, I'm going to turn everything that I turned off back on. Okay, just . . . " and he started muttering to himself, but Alecin could not understand what he was saying. "Now, I'm hacking into the security cameras," he explained, "I bet there's one focused on the . . . thing, and we can see if there was something around it that we missed. Here we go," he said when he had finished. Alecin walked over and looked at his screen over his shoulder. The camera was rotating slowly. When it rotated to where the key had been . . . the key was still there. Behind unbroken glass.

"How the . . . ?" they said in shocked unison.

"How could it possibly still be there?" Alecin demanded. "It's right here," she said, gesturing to the part. "And how can that glass not be broken? I heard you break the glass. I *saw* you break the glass."

"This must be an old feed," George concluded. "That's the only reasonable explanation. I must have hacked into an earlier feed."

"Wait," Alecin ordered as George started to put his phone away. "See that guy's phone." She pointed to one of the people on the screen who was taking a tour. "Can you zoom in?"

George zoomed in until they could see the time on the guy's phone.

"It's right." George stammered. "How can it be right?"

"Maybe it's from yesterday?" Alecin suggested. "I mean, it was," she checked her phone, "4:24 p.m. yesterday, wasn't it? It could just be from yesterday, right?"

"No," George said quietly. "Every night, the day's feed is downloaded to an external server. This camera wouldn't have access to it."

"Wait!" Alecin was still looking at George's phone. "The key is upside down."

"Are you sure?"

"Positive. It was the other way before."

"This makes no sense. How could it be there? And upside down? What the hell is going on?"

"I have no idea."

They were both silent for a moment.

"Whatever is going on, we need to get out of here," George said decisively. "Even if they aren't looking for us, we still need to get somewhere safe, where we can talk." He looked around them. There was no one. But he saw security cameras hidden discreetly in the trees. He took his jacket off, held it over Alecin, and then used his body to block any possible view of her. If anyone saw them, it would just look like they were a couple who were making out.

"Put it in the box," he said quietly. "Do it quickly."

Your capacity for stating the obvious is superb, Alecin thought. Did he really think she needed to be told to move quickly? But she didn't say anything and focused on getting the part into her box.

"Glasses, too," George instructed.

She'd forgotten she was still wearing them. She took them off and added them to the box.

Once her box was back in her backpack and George had his jacket back on, they turned to leave. And then the guys from the parking garage at the Bell were suddenly there. Again. *Dammit*, Alecin thought.

The guys had emerged from between the trees. They all looked like they had fallen asleep on a beach. Every bit of their skin was lobster red. *That's got to hurt*, Alecin thought smugly. They all wore dark sunglasses, apparently taking no chances this time. And they had guns pointed at them again.

"Hand them both over," Scarface snarled.

"Look, fellas," George began.

"Just do it!" Scarface snarled.

Alecin thought he sounded just a bit scared. "And I don't know what kind of voodoo magic you got going on, but don't try anything like before again."

Alecin and George exchanged glances. Voodoo magic? This guy doesn't know anything.

Far from the dark garage of last time, this time, they were in the bright sunlight, and George could see that they were each wearing earpieces. "Who's in charge?" George demanded. "It's obvious it's not *you* dumbasses. Do you even know what you're supposed to get?"

"Shut up!" Scarface yelled. Then, he seemed to listen for a second. "Mr. Smith says to hand over a box. Now." Scarface was obviously confused about why he was suddenly trying to get a box. When Alecin and George didn't move, Scarface nodded at the guy on his left. The guy walked over and began to punch George in the face repeatedly, and it seemed like he was just going to keep going.

"Stop!" Alecin screamed after George had been punched several times. "I'll give you what you want. Just stop hurting him!"

"No!" George yelled and was punched in the gut for his effort.

"I have to, George. I'm sorry. It's not worth your life. Once they get the box, they'll open it and get what they want." George nodded almost imperceptibly, understanding what Alecin was saying. It was okay to give them the box because there was no way for them to open it. Alecin slowly took off her backpack and pulled out her box. She walked halfway to Scarface, placed the box on the grass, then turned around and walked back.

"Get it," Scarface ordered the guy to his right. The guy obeyed and brought it over to Scarface. Scarface put his gun behind his back and looked all over the box, turning it front to back and side to side. "How the hell do you open this thing?" he asked.

Alecin and George said nothing.

"Well, I know one sure way to open it." He threw it to the ground with all his strength. And nothing happened. He stomped on it. Still nothing. Shaking his head, he walked a little bit away from the box, took out his gun, and shot the box. The bullet ricocheted off the box and hit Scarface in the chest, knocking him down and out. While the other two guys were focused on Scarface, George pulled out a gun from behind his back.

Where did he get a gun? Alecin thought.

George quickly fired four shots. Each shot found its mark, hitting each of the remaining bad guys twice in the chest. They went down immediately. George grabbed the box, grabbed a shocked Alecin's hand, and ran.

When they got to the car, Alecin got in and sped away. When she looked over, George was on his phone. "Are you kidding me? You're on your phone. Right now?!"

"There were security cameras back there. I prefer no one see me shoot those guys. Or anything else that happened. I need to delete the feed before someone sees it."

Alecin let him be. He was right. It would definitely be better if no one saw him shoot those guys. She had a million questions, but she'd wait. As soon as he put down his phone, she launched into a tirade. "I can't believe you killed those guys. I mean, I know you had to do it. You didn't have a choice. But, I mean, I just didn't think the quest would include murder."

"I didn't kill them," he said simply.

"What?!" Alecin yelled. "I saw you shoot them. And chest wounds are usually pretty fatal. All the heart and organs and stuff are there."

"Really? You didn't notice. I thought you would have noticed. You notice everything else. They were wearing body armor, and I hit them center of mass." George said. "So, they just got knocked on their ass for a few minutes, and they'll each have a big bruise. But they'll live. That middle guy too."

"Scarface."

"Scarface? Oh, because of the "—he traced his finger down his face—"ya, that works. Scarface hit himself center mass too. They'll all live."

"Oh, good. I mean, if it was between them or us, definitely them, but I'm glad it was no one. And just where did you get a gun? And why didn't you tell me you had a gun?"

"Alecin, you are yelling."

"I am not yelling," Alecin yelled.

George just looked at her.

"Fine. I'm yelling. But where did you get a gun? We flew here. You didn't check anything. How did you get a gun?"

"I know a guy," he said calmly.

"Of course you do." She was silent for a moment. "But why didn't you tell me you had a gun?"

" 'Cause I was hoping I wasn't going to need to use it. And I didn't want to upset you."

"Okay. New rule. If one of us is packing, the other should know."

"I'm sorry. Alecin, from now on, every time we leave the house, I will be packing."

Alecin blew out a breath. "George," she said in the same tone, "from now on, every time we leave the house, *I* will be packing."

"You have a gun?"

"No. I don't have *a* gun. I have *several* guns. But my favorite is my Walther PPK."

"Because it's the gun James Bond uses?"

"Well, I like to do some things the old-fashioned way. *Sky-fall*," Alecin explained when George looked blank. "It's one of his best lines from *Skyfall*. I love James Bond movies."

"The new ones or the original?"

"Both. I've seen every James Bond movie ever made. Sean Connery, though, will always be the best James Bond. Though I do like Daniel Craig," she added thoughtfully.

"Okay. But do you even know how to shoot a gun?"

"I find your lack of faith disturbing. Did you forget that I was in the Navy? Learning how to shoot a handgun is required training. I'm an expert marksman. Got the ribbon and everything."

George was silent. He didn't think he'd ever heard a woman say anything so sexy in his entire life.

"How did *you* learn to shoot like that, though?" Alecin continued. "I mean, those were really good shots. I'm not sure *I* could have made those shots."

"I do competitive shooting as a hobby."

"Of course you do."

They drove in silence for a while.

"How did they find us?" she asked at last. "I mean, we were so careful. How did they find us?"

"I've been thinking about that, and I can't . . ." He paused. "Oh, I am such an idiot!" he yelled. He slapped his palm on his face and then screamed. He forgot he had recently had his face used as a punching bag.

"You figure it out?"

"Yes. I can't believe I was so stupid. It's our phones. They tracked our phones. I didn't think they had the resources to track our phones, but they obviously do. Pull into the next parking lot."

When she had, they both got out. "We need to destroy them quickly. They're probably on their way here."

"Destroy them? Can't you just do your George thing and make it so they can't track them?"

"I already disabled *most* tracking programs on our phones, but that must be how they're tracking us, so I don't want to risk it. We need to just destroy them."

"Why can't we just erase them? Then drive off and throw them out the window? They always do that in the movies."

"So they can recover them and recover all our data and stuff? I don't know about you, but my life is on my phone. I'd rather them not have all that data on me. No. Destroying them is much safer. Here." He grabbed her phone. He put his phone under one tire and her phone under another. "Let's go."

They got in the car, and Alecin drove over both phones several times. When they looked at them after the last time, there was nothing but piles of junk. Alecin couldn't come close to recognizing any part of her phone. "Good?" Alecin said.

"We're good. Let's get to the airport."

"The airport. Why?"

"So we can go back to Tennessee. We can't drive there. This is a rental. And anyway, it would take too long to drive."

"But my house is less than a half-hour away. And it's under my parents' name. If the bad guys check the records, they won't find any address for me. And I have my own room for doing the stuff. Seems ridiculous to fly all the way back to Tennessee."

George thought for a moment. "You're right. Sorry. I forgot you lived near here. Let's go to your place. And what is *that*?" he asked, pointing.

Alecin looked to where he pointed. He was pointing at the Air Force Memorial that was just off the freeway. The memorial was supposed to look like three planes that took off from the ground, but to Alecin, it always looked like the three hairs people draw on babies' heads when they draw babies. She shared this with George.

"You're right! That's exactly what it looks like!" George exclaimed. "Okay," he said, settling back. "In honor of the Air Force, let's hurry and get to your place. I feel the need—the need for speed."

"*Top Gun* was Naval aviators. Not the Air Force."

"Oh yeah. Navy. Okay. How about 'You can't handle the truth!'" George said, imitating Jack Nicholson.

"You know, being in the Naval JAG Corps was just like that movie. I can't tell you how many times I had to prosecute somebody because they ordered the code red, which I always thought was odd since there was no such thing." She paused. "So, who do you think the bad guys are?"

"I think that's probably a discussion we should save for a secure space. I didn't have time to check this car before we left Mount Vernon."

"Wait, do you think they know this car? Do you think they bugged this car? George, what if there's a tracker on this car?"

"They might know this car. We don't know how long they've been following us since we got to DC. That's good thinking. We need to ditch this car. Do you know how to steal a car?"

"No. And we can't steal a car. Besides, I have a better idea." Alecin used the car's navigation system to find the closest police station.

"Police? Why are we going to the police? We can't turn the bad guys into the police, Alecin. We don't know who they are. And the police will want to know why they are chasing us and how we got away. And they'll want to know about that recent shoot-out."

"I know that, George. We aren't turning the bad guys into the police."

"Then what are we doing?"

"I'm not going to tell you."

"Is this to get back at me for not telling you about the gun?"

"Yep."

Alecin parked on the street near the police station. "You know there's a parking lot . . ." George began. Alecin turned and glared at him. ". . . and never mind," George concluded.

"Stay here," she told him and walked into the police station. She came back a few minutes later. "The police are ordering us an Uber. We need to wait over there." She pointed. "We'll leave this car here. I doubt the bad guys will want to come near here. When I get home, I'll call the rental company and tell them where it broke down and where it is." She began gathering up her bags.

"What did you tell them?"

"Doesn't feel good not knowing what's going on, does it?"

"Touché."

George wisely decided not to ask anything else. Alecin leaned in the driver's side door and popped the hood.

"What are you . . ." George began and then, remembering his decision from a few minutes before, stopped talking.

Alecin pulled one of the leads off the car battery and shut the hood. "Let's go. They should be here soon."

CHAPTER 17

Early the next day, Alecin and George sat in Alecin's Guardian room. George had resisted Alecin's urging to go to the ER, so she had done the best she could to patch him up. Alecin thought he looked marginally better.

The night before, George had insisted they stop at a cell store. He had wanted to get a new phone as soon as possible. Alecin almost thought he was going to start having withdrawal symptoms if he had had to go much longer without a phone. They used a fake credit card in their aliases' names to set up the telephones. George assured Alecin that his guy was good and there was no way the card could be traced back to them. George had also bought some items that Alecin didn't recognize. By the time they took another Uber to Alecin's house and ordered a pizza—because they had both been starving—they had both been exhausted. They had both dropped like stones into bed without discussing the newest part of the Appello or their latest bad guy encounter. Now it was time to do both.

"I'd really like to know who this Mr. Smith character is,"

George began.

"Yeah, it'd be nice if we could stop calling them 'bad guys.'"

"I was thinking more that it would be nice to know who they are so we can stop them from trying to kill us."

"Know thine enemy, George."

"I think Sun Tzu meant more about knowing your enemy's *motivations* and stuff. Not so much their *names*."

"So, what do you think their *motivations* are?"

"You mean, do I think they are in the loony alien conspiracy camp or the greedy bastards camp? I think the latter. They seemed way too resourceful to have been financed by a bunch of all-aliens-are-bad conspiracy loons."

"Crazy people can be quite wealthy sometimes. Look at Bernie Sanders. That guy is bat-crap crazy, but he's got lots of money. Which I always thought was weird because he thinks everyone should be poor."

"Crazy politicians aside. I think it's more likely that greedy bastards are going to have the money to finance an operation like this."

"I agree. Besides, I didn't really get a religious fervor-type vibe from them as you would expect from loony alien conspiracists that were ready to resort to murder. I got more of a greedy-bastards vibe. They seemed more intent on getting their grubby little mitts on the parts of the Appello than on destroying them."

"Well, narrowing them down to greedy bastards doesn't really narrow them down much. There's a lot of greedy bastards in this world."

"I know. I have no idea where to even start trying to figure out who they are."

"I may have some thoughts on that. With those parts I picked up last night, I think I can put together some kind of device that would allow us to track their communication signals the next time we encounter them."

"What if there is no next time?"

"Then I guess it really wouldn't matter who they are 'cause

they would have failed."

"Fair point."

"How long will it take to put that kind of device together?"

"I'll need most of a day—maybe a little longer. I'm kinda trying to cobble together a Lamborghini from the parts of a Camry. It's not that easy."

"Okay. Well, we don't even have the clue yet, and we don't know when we will get it or how long it will take us to figure it out. So, I'm guessing we can probably give you that day before we go after the next part."

"Speaking of Appello parts," Alecin said, pulling out the latest part. Then, they both sat, staring at it.

"I keep expecting it to do something so that it can tell us the clue to the next part. But it's not doing anything." Alecin sighed.

"Well, last time we got the clue with the part. Maybe that's not the way it happens every time. Maybe we have to find the clue by itself."

"But it seems like it should still be near the part, though. I mean, we only got one clue to one place."

"Good point. So, here's a question that's been bugging me. If the key that was at Mount Vernon is that," George said, gesturing at the part, "then what happened to the real key? I mean, there was an actual key to the Bastille, right? So, where is it?"

"On display at the home of the President of Kalec?" Alecin suggested in an overly helpful voice.

"Maybe when we call them, we should ask them to bring it back. I'd like it back at Mount Vernon."

"Sure, we can include that in the call. Anything else you want besides a key and help saving humanity from certain destruction? Maybe a new toaster?"

"No. I think the key and salvation about covers it."

"Okay. Good."

"I wonder," Alecin said after a moment, "if the real key is the key that's there now?"

"How could it be the real key? The real key is solid iron and weighs more than a pound. How could it just appear? I mean, I know the Kalecians can beam stuff around anywhere, but there are no Kalecians here as far as I know."

"Maybe they beamed it before they left. They put the real key there and then covered it with their replica, and when we took the replica, it sort of triggered something, and then the real key appeared. Like it was always there, but it was invisible, and then it became visible. But somewhere along the line, the replica got flipped over, and the original didn't."

George went to his computer. "You know, I'd really like to get another look at the key there now. Maybe if I can get a look at it with the bigger screen of the computer, I can see something."

"Or," suggested Alecin, drawing out the 'r,' "we could just go back there."

George stopped. "We can, can't we? Wait, we don't have a car. We can't use an Uber. I mean, I don't think the bad guys will be there, but if they are, we can't very well stand around waiting for an Uber while they try to kill us."

"Or," suggested Alecin, drawing out the 'r' again, "we could just take my car."

"I thought your car was at the airport?"

"It was. I had somebody go get it last night. There's an app for that, you know."

"Then what are we waiting for? Let's go."

"George, it's 7 a.m. Mount Vernon doesn't open until 9."

"Well, bugger it."

"Bugger it?"

"Ya. I lapse into British slang when I'm tired and hungry."

"Weird, but okay. Why don't you start working on your thing? I know a good place. I'll get us some breakfast."

"Do they have pancakes?"

"Of course."

"Good. Cause I was really wanting some pancakes."

★ ★ ★

After pancakes, George and Alecin once again found themselves at Mount Vernon. They had decided that the bad guys probably wouldn't be there because they wouldn't expect them to come back, but they were keeping an eye out, just in case. George's device wasn't ready yet. They had considered leaving Alecin's box at her house, so the parts would be safe, and just bringing George's box for anything they might find. But they decided they didn't want to let the Appello parts out of their control. Instead, this time, they *both* brought their guns.

They started a tour of the Mount Vernon mansion for the third time in two days. Once again, Alecin had the special glasses on. As they went through the house, the guide talked about how much renovation work had been done on the house over the years.

"What if one of those renovations removed the clue?" George whispered.

"Let's hope not because if they built over it, they won't come," she whispered back.

"Nice one, Ray. I hope you have your glove ready because we are gonna have to go the distance on this one."

When they got to the key, they looked everywhere around it. They found nothing.

"I think I'm going to have to touch it," Alecin whispered.

"We can't touch the key. It's behind that glass. You want to steal . . ." George looked around guiltily to see if anyone had heard him, "You want to take the thing out of the thing . . . *again*?"

"Not the key itself. Just around the key. Like when I was at the place with the headstone. I had to touch the ground around it before I found the thing."

"That guide is *not* going to let you touch the wall."

"She will if she doesn't know I'm touching the wall."

"She's going to notice if you touch the wall, Alecin."

Alecin smiled mischievously. "Not if you're having a heart

attack."

"But I'm not having—"

"Oh my gosh!" Alecin screamed, "Help! My husband can't breathe!"

George glared at Alecin and then did his best to fake a heart attack. Then, he discovered that when you fake a heart attack, you have to keep doing it until the ambulance comes, and then you still have to keep doing it until you get to the ER. And only then can you slowly make a miraculous recovery.

After a few hours in the ER, the doctors gave George a clean bill of health and told him that he had just had a panic attack and that he should take up yoga or something for stress relief. George didn't think he had ever been so embarrassed in his life.

When they got back to Alecin's house, George said nothing, simply pointing upstairs. Once they got inside the Guardian room, George unleashed his last several hours of frustration on Alecin.

"I hope you're happy! They stuck me with a needle six times! Twice in the ambulance, when the ambulance was bouncing around so much, the needle kept moving! While he was sticking me with it! I hate needles! And they carried me out of Mount Vernon on a gurney! A *gurney*! Do you have any idea how embarrassing it is to be carried out on a gurney when you don't even need a gurney?! And it was all for nothing! We don't even have the clue . . ."

He trailed off when he saw Alecin's face. "You got the clue?"

Alecin walked over to her box, opened it, and took out the clue.

"When? I never saw—"

"Well, you were focusing on faking a heart attack. And everyone else was focusing on you. I'm sorry. But come on, *I* had to pretend to nearly faint and vomit yesterday."

"You didn't have to go in an ambulance," George mumbled under his breath.

"The important thing is, we got the clue, right?"

"I guess so," George said, very close to pouting. "Look, I know a few hours of embarrassment is nothing really when the fate of humanity is on the line. Just no more giving me a fake heart attack unless I know about it. And no other fake medical emergencies unless we agree. Okay?" Alecin nodded.

"So, how did you get the clue?" George asked after a moment.

"Let me explain. No, there's too much. Let me sum up."

George laughed reluctantly, and Alecin was glad he wasn't mad at her anymore.

"I moved my hands all around the key while you distracted everyone. When I touched the bottom of the glass case, an envelope just slid out from the space between the case and the wall."

"Well, one thing is for sure. They are never letting us back on Mount Vernon."

"Not until your family takes it back. Anyway, here's the clue." They read it:

UNDER A SEA OF TEA
E PLURIBUS UNUM

"What do you think—?" George began, then trailed off when the doorbell rang. They both froze and exchanged questioning glances.

"Were you expecting anyone?" George asked.

"No. No one even knows I'm here."

"Where do they think . . . never mind. Do you have a security camera? Can you see who it is?"

"I have a security camera, but it was synced with my old phone. I haven't set it up with Jessica's phone. I thought that would lead them from Alecin to Jessica."

"Right. Okay. Well, what should we do?"

The doorbell rang again.

"I guess we should answer the door," Alecin said.

George and Alecin went to the door. Alecin was carrying a gun in her shoulder holster, which was hidden by her jacket. George had his gun in hand and was hiding behind the door.

"Ready?" Alecin whispered. He nodded.

Alecin opened the door. A man and woman, both wearing suits, stood on the porch. After years in the military, Alecin recognized their stance. Military and law enforcement always stood the same way. She could also see the slight bulges under their jackets where they carried their weapons. Alecin's first thought was that they were police. But then she looked at their shoes. *Too nice for local police*, she thought. She concluded they must be federal officers. She decided her best option would be to play dumb, at least until she knew what they wanted.

"Hi. Look, if you're selling something, I'm not interested, okay?" Alecin said, pouring into her words all the Southern charm she had learned from April.

"We aren't selling anything, ma'am," the woman replied. They both showed her their badges. "I am Special Agent Hansen, and this is Special Agent Wilcox. We're with the FBI. Do you mind if we come in?"

"What's this about?"

"We'd just like to ask you a few questions. It won't take long," SA Hansen said.

"Um, I guess so," Alecin said, going for bewildered but slightly curious, and she stepped back to let them in.

Alecin led them to what her family called the receiving room. It had a marble fireplace at one end, with a large family portrait hanging over it. There were two impressive couches and an antique coffee table that formed a seating area. The walls were painted a pale blue. Everything in the room was expensive and elegant. Alecin's family never spent that much time in this room. It was the room they used for receiving guests, and that was pretty much it.

Walking in, Alecin sat on the couch on the left. The FBI agents sat opposite her on the other couch. Once everyone was seated in the living room, Alecin asked if they wanted any coffee or tea, just like she had learned in that stupid finishing school. The agents declined.

George then walked in as if he had just come from upstairs. He had decided playing dumb was their best option, too. "Hey honey," George said to Alecin, "what's going on?"

Alecin stood. *Honey? Okay, guess we are going for playing a couple. I can play that.*

"Babe, this is Special Agent Hansen, and this is Special Agent Wilcox. They're from the FBI. This is George Washington. He's a friend of mine."

"The FBI?" George asked, aiming for mild concern. "Has something happened?"

"Mr. Washington, how fortunate to find you here. We were hoping to speak with you as well," SA Wilcox said, avoiding George's question.

"Really? What about?" George asked, moving in to sit next to Alecin and taking her hand. Alecin was a little surprised he was holding her hand, but she did her best not to show it.

"I'm sure you've heard about the crack in the Liberty Bell being mysteriously repaired," SA Hansen began.

"Yes, we heard about that when we were on our way back from Philadelphia. It's so crazy. You know we were there the day it happened?" Alecin asked, her voice dripping with feigned naïveté.

"Yes. That's why we're here, actually," SA Hansen said.

"Really? I don't understand. The FBI is investigating the Liberty Bell being *repaired*?" George asked. "I would think that would be the park service or something. Why is the FBI involved?"

"Well, the Liberty Bell is federal property. And its sudden repair was . . . unusual. The FBI takes an interest in the unusual," SA Wilcox said.

"Wait, are you two like Mulder and Scully, investigating X-files?" George asked. "The truth is out there," he said, smiling.

"No." SA Wilcox and SA Hansen said together, clearly unamused. George cleared his throat.

"But what does any of this have to do with us? I mean, it was still cracked when we saw it," Alecin asked.

"Well, it may be that you are one of the last people to have seen it before it was repaired," SA Wilcox explained.

"Really? How exciting." Alecin said, really trying to sound as naive as she could possibly manage.

"We'd like to show you some security footage if you wouldn't mind," SA Hansen said, making it clear that she wouldn't care even if they did mind.

"I don't understand," George said, "If you have what happened on camera, why do you need us?"

"As it turns out," SA Wilcox said, "there was a mysterious glitch where all of the security cameras turned off right before the Bell got repaired."

It took all of Alecin's self-discipline not to look at George. She concentrated on making her face look bewildered. She could feel SA Hansen and SA Wilcox studying her, looking like they suspected something. It was making her very nervous.

"That's unbelievable," George said, hoping he sounded innocent. He could tell Alecin was nervous but hoped that only he could tell—because he knew her. *Come on, Alecin,* he pleaded silently. *Where's that poker face I know you can do?*

SA Hansen produced a tablet and turned the screen toward George and Alecin. The tablet showed four different views of the Liberty Bell visitor's center. George and Alecin watched themselves walking around the Bell, looking at it intently. It was still cracked. Then, the cameras all went to snow. When the cameras came back on, Alecin and George were gone, and the Liberty Bell no longer had its infamous crack.

"Do you remember what you did after the cameras went off?" SA Hansen asked.

"Well, um, I think right after that, I mean right after what you saw, we left. I think it was about to close. And really, how much can you look at a bell?" Alecin joked.

"And you didn't see anything unusual?" SA Wilcox asked, ignoring her question.

"Well, there was that one guy, remember George?" Alecin said.

"What guy?" SA Hansen asked, very interested.

"He's on the video. It was just weird how he was there all alone, and he really didn't seem that interested in the Bell. You can even see that on the video," Alecin pointed out.

"That does seem weird." SA Hansen agreed. "I want to show you something else that seems weird." SA Hansen took the tablet, worked on it for a few minutes, then turned it back to George and Alecin. They saw themselves in their rental car, speeding by. And then saw themselves speeding by again from a different camera.

"You were going awfully fast, Mr. Washington. Why was that?" SA Wilcox asked accusatorially. Alecin wondered why they thought George was driving but decided it was best not to mention anything.

"To be honest, I wanted to get away from that guy Alecin mentioned. He had really creeped me out with the way he kept looking at Alecin. And I thought I saw him in the parking garage, too. I thought he was following us. I didn't know what he wanted, but I wasn't going to give him a chance to hurt Alecin. Once we got a few miles away, I slowed back down."

"And then where did you go?" SA Hansen asked.

"To the airport," Alecin said.

"Yes, our records show that you and Mr. Washington both flew into Philadelphia that day, went straight to the Liberty Bell, stayed there less than one hour, and then flew back to North Carolina that night. That is very unusual. Can you explain that?" SA Wilcox asked.

"It was my fault," George said quickly before Alecin could say anything. "I had wanted to surprise Alecin with a trip to Philadelphia. We had planned to stay for a few days. See the sights. The Liberty Bell was going to be our first stop. We just love all that historical stuff. But after we left the Bell, my security guy at my house in Tennessee called and told me that there had been a break-in, so we rushed back."

"That is unfortunate. I hope everything was okay," SA Hansen said without an ounce of concern. "Would you mind showing us your phone so we can just verify that you received that call?"

"I would, I mean, I wouldn't mind, of course, but I lost my phone yesterday. No idea where I left it," George said, hoping for sheepish.

"Hmmm," SA Wilcox said, "what unfortunate timing."

"Yeah, tell me about it," George laughed. "I'm just having a really bad week."

"Certainly seems that way," SA Hansen said, and it was clear she didn't believe him at all.

"Well, I hope we have helped. But I'm afraid we need to get going. We have some early dinner reservations," Alecin said, standing up.

"Just a couple more questions, Ms. Hamilton," SA Hansen said, and Alecin reluctantly sat back down. "If I could just get you to look at one more video."

George and Alecin watched themselves touring the house at Mount Vernon, and when they got to the room with the Bastille Key, the screen went to snow. When the camera came back on, they weren't there anymore, and they saw just for an instant what appeared to be the glass closing in on itself in the Bastille Key case.

Then, the camera changed, and they saw themselves in the garden. After a few minutes of them talking, it looked like they started to make out, and then again, the screen went to snow. When the camera came back on, Alecin and George were no longer there, but there was a body lying on the ground. Alecin and George didn't have to feign surprise at seeing the dead body.

"It's unusual how the cameras keep glitching around you two," SA Wilcox said suspiciously.

"What do you mean?" Alecin asked innocently.

"I mean at the Bell and then at Mount Vernon. And then strange things seem to happen when the cameras are glitched. The Bell suddenly got repaired. And if you watch closely, it looks like the glass around the Bastille Key is . . . reforming, just when the camera comes back. And when we compared this footage to earlier footage, the key is upside down. It just seemed to have flipped over all by itself." SA Hansen said.

"Yeah, that's weird, but I'm afraid I don't follow you. We were at the Bell, yes. But when we left, it was still cracked. And that's not us at Mount Vernon. I mean, they look kind of like us, I guess, but I haven't been to Mount Vernon in ages. And I know that that can't be George because he was here with me." Alecin pretended to be embarrassed. "We just started dating a few days ago, and we have been spending all our time together, most of it here. Isn't that right, honey?"

"It certainly is, sweetheart," George said, putting his arm around her.

"So, you're saying that's not you two on the camera at Mount Vernon, either by the key or in the garden?" SA Wilcox confirmed.

"Of course, it isn't," Alecin said firmly.

"What about the man lying on the ground in the garden when the camera came back on? Do you recognize him?" SA Hansen asked.

"No," Alecin and George said in unison.

"His name is Steven Kennedy. He works for Innovative Space Solutions. You work at SpaceX, isn't that right, Mr. Washington? Isn't ISS one of the biggest competitors of SpaceX?" SA Hansen asked.

"I work at SpaceX, yes, but I've never considered ISS to be much competition. How did he die?" George asked with genuine interest.

"We're still looking into that. Well, thank you very much for your time. We'll be in touch if we have any more questions."

"Just to let you know," Alecin said as everyone stood, "we're leaving tomorrow. Taking a road trip to see some of the historic sites of America. As George said, we're both history nuts. But we'll have our phones with us. George's new phone is getting here early tomorrow. He ordered a new iPhone from Apple. It'll be the same number. Sorry. I tend to babble, don't I, honey?" Alecin looked at George.

"Just one of the many things I love about you,' George said and kissed her cheek. She tried not to look surprised by this. "She just wanted to make sure you knew that we wouldn't be *here* for the next week or so. But you can call our cells if you have any more questions. We really hope you figure out what happened with the Liberty Bell. We've been wondering about that ourselves."

"George thinks aliens did it," Alecin said, giggling.

"I just said it was possible. Not that they *did* it," George said with mock indignation.

"It's nothing to do with aliens," SA Wilcox said definitively. "Again, thank you for your time. We'll contact you if we have any further questions."

Once the special agents had left, George and Alecin turned to look at each other, then ran to the Guardian room. Once inside, Alecin turned to George. "Holy shit! We certainly left quite a trail, didn't we? How could we have been so stupid?"

"Now, in fairness to us. We couldn't have known that getting the part from the Liberty Bell would cause it to fix itself and launch an FBI investigation. We also couldn't know that the Bastille Key and case would 'magically' reappear after we took it and be upside down. Though, on the whole, I think that's a lot better than a broken case and a missing key. I'm more interested in the fact that Scarface is Steven Kennedy."

"Do you think that means that ISS is the one who has been trying to kill us and get the parts?"

"I think there's a pretty good chance. But I don't think they're trying to kill us. I think they really want the Appello parts, and we happen to be in the way."

"We have a lot we need to talk about and do. But before we do anything else, we need to get out of here." Alecin said in a tone that brokered no argument.

"Agreed. We need to go totally off-grid. We can't do another thing as Alecin and George."

"Agreed. Let's pack up what we need—just the bare necessities. We can just buy whatever else we may need. But we should hurry. They may be back any minute to arrest us, and we can't do anything if we're in federal prison."

"Where should we go?"

"I've been thinking about that. I had a chance to think about the clue while you were being treated for your fake heart attack. I think we need to head to Massachusetts. I think the next part is at Boston Harbor."

CHAPTER 18

Eight hours later, Alecin and George were in a cheap motel somewhere north of DC. It wasn't the kind of place Alecin usually went when she needed a place to stay, but this kind of motel was anonymous, and they wanted anonymity. They hadn't wanted to draw attention by getting two separate rooms, so they had gotten one room but with two beds. The room was plain with white painted walls and no decoration. A flowered bedspread straight out of the '70s covered each bed.

George had run his magic wand over the room just to be sure there were no listening devices, and he had his white noise machine going. He had also disabled the audio function in both of their computers, just in case. And they decided it was best just to keep their new phones in the car. After everything they had been through, they were determined not to make any more mistakes.

George had insisted that they buy a few Wi-Fi mobile devices on the way. He didn't want to share the motel Wi-Fi with a bunch of strangers. They had also picked up an untraceable prepaid cell phone—a burner phone—that they could use to check Alecin's and George's voicemail in case the FBI called them. George had finished assembling his device to track the bad guys' communication, so they were ready in case they showed up again.

One of their mistakes, they had decided, was going after the Appello parts looking like George Washington and Alecin Hamilton. So, at the moment, they were both finishing dying their hair. Alecin came out of the bathroom after washing the last of the dye out of her hair and asked George, "How do I look?"

"I think you look great as a redhead."

"You're pretty cute as a blond," Alecin said nonchalantly. "I think I'll need to get some wigs or something, though. Not much I can do to change my short hair. I can't cut it much shorter. What are you doing?"

"Trying to find out everything I can about ISS. The CEO is this guy named Robert Jackson. He is *not* a good guy. It looks like he helped build this company through whatever means possible, whether ethical or even legal or not. He definitely would have the moral bankruptcy needed to come after us and the resources to do it. I think it's safe to say that he's our mysterious head bad guy."

"Good. It's good that we know at least that much. That FBI visit was not fun. But it may have been worth it just to find out about this Steven Kennedy guy. How do you think he died? He was wearing body armor like the other two, wasn't he?"

"Yeah, he was. I don't know. He didn't look like he had been shot. I didn't see any injuries of any kind. Do you think the bullet ricocheting off the box did something . . . Kalecian to him?"

"Maybe. I've never shot at my box, and I'm not interested in trying it. So, who knows what the effect would be? I bet none of the ISS guys will try to shoot at one of our boxes again. But back to this Jackson: what can we do now that we know who's coming after us?"

"Well, a little hacking and I found some not very legal activities that Mr. Jackson has been involved in, I mean, other than trying to kill us and destroy humanity. If the FBI got an anonymous tip about these activities, it might be enough of a distraction for him to give us time so that we can finish our quest. Or at least long enough for us to figure out how to keep him from killing us."

"That sounds good. Let's do that."

"Already done." At Alecin's glare, George put his hands up. "Hey, it's not like you get an indefinite free pass when you hack. You have to get in and get out. I had to act quickly."

Alecin considered. That sounded reasonable enough. "Okay. You're excused . . ." She pointed at him. "This time. Now," she continued, "we got out of Dodge. We found out how to hurt the bad guys, at least temporarily. We dyed our hair. What's next on our to-do list?"

"Well, I know it will take longer, but I think we should drive everywhere from now on. Flying is just too easy to track."

"I had reached that conclusion too. And I know we need to ditch my car since it can be traced. How do we get a new car?"

"We buy it."

"What?"

"I've been thinking about this, and whatever we do, we can't just leave your car here. They could find it, and then we will have to explain why we left your car here and how we got to Boston. I think the best option is to take your car in and trade it in for a new one. Even in 2024, it still takes a few weeks for registration paperwork to catch up. That should be all the time we need. If the FBI is still looking for us, they won't know to look for your new car for a few weeks. And, should we have to explain it in the future, we can just say that we decided we wanted a better car for our road trip."

"That's just brilliant. All right. We'll do that in the morning. Oh, that reminds me. I've been wondering, how did you pay the hospital bill? Do Tyler and Jessica have health insurance?"

"Are you kidding? In today's market? No. I told the hospital that I got my health insurance through my job, and if they found out I had a panic attack, it wouldn't be good. So, I just paid out of pocket. They seemed more than happy to take Tyler's credit card."

"Good thinking. Well, we still need to figure out the rest of the clue. Hopefully, we can do that on the way to Boston."

"There's just one more thing I want to go over before we turn in for the night," George said, walking over to her.

"What's that?"

George pulled Alecin to him, looking intently at her. If she pushed him away or told him to stop, he would. But she didn't.

As the moment and the meaning hit home, Alecin simply said, "oh."

George cradled Alecin's face in his hands and crushed his mouth to hers. Through her shock, Alecin briefly remembered seeing some movie where a woman says she wants to be kissed so passionately that her leg kicks back. This was one of those kinds of kisses. A war raged in Alecin between her sensible side that told her to stop this and just focus on the mission, not let anything get in the way, and the side that had wanted George to kiss her since she saw him get off that stupid motorcycle. The sensible side lost.

When George reluctantly pulled back, he laid his forehead against hers. "I've wanted to do that since I saw you on that trail at Kings Mountain."

"Really?" was all Alecin could say. She thought George thought of her as a friend or a partner with whom to complete a duty. She had never considered that he might actually have feelings for her. *But wait, did he have feelings for me? He hadn't really said that, had he?* Alecin reminded herself. He had just said that he had wanted to kiss her.

"George," Alecin began, pushing him away, "I don't . . . I mean, I never . . . I just . . . I don't do casual relationships. At all. If that's all this is, I'm sorry, but no. I'm not interested."

"Is that what you think this is?" George asked carefully.

"I don't know what to think. We've known each other for what—four days?"

"And we've been together almost constantly the whole time. Don't tell me you haven't felt anything. I know you have. I've seen it. I've felt it."

She looked at him in surprise. Was she really that transparent? "I'm not going to tell you that," she agreed. "I would be lying. But I really don't think you want from me what I want from you, so what's the point?"

"And what is it that you want from me?" he asked, taking her hand.

Dammit. She really didn't want to tell him the truth. She didn't want to deal with that pain right now. But she looked into his eyes. He looked like he sincerely wanted to know. He deserved the truth, she thought. He deserved to understand why she was turning him down.

"I don't do casual relationships," she explained again. "I know I'm considered old-fashioned, but I don't believe in dating around or playing the field. I believe that the purpose of dating is to find the person you want to marry. I know that a lot of people don't believe that anymore, and frankly, I think that's part of the reason we're on this quest. People have lost their respect for and belief in marriage and in family. But I haven't. So, if I don't think a guy is marriage material, I don't date him, and I can usually figure out I don't want to marry someone by the third date."

She took a deep breath. "I want much more than a casual relationship with you. I love you. I'm in love with you. I have loved you since the moment you got off that stupid motorcycle and looked at me with that look you have." *And that was that,* she thought. *Now he knew.* "But it's okay if you don't love me back. I don't expect you to. I just thought you deserved to know why I have to say no to a casual relationship. That's just not something I do. And it's not what I want. With you." She stared at the ground. She just couldn't look at him right now. She didn't want to watch him as he tried to figure out how to let her down gently.

"Alecin Hamilton." George took both her hands in his and brought them to his chest. "Look at me." When she did, he continued. "I have always been much too intelligent to believe in love at first sight or that you could fall in love with someone in a moment. But then, I saw you. You changed everything I thought I knew about falling in love. I love you too, Alecin. I'm in love with you, too. I've loved you since I saw you put creamer in your diet coke, which I still think is really weird, by the way."

"You're in love with me?" Is that what he had said?

"Very much so. Everything that you said about marriage and family—same goes. I've always believed that. And I haven't dated a lot because until I met you, I'd never met any woman with whom I could see spending the rest of my life. But you . . . I just can't see spending the rest of my life *without* you."

"You really mean that?" Alecin asked cautiously.

"Alecin, you're it for me, so I really hope I'm it for you because if I'm not, I'm just going to have to change your mind about that."

She smiled. "You don't have to change my mind about that. I can't see spending the rest of my life without you either, and I'd rather not try."

"Do you really mean that?" George asked, pulling her toward him. "Because I know we've only known each other for a few days, but I've been looking for you for my entire life. You're what I want, and I'm the kind of guy who goes after what he wants. My feelings for you aren't going to change a week from now or a month from now, or ever. And I just don't see any reason to wait. I'm going to love you for the rest of my life. I know it."

"I'm glad you feel that way because you're what I've been looking for my entire life too. You're what I want, and my feelings will never change. I know it, too."

"I'm really, really happy you feel that way. If that's how we both feel, I don't see any reason to wait a socially acceptable time period to have what we both want. Not when we both know. I mean, if you didn't know, I was going to be okay with waiting for you to figure it out. But you do know. And I know. So, why should we wait? There's no reason to wait."

Where is he going with this? Alecin thought.

George took a deep breath. He had been prepared to wait, but now he didn't see any reason to. Waiting was inefficient, and he hated inefficiency. But he wasn't sure how she would respond to what he was about to do. He knew he was taking a significant risk. But he decided it was a risk he was willing to take.

George took her hand and got down on one knee, and Alecin could swear her heart had stopped beating and that she had stopped breathing. What was he doing?! "Let's get that fake wedding ring off of there." He took the fake ring off her hand and threw it across the room. He then pulled a chain out from under his shirt and took a diamond engagement ring off it. "Alecin Hamilton," he said, holding the ring up to her, "you are the love of my life. Will you marry me?"

Alecin just stared at him. *What the hell is he doing?* she thought. *This is too soon,* Alecin's sensible side screamed. *You haven't even known him a week,* she told herself. *What's the hurry?* She hadn't been expecting anything, but she had hoped that maybe he would love her too and that maybe, someday, months from now, he'd want to marry her. But, Alecin thought, her feelings weren't going to change from today until then. She knew she wanted to spend the rest of her life with him right now, and so did he, so why wait to start their lives together? They had already waited so long to find each other. When you know, you know, and she had no doubt. So, she told her sensible side to shove it.

"You're the love of my life too. Yes, I will marry you."

George's heart had stopped beating when he asked the question. They'd known each other four days, and he was convinced she'd think he was crazy. But he already knew he wanted to marry her, and if she meant it that she already knew she wanted to marry him, it made no sense to wait. It seemed like it took her forever to answer. But finally, she said yes. She was going to marry him. At that moment, he felt like the luckiest man alive. He began to breathe again. He put the diamond ring on her finger and with a smile he just couldn't stop, he stood and kissed her.

Alecin couldn't ever remember being as happy as she felt at that moment. But there was one nagging little question.

"George, why did you have an engagement ring under your shirt?"

George laughed. "Well," he pulled her down to sit on the bed, "remember how I said how I've loved you since you ordered coffee creamer in your diet coke?"

"Yeah . . ."

"That next morning, when we were sitting together on my deck, drinking coffee and looking at the Smoky Mountains, I realized that I wanted you by my side for the rest of my life. I just knew it. So, I called my mom, and when my brother came over to help us, he brought my great-grandmother's engagement ring with him. I've been carrying it around, waiting for the right moment. This was the right moment."

"I think that is the most romantic thing I've ever heard in my life."

CHAPTER 19

When Alecin woke the next morning, it took her a minute to remember where she was, and when she did, she remembered the night before and smiled. Opening her eyes, she saw George sitting on the side of the other bed, watching her. "There she is," he said, smiling. "Good morning, Fiancée," he said as he moved to sit on the bed with her.

Fiancée, Alecin thought. She liked the sound of that, but still, it would take some getting used to.

"Were you watching me sleep?"

"Why? Is that weird?"

"That's a bit creepy, yeah. I've just never had someone watch me sleep before—you know, since I was a kid."

George laughed. "Don't worry. I wasn't actually watching you. I just woke up, and I was trying to figure out how to wake you, given your rule not to wake you unless the house is on fire or—"

"—someone is in need of medical attention. I guess, under the circumstances, that rule is *temporarily* suspended."

"So, tomorrow morning, I can wake you up doing this?" he

asked, kissing her softly.

"Most definitely," Alecin murmured against his lips, putting her arms around him. "Okay," she said, suddenly pulling back, "we are going to need to set some rules. No kissing . . . or hugging . . . or staring into each other's eyes . . . or marriage talk during the day when we're supposed to be focused on our quest."

"Good plan. Very sensible. When do those rules start?"

"In ten minutes," Alecin said, pulling him to her.

"I was hoping you'd say that."

Alecin sat cross-legged on the bed. She looked at her hand. The ring had looked so beautiful on her hand, she thought. This fake wedding ring that she and George had found after quite a bit of searching just wasn't the same at all. She pulled the ring out on the chain she now wore. *But I am still wearing it,* she thought happily. *Enough looking at jewelry,* she ordered herself.

Using her laptop, Alecin began searching for everything she could find about Boston Harbor and the Boston Tea Party. *Sea of tea,* she thought. *That* has *to be Boston Harbor.* She couldn't think of any other seas that would have ever had tea in them. But what did the *under* mean, though? Maybe there was some kind of sign or something that said, "Boston Harbor," and she had to look under it? And what did E Pluribus Unum have to do with anything? She was growing increasingly frustrated when George walked in. He had gone out in search of decent coffee and some kind of breakfast pastry—no raisins Alecin had insisted.

George held a container with two large cups of coffee and a bakery box.

"You wouldn't believe how far I had to go to find decent coffee. That theory about there being a Starbucks on every corner obviously doesn't apply here." He put down the bakery box and brought the coffees over. "I got you a fancy coffee with lots of cream and sugar in it," he said, handing her one of the cups.

She took a sip. "It's perfect. Thanks. So, what's in the box?" He brought it over to her.

"The only kind of breakfast pastry I could find was donuts. But I didn't know what kind you like, so I got a dozen different ones. I did the math. Statistically, you should like at least one of these."

Alecin smiled as she picked up a cake donut with chocolate frosting and chopped nuts, one of her favorites. *Leave it to George to apply math to breakfast*, she thought. Watching which donut she picked, George made a mental note and filed it away in the part of his brain he was calling, "Things I need to know about Alecin." Grabbing a chocolate bar donut, George put the box on the dresser and sat down with her.

"I know we're trying to stay under the radar, but I think tonight we need to at least upgrade to a room with a table or a desk. Only having the bed is really inefficient."

"We can do that," he replied, biting into his donut. "Why don't you tell me what you found while I've been out."

"I've been thinking that all of our mistakes have been because of Newton's third law."

"For every action, there is an equal but opposite reaction?" he asked, fascinated. She had the most amazing mind, but sometimes she didn't seem to make much sense.

"Well, not so much the opposite part. But more, for every action, there is a reaction . . . the cause-and-effect thing. We've been acting as if, regardless of our actions, the rest of the world would remain static, as if we were operating in a vacuum. Like, when the government decides to reduce the price of milk in school lunches. And they think, hey, cheaper milk for kids, that's good. But what they don't realize is that they have initiated a cause for a cascade of effects. When the price of milk goes down in schools, the demand goes up. But there's no stabilizing increase in price because the government has set the price of milk for kids. So, the increased demand makes milk producers raise the price of milk generally. And then some businesses that use a lot of milk, like a bakery, see a reduction in their profit margin, so to make it up, they fire Tony, the delivery boy."

"I follow you. Making it so little Johnny can pay less for his milk results in Tony losing his job. That has always driven me insane about government actions, especially pure feel-good ones. It's like they do not understand the basic idea that if you change a human being's environment, he will alter his behavior. Raise corporate taxes in one state to raise more money? Too bad that the raise in taxes makes that corporation move to another state. Now you've lost all those jobs and all that tax income, and you're worse off than you were before."

"Exactly. That drives me crazy too. Now, we can't predict all the consequences of our actions. But we can predict first- and second-order effects. And we haven't been doing that. We should have thought about how if something went wrong at the Bell, the FBI or police or whoever, may check into it and us. We *should* have covered our tracks, so we didn't leave that highly suspicious trail like we did.

"So, before we get to the Harbor, we need to do more than try to figure out the clue. We need to figure out the first and second-order effects of our actions. We should try to anticipate what could go wrong and plan for every contingency so that if something does go wrong, there's no trail back to us.

"We should have been doing that all along. No more flying by the seat of our pants in getting parts and clues. Once we figure out where the part is, we need to have a plan to try to get it and the clue with the least number of effects that will lead back to us. Okay then, what are the contingencies we need to plan for at the Harbor?"

"I don't know. I only got this far, and then I got distracted, and I started to try to figure out the clue, which was stupid. We can try to figure out the clue in the car. Before we head out, let's plan for as many realistic contingencies as possible. We don't want to go anywhere near Boston until we know what we're doing."

"Jessica," George said quietly, "I just don't think the force is with us today."

Alecin had to agree.

Since arriving in Boston, they had searched through the entire Boston Harbor Tea Party Ships and Museum, which seemed to be the only place that held anything from the actual Revolutionary War Tea Party. They had been excited to learn that the museum held one of the known tea chests from the original event. But that had been a bust.

They had reviewed every inch of the Old South Meeting House on the corner of Washington and Milk Streets, which had become famous as the location of the meeting that preceded the Tea Party. Although they hadn't held out much hope of finding something there. Even though the building still stood, it had come close to being demolished in 1876. They didn't believe the Kalecians would choose a building that they couldn't be confident would survive.

Even though Boston Harbor was immense, they confined their search to within one mile of the official marker of the Boston Tea Party, on the corner of Congress and Purchase Streets. They had searched that area of the harbor for anything that said "Boston Harbor"—and looked like it could be 240 years old—under which they could look to find the Appello part and the next clue. But they found nothing.

They returned to Alecin's new car, which they had purposely parked far away from any video cameras. They had gone with George's plan, and Alecin had traded in her car and upgraded to the newest model. It was ridiculously overpriced, Alecin had thought. But the supply chain for microchips needed to make new vehicles was still in chaos. The reduced supply of new cars—plus the massive inflation the country had been experiencing the last four years—had made the price of the new vehicle astronomical. Although she could afford it, the principle of paying that much for a car annoyed her. She had to remind herself continually that she had no choice—the fate of humanity was on the line.

George had thoroughly scanned the new car, just in case. They were taking no chances.

"Maybe we're looking for the wrong thing," George suggested. "I mean, *harbor* isn't synonymous with *sea*. Maybe we should be looking for the word *sea* to look under."

"You're right. *Harbor* isn't synonymous with *sea*, but I was . . . " Alecin stopped.

"What? What is it?"

"*Harbor* isn't synonymous with *sea*."

"I know. That's what I just said."

"The clue was 'under the sea of tea.' We've been looking in the harbor. We need to look under the sea! We need to look under the water!"

George wasn't so convinced. "Do you really think the Kalecians would have hidden something under the water? I mean, how could they know that humans would develop scuba diving or any method of being underwater? It's not like anything like that existed in 1797."

"I don't know. Let's go check into a hotel. I have an idea. I want to check something."

When they were in the hotel room, Alecin filled the bathtub with water. Then, she put on her Kalecian glasses and stuck her head in the water. She stayed underwater for so long that George was beginning to think she had drowned. Then, she came back up. She took off the glasses and told George, "You've gotta try this." So, George put the glasses on and put his head in the water. It was like there was a bubble or something around his head. He could breathe easily. He could see everything. He actually didn't feel the water at all.

"That's amazing!" he said, raising his head back up. "Do you think they just create the bubble-like thing around your head, or is it your whole body?"

"Let's find out," Alecin said, grabbing the glasses. With her clothes still on, she stepped into the tub and put her head and as much of her body as possible under the water. She came up after a few seconds. "It's just the head, from the shoulders up. From the shoulders down, it feels like it normally would."

"I don't think the Kalecians would have given those glasses . . . underwater breathing powers unless they needed to, unless there were something you would need to get to underwater. I'm convinced." He grabbed Alecin's bag and tossed it into the bathroom. "You need to get into some dry clothes. And I need to find a place to rent a boat and some scuba diving gear."

The next morning, Alecin and George were on their rented boat, in wetsuits, arguing. "You're the Chosen One. I think you need to wear them," George told Alecin in a tone of voice that made it clear that he thought she was being unreasonable.

"They worked just fine for you before, and I have much more experience diving than you do. I've been diving with my grandmother since I was five years old. It makes more sense for you to use them," Alecin replied in the same tone.

"I have plenty of experience diving. I'll be fine. And what if we can't find the part and the clue unless you're wearing the glasses?"

"Let's just give this forty-five minutes. That's our max air anyway. If we don't find anything by then, we will switch off."

"Fine, but you watch your air closely. And watch out for boats and stuff. This is a busy harbor."

"I will," she promised. "Hey," she smiled, "this was our first fight as an engaged couple."

238 K. B. CONDI

"It was, wasn't it?" The thought made him smile.

"You know what that means, don't you? We have to kiss and make up."

"Well, if that's the rule . . . ." George smiled as he moved toward her.

Alecin put her hand up. "But no kissing when we are supposed to be questing, remember?"

"Seems you have a conflict in your rules there, darling," George said as he drew her into his arms.

"Well, the no-kissing-while-questing thing was more of a guideline," Alecin said with a smile.

"I completely agree," George said as he kissed her.

Making up kiss done, they completed suiting up and flipped off the boat into the water. They had anchored their boat as closely as allowed near the location of the Boston Tea Party. But the sea of tea had a tremendous amount of search area, so they expected it to take a while for them to find what they were looking for.

No more than five minutes after they entered the water, George gestured for them to surface.

"Did you find it already?" Alecin asked, surprised.

"No, but when we're in the water, I can feel this . . . I don't know . . . like something is pulling me. It's not strong, though."

"I felt something like that before. At Kings Mountain. Can you tell in which direction it is pulling you?"

"As I said, it's not a strong pull. But yeah, I think I can tell. I think I can follow it."

"Then I'll follow you."

They descended back into the water. The pull led them close to the harbor walls. After a while, George began to wonder if they should have brought tools for digging into the harbor walls. If they needed them, they would need to go all the way back to shore to get them, and that would take a lot of time. And it was inefficient, George thought. He hated inefficiency. He continued to swim toward the pull, keeping an eye out for anything. Alecin swam along beside him. It was almost time to switch off, George thought with relief. He would feel much better with Alecin wearing the Kalecian glasses.

Then, George felt something tug at his right hand and looked at Alecin, thinking it was her trying to get his attention. But she was still looking around. He looked down and gasped. Fleetingly, he thought he was very grateful he had the glasses on because he was pretty sure he would have choked on some seawater if he had gasped like that in a scuba mask. There was an Appello part in his hand! It was just suddenly there. He noticed he was gripping it as if his life depended on it. Not just his life, he thought, all of humanity.

Then, he felt something tug on his left hand. When he looked, there was a small gold envelope in his hand. In the back of his mind, he wondered how an envelope could be in the water. But it didn't matter. He had found them! As quickly as he could while keeping a firm grip on the part and the clue, he swam over to Alecin. He reached out and touched her shoulder with the part. When she looked over, he held up the part and the clue, a huge grin on his face in his little bubble. Alecin grinned in return. She gestured for them to return to their boat as quickly as possible. That part of their quest was done.

When they got to their boat, Alecin told George to let her go up first. She got out and then immediately turned to him. She took the part and clue from him so he could climb the ladder out of the water. Once he stood on the deck, she threw her arms around him, part and clue still in hand.

Then, her heart stopped. "I'll take those," a voice said behind her. She turned and saw Robert Jackson—she recognized him from his picture on the website George had shown her. He was tall, and under other circumstances, Alecin would have thought he was attractive. He had let his hair go silver, and it was cut in a style that gave him an aura of wisdom. His expensive dark suit was complemented by a shiny, obviously expensive watch and leather shoes that looked entirely out of place on a boat deck. He was standing there in his expensive suit and *smiling* at her. Like they were friends or something. But the smile didn't go to his eyes. His arrogance and greed came through clearly in his eyes.

There were two men on either side of him, each with a gun pointed right at them. Two she recognized as the men George had shot at Mount Vernon. She didn't recognize the other two, but they didn't look altogether different. They were all heavily muscled and dressed in black, with close-cropped hair and dark sunglasses.

Looking at them, Alecin thought, *shit, how the hell*, and *sorry, Grandpa*, all at the same time. Then, she kicked herself for not bringing her guns. They had known they couldn't take them in the water, and they hadn't wanted to leave them on the boat unattended, so they'd left them back in their hotel room. *Dammit!* But since they had the same thought about their Guardian boxes, they, at least, weren't there for this Robert guy to steal.

"Don't hurt her, Robert," George demanded.

Robert? Alecin thought. There was something about his tone that was just not right. She looked from George to Robert and back again. And what she saw shocked her.

"You know him!" Alecin cried. She couldn't believe it. This guy that was trying to kill them and destroy all of humanity was someone that George knew, and from what she could tell, knew quite well. Her heart raced, and she suddenly felt cold all over her. And a little dizzy. All she could think was that George had fooled her and betrayed her. She swayed.

George reached out to grab her. "Alecin!" he shouted with concern.

But it was a fake concern, Alecin thought. It was all a lie. It was all nothing but a damn lie.

"You know him! You know him! How could you!?" She shook off his hold and raised her hand to slap George across the face, but then she realized she still had the envelope with the clue gripped in her right hand. She wasn't willing to let it go, so she couldn't slap him. She didn't know if she was more shocked or angry or hurt, but she was pretty damn sure she was pissed that she couldn't slap him.

"You didn't tell her, George?" Robert asked mockingly. "Tsk, tsk. Now that's just not nice."

"Let her go," George demanded, then changed his tone. "Just let her go," he pleaded. "We can settle this, Robert. Just you and me. She doesn't need to be a part of it."

What is he even saying? Alecin thought. "What is going on here? How do you know him? *Why* do you know him?" Alecin demanded with her voice full of panic.

George looked at her. "Alecin, I'm sorry . . . I never meant . . . I would never . . . I just . . . I'm sorry . . ." he trailed off.

He didn't know what he could say to her right now. He didn't think there was anything he could say except that he was sorry.

Alecin said nothing in response. She had nothing to say. She had never felt so betrayed in her life, and by the man she loved! The man she had just agreed to marry! It was just too much. She was speechless.

"Let her go," George demanded again. "Come on, Robert. We can settle this."

"I'm afraid I can't do that," Robert told George. Then, he looked at Alecin. "Don't be mad at George," he said pacifically. He looked back to George and said pointedly. "He really didn't know what he was doing."

"How did you find us?" George demanded.

"I don't have to explain anything to you!" Robert bellowed at George. Then, he seemed to regain control and calm down. He casually brushed at the lapel of his suit. "But I will. I think she should know just what kind of man you really are. And I want you to know. I want you to know how I beat you." Anger. Derision. Hurt. Pride. Robert's voice combined them all.

"You see," he began, sounding as if he was telling a story over dessert after a friendly dinner, "when you decided to leave me and go to that other company . . . well, at first, I have to confess.

I was hurt."

"I had taken him under my wing," Robert explained conversationally to Alecin, "nurtured him, taught him. He was my protege. I loved him," he finished angrily. Then, he turned back to George. "But that didn't mean anything to you, did it?" he asked, bitterness and hurt dripping from every word.

"I didn't mean to hurt you, Robert. Let her go. I'll come back to ISS. It can be just like it was before, I promise. Just let her go," George pleaded.

"It's far too late for that," Robert said in that same hurt and bitter tone.

"Anyway," Robert continued in his previous conversational tone, "I decided I could use your betrayal to my advantage. I knew you were much too honest to ever be a spy for me. But then I realized I didn't need your cooperation at all. If I could know where you were and could listen in on some of your conversations, then I expected I could learn some of the secrets of that detestable company."

"You son of a bitch!" George screamed, realization dawning. "You put a tracker in me?! And a bug?!" He made a move to lunge at Robert but then stepped back when Robert's goons raised their guns at him.

"I did, yes," Robert said pleasantly, smiling with pride. "And was I ever surprised by what I heard! Imagine aliens coming to Earth and leaving their technology! Technology that could advance humanity to an undreamed-of place. And all I had to do was get my hands on it, and the future, the fame, the money . . . it would all be mine. It was almost too good to be true. I almost didn't believe it. But the more I listened to you, George," he smiled at George, "well, let's just say you were very convincing. You really should not talk to yourself so much. It's not healthy."

"That technology isn't here to make you rich, asshole," George snarled through clenched teeth. "It's here to save humanity. Do you even get that, you heartless prick?"

"But really, they didn't come here to help us," Robert explained, as a teacher may explain a very simple problem to a confused student. "They came here to *control* us. To rule over us. If I can use their technology to advance humanity so that we can't be controlled, well, then I'll be the savior of humanity. Which would be a valiant cause, I admit. But let's be honest. I'm in it for the money.

"It's been so hard," Robert whined, "waiting for that vote, for the Guardians to finally start looking for this technology. I was getting too impatient. So, I had to move things along. A couple of presidential assassinations, and voila." He twirled his hand in the air and sighed with a smile Alecin could only describe as fiendish. "I had Guardians out gathering up my treasure. I only wanted one. I thought I would just need to wait until the first one was found, and *take it*." He mimed taking something from someone.

"But you two," he said accusatorially, pointing at George and then Alecin. "You two have just kept getting in my way. The tracker has been very good. Unfortunately, my bug in you," he said to George, "only lasted a few months. It was very good. It could even get around those so-called *precautions* you put in your 'Guardian'"—mocking air quotes—"room. But we'll have to keep working on it. It stopped working way too early."

"When?" George demanded. "How did you get that stuff in me? Where are they?"

"Why on earth should I tell you where they are? Then, you would just take them out. And I took such care to make them so hard to find. No bigger than a grain of rice," Robert said proudly. "And as to how? Well, that's just a trade secret, George." He walked over to George and looked him in the eye. "And you don't get to know *my* trade secrets anymore," Robert said coldly, punctuating his statement with a punch to George's gut.

"You don't know how long I've been wanting to do that," he said nonchalantly, returning to his men. "As to when, it wasn't hard. I just invited you to dinner. You were so eager to make amends. And I slipped a little something into your drink. While you were out, I had someone come in and place them. And you just thought you had fallen asleep and were none the wiser.

"Well now," Robert said, clapping his hands together in delight, "now that that's done, here's what's going to happen, George. My men are going to take Alecin here to someplace very unpleasant and where you will not be able to find her. Then, you're going to go get all that alien technology for me—*all* of it, George—the stuff you already found and the stuff you know is out there. And you're going to bring it to me. When you do, I'm going to kill you. But I will let Alecin go back to her little life unharmed."

Alecin gasped. She didn't know if she feared more for herself or for George.

"Look, Robert, just let her go now. I'll bring you everything. You have my word. You can track me. There's no reason to use her just to hurt me," George pleaded. By now, he couldn't even bring himself to look at Alecin.

"Wrong, George," Robert said menacingly. "I have every reason to hurt you. And if I must hurt her to do it, I will.

"What are you waiting for?" Robert yelled at his men. "Grab the thing and grab the girl. Let's go!"

The two men on Robert's right moved toward Alecin while the two to his left kept their guns trained on George. One of the men grabbed the part Alecin still held in her hand. As soon as he touched it, he dropped like a stone. Looking in bafflement at his colleague, the second man also tried to grab the part from Alecin's hand but had the same reaction.

Robert and his men had their attention focused on the men on the ground. George seized the opportunity. He grabbed Alecin's hand and they jumped into the water. Alecin put her mask back on, and they both descended into the water as quickly as possible. They could hear bullets hitting the water above them.

George didn't know where to go, but he knew he wanted Alecin as far away from Robert as possible. Alecin swam toward the

Boston Tea Party floating museum. It was the summer tourist season, and the museum was one of the most popular places in the harbor. Alecin hoped that even Robert wouldn't be foolish enough to pull a gun on them in the middle of a crowd.

Once they were close to the museum, Alecin and George found a place where they could pull themselves out of the water, to the shock of the tourists visiting the museum. Alecin wondered if they were more shocked to see two people come out of the water or to see a person come out of the water in just a wetsuit and weird-looking glasses. She couldn't wait around to find out.

As soon as she was on shore, Alecin put the clue envelope and Appello part in the pockets of her wetsuit and started tearing off her dive equipment. She threw it all in a pile on the wharf. George added his flippers to the pile.

"We have to get back to the hotel," Alecin said, struggling to catch her breath as she tore off her diving equipment. "We have to get the boxes."

"I know. You go. I'll lead them away. They can only track me. They'll follow me. Alecin, I'm so sorry." George couldn't think of what else he could say.

"George . . ." Alecin let his name hang in the air. George looked at her, and his heart broke at the look of hurt and betrayal in her eyes. *I'll never be able to make this right*, he thought, *but I can keep her safe.* He handed her the glasses. "Run!" he yelled. Then, he disappeared into the crowd.

CHAPTER 20

Alecin added the glasses to her pockets and ran. She ran as fast as she could, ignoring the stares she got from people surprised to see a woman running through the streets in nothing but a wet suit. In the back of her mind, she thought she would never be able to explain *this* to the FBI. When she got to her car, she was thankful that they had upgraded. This newest model didn't require her to have a key at all. Using her code and handprint, she got in the car, and using her thumbprint, she started the car and sped off.

Alecin drove to the hotel as fast as she dared, watching in the review mirror for any hint that she was being followed. Every time her thoughts turned to George and tears threatened, she clamped them down. *Not now*, she commanded herself. *Not now!* She needed to focus.

When she got to the hotel, she grabbed the room keys out of the car console and raced up to her room. Once in the hotel room, Alecin quickly changed out of her wet suit. Her heart shattered when she saw the engagement ring she was still wearing around her neck. *No time for that now*, she scolded herself.

She pulled out her box and put the glasses, clue, and part in it. After a moment's thought, she took off her engagement ring and put it in the box too. She didn't want to lose it, but she really just couldn't look at it right now. And she certainly wasn't going to wear it. She grabbed her holster and shoved it on, slamming her gun into it. If Robert and his goons showed up again, she thought, this time they were in for a surprise.

Alecin threw all the computers, George's bug-finding wand, the white noise machine, and the rest of the weapons in a bag. She thought that if those assholes came here, she didn't want to leave anything behind that may help them. She grabbed the bag with the electronics and weapons, her backpack that had her box, and George's backpack that had his box. And her satchel, just because the thought of Robert pawing all over her pretty embroidered satchel pissed her off. She left everything else. Her hands were full, and she certainly wasn't going to take the time to make two trips.

After a quick check of the room to be sure she had not forgotten anything important, she rushed back to the car. Once she started it, she just sat for a moment. She realized she didn't know where to go. *Anywhere*, she decided. She just needed to not be there. She started driving.

Two days later, Alecin sat alone in a hotel room. She wasn't quite sure where she was. Once she left Boston, she had driven north for a while, then west—or was it east? She couldn't even remember. She had just driven aimlessly until she was too tired to drive anymore.

When she had been too emotionally spent to drive any farther, she had pulled into one of those all-in-one travel stops that the east coast states seem to favor. The stop had several gas stations, so motorists could fill their tanks, and Alecin did just that.

There was also a large building that housed restrooms, a food court, a convenience store, and a gift shop for those who had neglected to pick up a souvenir for someone on their list. Alecin had parked outside this building, then had just sat in her car. *Think Alecin,* she had ordered herself. She had been determined to keep her mind focused on her mission, and how to fix the mess she had created by trusting George.

Robert had known her and George's boat, she thought, which meant he could find out where they had rented the boat, and that would lead him to Jessica and Tyler. So, Jessica's and Tyler's cell phones had had to go. Alecin had flushed them both down the rest stop toilet. Paranoid, she had thought, but then she had a right to be.

She had picked up some coffee and briefly had thought she should get food, but she just hadn't had any appetite. When she had returned to her car, she had run George's wand over it. She hadn't been quite sure what she was looking for, but she had also tried looking for tracking devices on her car. When she had thought of how George would have known how to find a tracking device, she had brutally suppressed the thought.

For two days now, Alecin had tried really hard not to think about George. She had to focus on the quest, she repeatedly reminded herself. But thoughts of him just kept creeping in.

It was her own fault, she decided. She should never have fallen for those good looks. If she hadn't been focused on how amazing his eyes were, she would have seen the deceit in them. Oh, he had played her like a fiddle, she thought angrily. Flirting with her and getting her to fall in love with him, just so he could use her.

If she ever saw him again, she had some choice words to say to the lying bastard. In her mind, she had spent a lot of time over the last two days rehearsing just what she would say if she ever saw him again. But she doubted she would ever see him again. He was probably already back home in Tennessee, she thought bitterly. He didn't care about her. He didn't care about being a Guardian. How could she have misjudged him so badly, she wondered over and over again.

Sighing, she tried again to get herself to focus on her mission. She read again the clue they had found in Boston.

HOUSE OF FOUNDATIONS

The last couple of days, she hadn't been able to focus enough to figure it out. And that pissed her off. She simply couldn't believe what a fool she had been. She was supposed to be good at observing things. She was supposed to be good at reading people. But she had completely misjudged him. She should have listened to her grandfather and trusted no one. It was no matter, she told herself. She had started this quest alone, and she could finish it alone, too.

She sat endlessly scrolling through sundry websites, hoping something would ring for her. Then, an actual ringing phone distracted her. Since *she* didn't talk to herself, she had seen no reason to leave the burner phone in the car. Without thinking, she answered it.

"Alecin, don't hang up," George said quickly.

Alecin's heart stopped. "What do you want?" she asked, keeping her voice flat and emotionless.

George swallowed the lump in his throat. He hadn't expected her to accept him back with open arms, but the pure hostility in her voice threw him off.

"Alecin, I love you. I know I've got some things to explain. But please. Give me a *chance* to explain," George pleaded.

Alecin was silent. She was so angry and so hurt. But she did want an explanation. And maybe, she thought, if he explained, she would be able to move on and focus on the mission. Plus, she had to give him his box. A Guardian couldn't do anything without his box. Not that he cared about being a Guardian, Alecin thought angrily.

George took the silence as a good thing since she hadn't told him right away that she never wanted to see him again. "I found the tracker and the bug that Robert had implanted in me and removed them. I'm clean. I made sure of it. Robert can't track me anymore. If he could, I wouldn't be calling. I wouldn't put you in that kind of danger."

"You mean you wouldn't put me in that kind of danger *again.* Because you did just that," Alecin said bitterly, "by lying to me."

Okay, I deserved that, George thought. He tried a different tactic. "Please let me try to explain. Just give me a chance. Please."

"Fine. Explain."

"Not over the phone. Alecin, please."

I'll meet you, you jerk, she thought, *so I can tell you to get lost in person. I want the satisfaction of throwing that stupid ring back in your stupid face.*

"Where? When?"

George breathed a sigh of relief. Maybe, he thought, just maybe, he hadn't lost her forever. "Where are you now?"

"I'm not sure." She walked to the room phone and checked the address on it. "I'm in Harrisburg, Pennsylvania."

"Is that where you need to be?" She knew what he was asking—if that's where she needed to be because that's where the clue had led her.

"No, I don't know where I'm supposed to be yet." *And it's all your damn fault,* she thought angrily.

"Just stay there. Give me the address. I'll be there in about an hour."

She gave him the address of the hotel.

"I'm on my way. I love you, Alecin."

Alecin just hung up the phone.

When she heard the knock on her hotel room door an hour later, Alecin struggled with the wave of emotion brought on by the thought of seeing George. *Just shove it down, she ordered,* as she had ordered herself countless times in the last hour.

Give him his stuff, tell him to get lost, and move on with your life, she commanded herself. Taking a deep breath, she opened the door. She wasn't sure what she'd expected to see, but this wasn't it. George looked like a little puppy that had been kicked and then put out in the rain. It didn't look like he had shaved in the last two days. Or even eaten. Misery was etched over every part of his face. She started to feel sorry for him, then decided he deserved it—every damn bit of it.

"Hi." *Brilliant start, George*, he chided himself. *Get it together.*

Alecin didn't trust herself to talk, so she simply left the door open and walked back into the room. George followed her and shut the door, and then didn't know what to say next. He had been practicing his speech the whole way here, but now that he *was* here, he didn't know where to start.

Finally, Alecin said, "I used your wand and checked this room. I'm pretty sure I did it right, but you can do it again if you want. And . . ." She listlessly gestured to the white noise machine.

George thought she sounded so tired and sad. He had done that, he knew. And he knew she hadn't deserved it. A fresh wave of guilt washed over him.

"So, we can talk about stuff," Alecin continued. "I brought your box. And I destroyed Jessica's and Tyler's phones. I used a different name and cash to check in here."

"Good," George said, rubbing his hands together. He was so nervous. He realized this was probably his last shot, and he couldn't afford to blow it. "That's all good. But I didn't come here to talk about Guardian stuff. Well, I guess I did, in a way. I wanted to explain. I thought . . . well, I *know*, I owe you an explanation."

"Okay." Alecin sat in a chair across the room. She had moved as far away from him as possible, George realized. "I'm listening. Explain."

Well, that was certainly blunt and to the point, he thought. She wasn't giving him an inch, and that scared him. But maybe, he thought, maybe if he explained. He took a deep breath. "So," he began, "Robert was telling the truth about all the stuff he said about our relationship. But you should understand that when I knew him, I thought he was someone completely different. To me, he was a great guy. I idolized him. And he had convinced me that we were a team, working together to build ISS into the world leader in technology and space exploration. Then, about two and a half years ago, I began to suspect that he wasn't the person I thought he was. I hacked into the ISS computer system and saw some files that Robert didn't want me to see. It wasn't anything illegal, but all of it was highly unethical. I knew I couldn't be a part of ISS anymore. So, I quit. Robert, as you saw, took it very badly. And I began to see the darker part of him. I decided to move on and just tried to put as much distance between us as possible."

When Alecin said nothing, he continued.

"I didn't know it was ISS that was coming after us until after the FBI came to see us. Please believe that. I didn't know until they told us that Scarface . . . Kennedy . . . whoever, worked for ISS. I mean, I had suspected it was Robert before then. I had kept tabs on Robert by hacking into ISS every now and then. I saw just enough to make me suspect he knew some of the story about the Appello and the Guardians, but I did not know how much he knew or how he knew it. But I thought . . . I *knew* that somehow, in some way, I had screwed up. I knew that he knew about the Appello and the Guardians from me. I didn't know how he knew. But I knew it was my fault.

"When the vote came in, I really wanted to be the first. I wanted to be the Chosen One. Mainly because I really wanted to do the quest, but a little because I thought, if Robert came after The Chosen One, I wanted it to be me. But I didn't really expect him to go after The Chosen One at all because the vote happened long after I left ISS, and I couldn't see how he could possibly know anything about it.

"When those guys came after us at the Liberty Bell, I suspected it was Robert behind it, but just because he was the only guy I knew who was a big enough asshole to do it and he had the resources to do it. But I didn't really believe it was him because, as I said, I couldn't see how he could know anything about the vote or the quest. And I had never known him to be violent. He was a manipulative and unethical son of a bitch, but I didn't think he was violent. And those guys at the Liberty Bell were definitely violent."

Alecin's poker face remained. George couldn't tell what she was thinking. But she hadn't thrown him out yet, so he plowed on.

"It never occurred to me that he would have put a tracker and a bug in my body without telling me or getting my permission. I knew he wasn't a good guy, but a tracker in my body was just not even on the radar. I never thought that even he would stoop that low. And I didn't see why he would ever have any interest in where I was.

"I didn't tell you I suspected ISS before the FBI came because, although I suspected Robert, I really thought it couldn't be him."

He had practiced this in his head, but it was still so much harder than he thought it would be.

"And I was embarrassed . . . I felt humiliated . . . that I had been duped by Robert for so long . . . that I had worked with him. I . . . I just didn't want you to know. I was ashamed. I convinced myself that it couldn't possibly be Robert, so there was no reason to tell you about him."

"Even if all that's true, George, why didn't you tell me the truth when you knew it was Robert? Why did you keep lying to me?" Alecin demanded.

"I don't know. I've been trying to figure it out. I think part of it is . . . well, ever since I became a Guardian, I have known that I would never be able to share that part of my life with anyone. And then I met you. But by then, I was just so used to the fact that I had to keep secrets from everyone, I guess I couldn't make the mental shift to being able to share my secrets."

"But being a Guardian means you *have* to lie. You take an oath that requires you to lie in order to keep it. You lie to protect all of humanity. You didn't *have* to lie to me. You had not taken any kind of oath to lie to me. You just chose to lie. And it wasn't to protect all of humanity. It was only to protect your stupid pride. And it almost got us both killed."

Wow, George thought, *that stung.* "I know. Like I said, maybe I just got used to keeping secrets." He paused and took a deep breath. "No. That's not it. That's no excuse. Maybe that's just what I tell myself. But the truth is, I didn't tell you because I was so embarrassed that I had been a part of ISS for so long. That I had played the fool for so long. And I felt mortified and guilty when we learned it was Robert because I knew that somehow, someway, Robert had gotten information about the Guardians from me . . . that the entire fate of humanity was threatened because I was an idiot. Because I had screwed up. And I just couldn't bear the idea of you knowing all that. I told myself I was protecting you, and maybe partly I was, but I was more protecting myself . . . protecting my stupid pride."

George went to her and took her hands in his. He got down on his knees so they would be at eye level. "I should have told you the truth. I'm so, so sorry. I thought about telling you, but I just couldn't bear the thought of you looking at me and being ashamed of me. But the look you gave me on that boat . . . that was so, so much worse. Please give me another chance. I will never lie to you again. Ever. Please."

Alecin pushed his hands aside and stood to pace. George knew her well enough to know that meant she was thinking and not to bother her. So, he stood and waited patiently. To him, it seemed like forever before she said anything.

"You broke my heart," she said matter-of-factly.

It broke his heart to hear that and to know it was true. He preferred her angry at him than to hear that. Then, she started to cry, and he thought, *Oh, shit, no. Not that. Anything but that.* He didn't think he could feel any worse, but seeing her cry made him feel so much worse. He would have preferred pretty much anything to her crying. Not knowing what else to do, he pulled her to him and held her.

"I know I did, and I wish I could take it back. I hate myself for that. Please don't cry, baby. Please," George pleaded, but she continued crying. He didn't know what to do. He tried to hold her, but she pushed him away. And that really hurt.

"When I realized that you and Robert knew each other, I thought . . . well, I didn't know what to think. But I have never felt that deep a betrayal," Alecin said tearfully.

"My love, I was an idiot. And a coward. And I lied." He pulled her back to him and lifted her chin so he could look into her eyes. "But I did not betray you. I would never—could never—betray you. I love you. I made a mistake. A horrible, awful, stupid mistake, but I'm still the same guy who you fell in love with. I promise."

She was quiet for a long time—an eternity, it seemed to him—but she hadn't pushed him away again.

"With whom I fell in love," she corrected, finally, and with the tiniest hint of a smile. But that was enough for his world to right again.

"With whom you fell in love," he said with a sigh, overwhelmed with relief. He had spent the last two days thinking he had lost her forever. He took her face in his hands.

When he kissed her, much of the hurt, misery, and anger Alecin had felt since that moment on the boat finally lifted, and she felt like she had taken the first deep breath she had taken since that moment.

But she stepped away again. "I'm still angry at you."

"Understandable."

"And I hate Robert."

"I understand that too."

"And I want you to promise me that we can schedule in some time after this quest so that I can yell at you some more because you deserve it."

"As you wish."

"Dammit. Stop trying to make me smile when I'm mad at you." She paused. "You know that movie with the line that says love means never having to say you're sorry?"

"Yes."

"It's bullshit. You're going to need to keep saying sorry. I need to hear it—I don't know how many more times, but more than I've heard it so far."

"Then I'll keep saying it." He took her hands again and pulled her back to him again. He just needed some kind of physical connection at the moment. "And I'll keep saying it. Know this, Alecin: you are the love of my life. This is true love. You think this happens every day?" He smiled at her, but she just continued glaring at him. *Dammit*, he thought. Why couldn't he make her smile at him? He just wanted to see her smile at him.

"And stop trying to make me smile by quoting one of my favorite movies. I'm mad at you."

"I know." He held on as she tried to pull away again. "But just because it's a line from a movie doesn't mean I don't mean it. You're my true love, and true love doesn't happen every day. You can keep yelling at me. I'll keep saying I'm sorry. I'll do whatever you need—whatever it takes for you to trust me again."

"I don't know what it will take." She took a deep breath and stepped away from him. "But right now," she continued, her tone becoming more weary than angry. "Right now, I need you. I haven't been able to make any progress since . . . well, for the last two days. I can't do this alone. We need to do it. Together. And the fate of all humanity is more important than this," she gestured from herself to him.

"Then let's do it. Together."

"Is there anything else you haven't told me?"

"You mean, do I have any other homicidal ex-bosses intent on killing us and destroying the world out there? No. It's just the one."

"Just so you know, if I have any homicidal ex-bosses intent on killing us and destroying the world out there, I'm not telling you."

"That's fair."

"And I want to know how you found the tracker and got rid of it."

George smiled. "I know a guy."

"Of course you do."

"Do you want to know more than that?"

She thought for a minute. "No. I really don't."

Then, George noticed something that stopped his heart all over again. "You aren't wearing my ring anymore."

"No. I'm not."

"Will you put it back on?"

"No. Not yet."

It's understandable, George told himself. It hurt like hell, but it was understandable. He just needed to give her more time, he assured himself. He'd get her all the way back; it was just going to take more time. Right now, there were more important things at stake. What was the fate of all of humanity compared to his love life?

"Okay." He blew out a breath. "Let's get to work. But first . . ." George grabbed Alecin and pulled her to him, holding on tightly. "I was so afraid I'd lost you forever," he murmured. "Let me just hold you a minute. I just need to hold you a minute."

"These last two days . . ." Alecin said quietly through tears.

"I know, baby. I know. Easily two of the worst days of my life. I was afraid I wouldn't be able to find you . . . that I wouldn't even have a chance to try . . . I'm so glad you kept that burner."

"I guess I was hoping you'd call. What took you so long?"

"Well, I had to see a guy about a thing. I called as soon as I could. But never again, okay? I can't go through that ever again."

"Never again," Alecin agreed. " 'Cause if you ever do something like that again, I'm just going to shoot you."

CHAPTER 21

"Foundations," Alecin repeatedly muttered, pacing the small hotel room. They had been working for an hour but so far hadn't gotten any farther than Alecin had gotten in the last two days, which was nowhere.

Alecin stopped pacing. "It's not the literal foundation of a house. A literal foundation is called *a foundation,* not *foundations.*" She stressed the "s." "I don't think that's what we're looking for. Do you think we're looking for something that supports a house, as a foundation does, but isn't a foundation?"

"Maybe we aren't looking for a literal house either," George pointed out.

"But so far, the clues have been pretty literal. A mountain of kings was literally Kings Mountain. Norris, or his bell at least, literally called John Hancock. The Bell didn't figuratively call him. And the sea of tea was an actual sea that had, at one time, a lot of tea in it. And we literally had to look under the sea."

"So, are you thinking that either the house is a literal house or the foundation is a literal foundation, and we just have to figure out which is which?"

"Maybe. I don't know." Alecin huffed in frustration. Part of her still felt like she didn't know anything anymore.

"Well, let's just go down that road and see where it takes us. Let's assume that the house is literal. Foundation can mean so many things beyond the actual foundation of a house."

"You mean, like how trust is the foundation of any relationship?"

"Ouch. Well, that hurt. But yes, like that."

"So far, all the clues have pointed to the beginnings of this country . . . things that would have been important to the country in 1797."

"Okay. So, in 1797, what would have been considered the foundation of the country?"

They looked at each other. "The *Constitution!*" they shouted in unison.

"And the *Constitution* was signed in the Pennsylvania State *House,* but the *Constitution* is just one thing. The clue says *foundations.*" Alecin again stressed the "s."

"You're forgetting. There was another foundational document signed in that house."

"The *Declaration of Independence!*" Alecin said, letting out a gasp.

"We need to go to the Pennsylvania State House," George declared.

"Well, it's called Independence Hall now. The name started to be changed when Lafayette came to speak there in 1824 . . ."

"Time and place, my love. Time and place."

"Right, sorry. Let's go."

By the time they got to Philadelphia, Independence Hall was closed. That meant they had to get a hotel room and wait impatiently for the first tour of the day the next day.

As they waited, Alecin held her hand up to block out the

early morning sun. The glasses may have had extraordinary powers, but they didn't include blocking out UV rays.

She and George hoped retrieving this part and clue wouldn't involve a felony, but just in case, they had taken precautions. They parked their car far from Independence Hall and made that their designated meeting point when they separated. They had taken separate Ubers to the Hall. Alecin wore a blond wig they had purchased the night before and a wide-brimmed hat. She looked like she was going to the damn Kentucky Derby, and thinking as much, she grimaced. Her face was covered with a mask that still, in 2024, wasn't tremendously uncommon. Her simple shirt was covered with a light jacket that also covered her shoulder holster and gun. She wore loose-fitting jeans and good walking shoes, just in case she had to run. George covered his hair with a ball cap and his eyes with oversized, dark sunglasses. He also wore a light jacket to cover his shoulder harness and gun.

Their personal safety against the FBI and Robert taken care of, they focused their attention on finding the Appello part and clue. The Hall that had been there in 1797 had largely been replaced with updates and refurbishments throughout the years. Most of the items in the Hall were replicas. With all that, they were unsure what they would find once they stepped inside.

"The Assembly Room is next," George whispered as they took the tour.

"I know," Alecin whispered back.

"That's where both the *Declaration of Independence* and *Constitution* were signed."

"I know."

"So, there's a good chance the part and clue will be in there."

"Babe?"

"Yes, my love."

"Shut up before I smack you."

George shut up.

When they walked into the Assembly Room, Alecin's eyes

immediately shot to the Rising Sun Chair. Among the many replicas, the chair was the actual original chair in which George Washington had sat during the Constitutional Convention. It was one of the most famous artifacts in the Hall. Although Alecin hadn't told George, she had been dreading that she would have to figure out a way to touch it, or worse, that she and George would have to steal it. When she looked at the chair and saw nothing more than a chair, she breathed a sigh of relief. She hadn't even realized she had been holding her breath. But her relief was followed quickly by worry. She had been almost positive that the part would be in the chair. If it wasn't there, where was it?

When they walked into the Assembly Room, George's eyes immediately went to Alecin's. He hadn't told her, but he feared the part would be in the chair too. He watched her closely to see her reaction to the chair. He saw her look at the chair and breathe out a sigh of relief. *Good sign*, he thought. He touched her arm and gestured to the chair, eyebrows raised in question. She shook her head. He echoed Alecin's sigh of relief, followed by the same worry.

They finished the tour without Alecin seeing any sign of the Kalecians. After the tour, they stood outside, away from anyone who could possibly overhear, and discussed their next step.

"Maybe we should go through again, and I'll wear the glasses this time. Just to put a second pair of eyes on everything," George suggested.

"Are you saying you think I missed something?" Alecin accused angrily. Then, she quickly regretted it. "Sorry. Sorry. I told myself I was going to put aside . . . everything and focus on the mission, but I guess I'm still working on it."

"It's ok," George said patiently. "And I don't think you missed anything. It was just a suggestion. The part has to be here somewhere. If you didn't see it on that tour, then where is it?"

"It may be in rooms that the tour doesn't include."

"I was afraid you would say that. I was really hoping to avoid a felony this time."

"Me too. Before we go there, let's make sure we cover all other non-felonious possibilities."

They were quiet for a few minutes as they each tried to think of other possibilities.

"What if," Alecin began, "it's not that it's *inside* the building—"

"—but *outside* the building! Alecin, that's brilliant!"

"You're just saying that because you are still groveling to try and convince me not to be mad at you anymore."

"You not being mad at me anymore is, at the moment, my strongest desire. That is true. But I really do think that's a brilliant idea."

Alecin wasn't buying it but decided it wasn't the time to argue the point. "Okay then. Where should we start?"

"In the immortal words of Maria in *The Sound of Music,* let's start at the very beginning. It's a very good place to start."

"As long as we don't have to solve a problem like Maria."

George grinned. " 'Cause really, how do you solve a problem like Maria?"

Alecin laughed. "Great. Now that song is stuck in my head."

They made their way to the door where they had begun their tour and slowly started to make their way around the building, trying to look at everything. As they walked, George took Alecin's hand. At her glare, George explained, "We're a couple strolling around Independence Hall. Holding hands helps sell it."

Alecin stopped glaring but didn't remove her hand. George gave himself a mental fist bump.

Alecin then stopped and looked intently at the wall on the eastern side of the building. "You know how in *National Treasure,* Nicolas Cage took a brick out of the tower at Independence Hall and found the parchment and glasses behind it?"

"Yeah."

"Couldn't have happened. The original tower on Independence Hall was made of wood and was demolished in 1781. Construction of a new brick tower that replicated the design of the 1750s tower didn't start until 1828. The Founding Fathers couldn't have hidden anything behind the bricks. They didn't exist."

Her voice changed to a whisper that only George could hear. "I only bring it up because the Kalecians *did* hide something in the bricks of the original Independence Hall, and they did it behind that brick right there." She gestured toward a brick that was straight in front of them and at about shoulder height. She took the glasses off and showed George. George immediately saw the brick to which she had been referring.

"Maybe it's not behind the brick, but it *is* the brick. Should we try touching it?" Alecin whispered when George handed her the glasses back.

"Well, not right now. What if it just transforms like that other thing did?"

"I didn't mean right now."

"How should we do this? We've learned that the FBI doesn't like it when the security cameras glitch at national landmarks. We may not want to try that again."

Alecin looked up. Although the morning had been bright and sunny, clouds now covered the sky. *It might rain*, Alecin thought, and that gave her an idea. "Let's go buy an umbrella," she said.

Twenty minutes later, Alecin and George returned to the same spot. They stood next to each other, and both leaned casually against the wall, looking around. George refreshed his memory on where the security cameras were hidden and their cycle. Alecin had George's Swiss army knife in her pocket. She hoped it would be enough if she had to dig the brick out. They didn't exactly allow patrons to bring construction tools into Independence Hall, so the knife was the best she could do. She had her box behind her feet so she could quickly put anything they found in it.

"You ready?" George whispered. She nodded. "On three." George watched the security cameras. "One. Two. Three." On three, in what he hoped looked like a casual act, George opened the solid-black golf-sized umbrella they had just purchased. He held it up so it covered him and Alecin from the security cameras. As soon as the umbrella was up, Alecin touched the brick. Nothing happened. *Shit*, she thought. Then, she waved her hand over it like she waved her hand over her box. The brick disappeared. She felt like weeping with joy and relief. She reached into the hole the now absent brick had made and pulled out an Appello part and another gold envelope. She waved again, and the brick reappeared. She quickly put the Appello part and envelope in her box, then stood up.

"Ready?" George whispered. She nodded.

As he kissed her, George slowly lowered the umbrella. George had convinced Alecin that kissing her would make any observers think he had put the umbrella up to avoid prying eyes from observing their public display of affection. The plan was to stop the kiss once the umbrella was down, casually gather up their things, and walk out. But when the umbrella was down, neither seemed to notice. And George put the umbrella back up.

After getting the Appello part and clue, Alecin walked back toward her car—their designated meeting place. They had parked on a residential street, where cars lined both sides, and there was not a camera in sight. They had wanted to avoid cameras and the all-seeing eye of law enforcement. As she walked, she began to think: *Did that seem too easy?* Her dad used to tell her that if you studied hard for a test, it would be the easiest test you ever took. *Maybe it was easy because we had a plan this*

time and didn't just wing it? she thought. *Or maybe it was easy because George didn't have a tracker in his body that allowed some homicidal maniac to show up and try to kill us and steal the Appello part,* Alecin thought bitterly.

Alecin was lost in her thoughts and not paying much attention when someone stepped from between the cars and into her path. She looked up and recognized Robert's face. She tried to scream. But one of his goons came up behind her and put his hand over her mouth to stifle her scream.

"Get her in the car!" Robert yelled. Alecin felt something pinch her neck, and then everything went black.

CHAPTER 22

George paced by the car. *She should have been here by now,* he thought for at least the hundredth time. It was already thirty minutes past their agreed-upon rendezvous time. *Something must have gone wrong,* he thought again. She wouldn't do this to him on purpose, would she? A thousand scenarios played in his head. She had been hit by a car. She had been mugged in the street. Or the one George didn't even want to think about; she had just decided to leave him. She had decided she didn't want him in her life anymore and had just left. *Well, if that's what she's done,* George thought, *too bad. I've got the Appello parts, and as long as I have those, she'll have to see me.*

They had only brought Alecin's satchel and one backpack on this retrieval. They had thought they would look less conspicuous if they only had one backpack. George, being a gentleman, had insisted that he carry it. The backpack held her box with all of the parts they had retrieved thus far in it.

But if she decided to leave, he thought, with fear racing throughout his body. He knew his woman. She was stubborn.

Once she made a decision, that was it. There was no changing her mind. *Please don't let that be it*, he thought. Then, he felt guilty for hoping that she had just been hit by a car.

He heard a cell phone ringing and realized it was coming from the car. It was the burner phone he had bought, so Alecin could call him in case something happened. He leaned into the car through the open passenger door and found the cell phone in the glove compartment. His first thought was that Alecin was calling to tell him it was over, and a wave of nausea washed over him. He answered with a weak hello.

"George, what's the matter, my boy? You sound positively awful," Robert said cheerfully.

George's heart stopped. He couldn't breathe. "Where is she, Robert? What have you done? I swear, if you hurt her, I'll—"

"Oh please," Robert interrupted, "don't waste my time making empty threats. We both know you wouldn't do a damn thing. Mr. Goody Two-shoes. Isn't that what I used to call you?"

"Where is she?" George asked again. *I've got the Appello parts*, George thought. *He won't hurt her as long as I have those.*

"Tricky little buggers, aren't you two? When the man I had stationed at Independence Hall let me know he spotted you two, I told him to follow Alecin. She was always the one holding my fortune. But you tricked me, didn't you? She doesn't have them. You do, don't you?"

"Yes." George found it hard to speak through his fear and rage.

"And you'll give them to me if I let her go free, won't you?"

"Yes. Just tell me where. I'll bring them."

"Now, that's a good boy. I'll text you an address. Be there in one hour. Bring them all, George. I know how many there are, and if you try to fuck with me, I'll kill you both. Do you understand?"

"Yes."

Robert hung up the phone. George pounded on the hood of the car. How could he have been so stupid? How could he have let her leave alone? He had underestimated Robert again! What an idiot he had been! The cell phone beeped, and he looked at the address Robert had texted him. *Okay, pity party over,* he thought. And he got to work figuring out a plan to save Alecin.

When Alecin came to, she looked around and thought, *Are you fucking kidding me?* She was seriously tied to a chair, in the middle of an abandoned warehouse, with bad guys with guns surrounding her. Couldn't Robert at least come up with an original kidnapping plan? Did he have to copy every kidnapping movie ever? Did he just watch a YouTube video on how to kidnap someone? Step one, find an abandoned warehouse.

She did *not* appreciate her role in this particular kidnapping cliche. She did *not* want to be the damsel in distress. Robert wanted the Appello parts. George couldn't let Robert have them. Her life meant nothing compared to the fate of all of humanity. Surely George must know that. She did not want him to rescue her. She did not want this particular movie to end with her and George dead and Robert having the Appello. She wanted George to stay as far away from there as possible. If she wanted out of here alive, she would need to make it happen herself. She wasn't going to wait around to be rescued.

Alecin took stock of her situation. They had taken her shoulder holster and gun. Those had been obvious. But then they must have figured she wasn't a threat because they had stopped there, so she still had her gun in her ankle holster. And she still had George's Swiss Army knife in her pocket. She moved her hands. Zip-tied to the chair. *Dammit,* she thought. She checked her legs. Also zip-tied to the chair. *Dammit,* she thought again. First order of business was to get herself untied, she decided. If only she could get that knife, she might be able to cut herself free.

As she tried to formulate a plan, Robert walked around and

stood in front of her. "Oh good, you're awake. I wanted to let you know, you needn't worry. George is on his way with my treasure, and then you and he can ride off into the sunset."

"Lies do not become us," she said through clenched teeth.

"What?"

"Stop lying to me. You aren't letting us go. You're going to kill us both. You fucking asshole!"

"Oh, come now. There's no need for name-calling. And you are mistaken; I'm not going to kill anyone."

"Stop. Lying. To. Me," she demanded.

Robert looked at her for a moment. "You're right. I am going to kill you both. How did you know that?"

Alecin sneered, "I'm psychic."

"Really? Then what's my future?"

"You will die a horrible death very soon."

Robert laughed. "You know, I kind of like you, Alecin. I'm almost sorry to kill you. But I know George. Once I get my fortune, he—and I'm guessing you as well—will not stop until you take my treasure away, and I can't have that."

"We have families. Powerful families. Wealthy families. And they won't stop until they find you."

"Nice try, Alecin. I know you Guardians guard your secrets. Neither of your families has any idea where you are. They'll never be able to trace your murders back to me," Robert said nonchalantly. Then, he checked his watch. "Well, Alecin, it's been lovely talking with you. But I must go now. Goodbye. Forever." He walked away, chuckling.

I really, really hate that guy, thought Alecin. She checked out her guards. She recognized two of them as the ones from the boat who had been knocked unconscious. Another two she recognized from the Liberty Bell. They were still burned, she noticed with some satisfaction. And the other two from the boat were there, too. *Six guys Robert?* she thought. Hardly seems necessary. She must scare him, after all. She got some satisfaction from that too.

She was still wearing the Kalecian glasses. *I wonder if they could help out here,* she thought. Then, the room seemed to explode in sound and bright light.

Alecin realized the glasses were good for something. They had kept her from getting blinded by the flash-bang grenade. She heard what could only be gunfire. And she saw smoke that could only come from a smoke bomb. She felt her hands being freed.

What the hell is going on? Alecin thought. *Who's throwing flash-bang grenades? Did George call the police?* Nobody was yelling that they were the police. *If they were police, they'd be identifying themselves, wouldn't they?* Whatever was going on, she decided, she needed to not be zip-tied to a chair. The second her hands were free, she grabbed the knife out of her pocket and cut her leg ties. Then, she grabbed her gun from her ankle holster, hit the ground, and began to crawl, waiting for the smoke to clear.

As the smoke finally began to clear, Alecin saw that all of the guards were down. Then she saw six people she didn't recognize, but she got the impression that they were the cavalry. And they definitely weren't any kind of law enforcement. She couldn't make any sense of what was going on. Then, Alecin's heart stopped. Robert was holding a gun on George, and George was holding a gun on Robert.

"Give it up, Robert. You've lost," George demanded.

"How dare you? This was *my* treasure."

"It was never a treasure. It was never yours. And it will never be yours."

Robert sneered. "Well, at least I get a consolation prize." And with that, he shot George twice in the chest.

Alecin heard someone screaming "no," but she didn't know where it came from. *Was that her?* She felt the gun in her hand and aimed it at Robert.

"You are going to die a horrible death very soon, just like I said you would, asshole!" Alecin screamed as she emptied her gun into Robert. And when her gun had emptied, Robert was undoubtedly dead. She had shot him in the head, at least twice.

She ran to George, pleading, "no, no, no" over and over again. But she wasn't sure if she was saying it in her head or out loud. She saw the holes in George's shirt where the bullets had entered. But there was no blood. *Why isn't there blood? Where is the blood? And why is my face wet?* Nothing was making any sense.

George opened his eyes. *Man,* he thought, *that really hurt.* He saw Alecin frantically running her hands all over his chest and crying. He smiled. "Aw, you do care," he said. At the sound of his voice, Alecin yelled his name. Then, she grabbed him and kissed him harder than she had ever kissed him before.

When the smoke had all cleared and the bullets had all stopped flying, George stood to the side, holding Alecin. Or really, Alecin was holding him. *Being shot while wearing body armor won't kill you, but it will hurt you pretty damn good,* George thought.

Mac, whom Alecin had determined to be the head guy of her particular cavalry—whoever they were—came over. "We're all good here," Mac reported. "No casualties except bad guys. No injuries on our side." Mac looked at Alecin. "Alecin, pleasure to meet you even though the circumstances aren't the best. I'm glad you're okay." Mac smiled at her.

"Thanks, Mac. Really. And please thank everyone else too."

"Will do," Mac told her. Then, he turned to George. "You want us to handle clean-up?"

"Yeah, Mac. That would be great. Appreciate the assist. Really."

"Well, I owed you one," Mac smiled.

"Hey, clean-up includes this gun," George said, handing Mac the gun with which Alecin had shot Robert, "and this one." He handed Mac his gun. He had managed to shoot a few of Robert's men at least.

"You got it," Mac said, taking the guns. He gestured to one

of his guys who came and got the guns. Mac then pulled a gun from his back. "We found this one in an office. It hasn't been fired, so it's clean. Do you want to keep it?"

"My Walther!" Alecin took her gun with delight.

"Guess so," George said. "We're going to get out of here, Mac. We'll take the car I drove here. You know how to reach me when and if."

"We'll make it happen," Mac said, then walked away.

Alecin helped George walk to the car. Once they were out of earshot, Alecin asked, "What did he mean by clean-up?"

"He meant they'll make sure the bodies, the guns, and the bullets are never found and that absolutely no evidence remains in that warehouse. In an hour or so, no one will ever be able to tell what happened here."

"Wow. I didn't know you had it in you to do all this."

"Your life was in danger. I couldn't do anything else."

"Thank you."

"Never go up against a Southerner when death is on the line," George quipped.

"Or get involved in a land war in Asia," Alecin smiled.

"Exactly."

"You do know he planned to kill us both, right?"

"Oh yeah. Robert may have fooled me once upon a time. And I underestimated him a lot as far as what he could do, but what he would do today? That I never underestimated." He paused. "Speaking of Robert, I didn't know you had it in you to empty a gun into a man."

"Your life was in danger. I couldn't do anything else."

"Thank you."

"Babe, how did you get six obviously highly trained security guys to stage a below-the-radar, probably completely illegal, hostage rescue, with what, an hour's notice?"

George smiled. "I know a guy."

"Of course you do."

When Alecin finally walked into their hotel room in Philadelphia, she was tremendously relieved. And then she panicked. "Where's my box?! I don't see my box?! You didn't bring it to rescue me, did you?!"

George took her hands and brought them to his lips. All he could think was that he'd gotten her back; she was okay. Ever since he got that phone call from Robert, he had been terrified of what Robert would do to her.

"Calm down. It's okay. I'm so happy to have you yelling at me again. I didn't take your box to rescue you. The risk was too high. But I didn't want to leave it here in the hotel room, unattended."

"Okay. Sorry. I had these visions of Robert's goons coming in and stealing it while I was being held hostage, and you were rescuing me. Where is it?"

"It's in the hotel safe. I know it's not the best option. But I only had a short amount of time to make things happen. I'll go get it now. I'll be right back. Don't get kidnapped again."

"I won't." She smiled. "I promise."

While she waited, she turned on the white noise machine and decided to run George's wand all over the room. Just in case Robert had been able to plant a bug while they had been gone. *Robert may be dead*, she thought, *but evil assholes like him were like cockroaches; if there was one, there was always more.*

She was just finishing when George returned, her box in hand. "I don't know about you, but I would just as soon get out of Philadelphia. Can we open this right now? Maybe we'll know where to go so we don't start heading in the wrong direction," Alecin said.

"One question first," George said, putting down the box and pulling Alecin to him. "Does staging an armed rescue and saving your life get me out of the doghouse?"

"No."

"Man, you are harsh."

"But," she continued, drawing out the word, "when Robert shot you, there were moments—some long horrible moments—when I thought you were dead. When I thought I had lost you forever. And now, well, I don't want to waste another minute of my life being mad at you. Life is too fleeting. It's just not worth it."

"So, all I had to do to get you to forgive me was die?"

"Well, you didn't actually die. You were only *mostly* dead," she smiled. "Mostly dead is slightly alive."

He chuckled, then laid his forehead against hers and blew out a breath. "I was so scared. Not about the guns or getting shot or anything but losing you. I don't know what I'd do if I lost you. I don't want to waste another minute of my life with you being mad at me, either."

"Stay right here. I just need to do one thing." She went to her box and took out his engagement ring. She handed it back to him. "Ask me again."

George looked at the ring but said nothing.

"What's wrong?" Alecin asked, her voice tinged with panic. Did he not want to marry her anymore?

George hesitated. He was about to break at least five different laws. But then he looked at Alecin. He couldn't risk losing her again. "My love, remember how you said that being a Guardian requires you to lie, but that's okay because it's for the sake of humanity?"

"Yeah," she said suspiciously.

"If there was this other thing that required me to lie to you, but it was for the sake of, let's say, hypothetically, national security, would it be ok to lie to you about that?"

Alecin folded her arms and looked at him. "If it hasn't bothered me before, why do you think it would bother me now?"

"You knew?" he looked at her, genuinely surprised. She just gave him that look she gave him when she thought he had said something stupid. And he had, he realized. "Of course, you knew," he said like it had been obvious—because, in reality, it *had* been. "So, that's okay, hypothetically?"

"I understand lies to keep secrets you have to keep. I understand that better than anyone. But lies that you choose to tell me? When you could tell me the truth. That's another story."

"Okay. Good. I just . . . I needed to be sure," he pulled her to him again. "I cannot lose you again."

"I can live with you just telling me you know a guy, hypothetically."

George smiled, and the last little bit of fear that had gripped him finally let go. He got down on one knee again and offered her his ring. "Alecin Kristina Hamilton, will you please marry me? I promise I will never lie to you again, with certain agreed-upon hypothetical caveats. And I will spend the rest of my life trying to make you happy. No caveats."

"Yes, I will," she said, smiling and letting that last bit of hurt and anger go.

George took the ring off its chain and put it back on her finger. And felt like he could finally breathe for the first time in four days.

"And this time," he said, holding her hand, "keep it where I put it, will ya?"

Alecin smiled. "I will."

CHAPTER 23

When Alecin and George read the newest clue, their plans for an early exit from Philadelphia went awry. The clue was just as cryptic as the others had been.

A CORNERSTONE FOR A CORNERSTONE

"Any idea?" Alecin asked.

"Hold on. There's something . . . but I just can't . . . it's a niggly."

"A niggly?"

"That's what I call it when something sounds familiar, but I can't remember how or why. I know it's there somewhere in my brain, just niggling to get out."

"Is it familiar enough to point us in a direction?"

"I feel like it may be . . . Washington DC?" He paused. "That's it! Washington. I remember now. I remember hearing about George Washington laying the cornerstone for the US Capitol building." He paused. "Alecin! It was said that he put an engraved silver plate under the cornerstone. Do you think?"

"Hold on, when did he lay that cornerstone?"

"I don't remember."

"Let's check." Alecin grabbed her laptop and thought about how she missed her smartphone and missed having the internet in the palm of her hand. *Perspective,* she chastised herself. *You just survived being kidnapped and you killed a man for this mission. Not having a smartphone is a small thing.* "Here. It was 1793."

"So, that's four years before they left. Do you think they would have hidden a part of the Appello that early?"

"Time is a big ball of wibbly-wobbly timey-wimey stuff."

"My love, why are you quoting *Doctor Who* to me right now?" George asked, confused.

"It's always the right time for *Doctor Who*. But I'm just saying maybe it wasn't early for them. Remember how they returned The Three to the exact same time as when they had been taken? They don't view time the same way we do. We assume time moves in a straight line. They don't."

"You're right. I'd forgotten about that. You are absolutely right."

After a few minutes of searching, George found something else that showed them that they were on the right track. "It says they don't know where the cornerstone is because they aren't sure if it was the cornerstone of just the Senate wing, which was the first building constructed, or of the whole building. And now they aren't even sure if it's still in the Capitol Building at all."

"How do they lose a cornerstone?"

"Time, I guess. The Capitol Building was burned down during the Civil War and had to be rebuilt. And since then, they've had to expand it and remodel it, and now no one knows where this cornerstone Washington laid is. They've looked for it by using metal detectors to search for the silver plate . . . *but* the metal detectors haven't been able to find it."

"What if," Alecin asked excitedly, "they can't find it because it isn't really a silver plate at all?"

"My thoughts exactly."

"And the cornerstone was for the congressional building. The legislative branch is one of the three branches of our government. It's definitely a cornerstone of it."

"A cornerstone for a cornerstone. I think we got it, Alecin."

"I think we do. And the best part of that? We get to get the hell out of Philadelphia."

When they got to DC, Alecin and George realized they had a problem. The clue specifically referenced the cornerstone, and they both believed that one of them would need to touch or wave their hand over the cornerstone to get the part and the clue. They would need to do something that required them to be in the physical presence of the cornerstone, at the very least. But nobody knew where the cornerstone they needed was, and they had had no luck in finding it. Not even the Kalecian glasses were helping.

"Well, this is a first," Alecin observed when they had given up for the day and were back in their hotel room. "We know, or think we know, the exact object hiding the part, but we just can't find the object."

"I don't think the Kalecians envisioned them actually losing the cornerstone."

"And did you hear that one guide we talked to? He said the cornerstone is probably underground by now. What are we going to do?" Alecin said, throwing herself back on the bed.

Looking at her, George knew what he'd like to do. He went over to the bed and lay down next to her. "Maybe we should do something to take our minds off of it. Come back to it fresh."

Alecin turned to look at him. "What did you have in mind?"

He smiled. "Let me show you."

The next day, George and Alecin decided they needed a new plan. George went out to grab some coffee and breakfast, and Alecin sat down with her laptop to figure out a new plan. But she came up with nothing and decided she needed coffee to get her brain to function.

When George returned, he said: "I have coffee, bagels with schmear, and a new plan. Which do you want first?"

"Coffee. Definitely coffee." She took a few sips and thought she could actually feel the caffeine waking up her system. "Now give me a bagel and tell me your plan."

"I set us up a meet with the chief of the Capital Guide Services—one of the few people in the Capitol who can give us access to anywhere and who would know the most likely places the cornerstone could be."

"How did you do that?"

He smiled. "I know a guy."

"Of course you do."

The chief of the Capitol Guide Services was a middle-aged man named Walter. Walter had a receding hairline and a friendly smile. Walter seemed more than happy to show them around and to share his—quite substantial—knowledge of the Capitol Building. He said he owed George's friend a favor and was happy to do it. He knew that George was a direct descendant of George Washington and thought that was amazing. He thought the fact that George was named after the first President was hilarious. He said his wife would never believe him, and George agreed to let him take a selfie with him and a picture of his driver's license to prove his name. Walter believed their interest was simply interest and curiosity about the actions of an ancestor. As someone who respected history—as he informed them—he appreciated their interest.

He asked about Alecin's strange glasses. She told him that she had a rare eye condition and that the glasses helped her to see. He expressed his sympathy and then proceeded to tell her about every member of his family who had ever had issues with their eyes. Alecin thought he was adorable.

Walter took them to the area where *he* believed the cornerstone laid by George Washington was. Walter pointed to a particular stone and explained to them all the reasons why he believed that it was the cornerstone. Alecin didn't see anything there, so they were less convinced, but they made all the appropriate noises. Walter next took them to the area where many believed the cornerstone was, and the whole scene replayed itself. There was one more stone that Walter thought be the cornerstone, so the group headed in that direction.

They walked along a passageway that had what were clearly construction stones lining the wall to the right of them. As they came around a corner, Alecin grabbed George. She subtly pointed to a stone in another corner, at the bottom. George raised his eyebrow in question, and she nodded. Then, she handed George the glasses. George shook his head and tried to hand the glasses back to her. She pushed his hands back.

"This is yours," she mouthed. To settle the matter, Alecin linked her arm through Walter's and subtly steered him away from George.

"Where are your glasses?" Walter asked.

"Oh, I have to take them off every once in a while, or I get a headache. Now I hear that Washington supervised the building of the Capitol Building himself. Can you tell me about that?" As a matter of fact, Walter could, and he began to do so. Extensively.

Once their backs were turned, George waved his hand over the stone he saw through the glasses. The stone vanished, leaving a hole in the wall. Although that's what he was hoping to happen, George still gasped.

In the bottom of the hole was the Appello part. The other Appello parts were placed by Kalecians, which was awe-inspiring. But as he picked up a part that George Washington, the first president, his many-times-great-grandfather himself, had actually laid, he thought that was awe-inspiring on another level. He took his box out of his backpack and quickly put the Appello part and the clue that had been beneath it in it, then put the box back in his backpack. He wished Alecin could have shared this with him and felt a twinge of regret as he waved his hand again to bring the stone back. But he was also profoundly grateful that she had been selfless and caring enough to give him this opportunity. *That's my girl*, he thought with a smile.

When he was done, he jogged in the direction they had been walking before he had stopped at the stone. He caught up with Alecin and Walter and fell into step behind them. Walter was discussing with Alecin all of the unique features of the Capitol Dome. George touched Alecin's shoulder to let her know he was back. When she turned to him, he nodded. Mission accomplished.

As soon as they returned to the hotel room, George grabbed Alecin. "Can I just tell you how happy I am at this moment to have gotten through that with neither of us committing any felonies, no one threatening us at gunpoint, and no one kidnapping you. I had no idea going on this quest would be so clown-watching-you-from-a-storm-grate terrifying." George hadn't realized how anxious he had been about this retrieval until that moment.

"And if you had known, would you have still asked to come with me?"

"Oh, in a heartbeat."

"Well then," she smiled, "shall the adventure continue? Should we see where we are to go next?"

"Definitely. I've wanted to open that envelope since I got it. Release the Kraken."

Once they opened it, though, they were confused. There

wasn't a clue. There was just a bunch of numbers. "Do you think we have to decipher it to figure out the clue? Why would they put the clues in a cipher now and not before?" Alecin asked.

"I don't think so. I don't think it's a cipher. But there is something familiar about those numbers. It's another damn niggly."

"But the clue has to lead us to a place, right? If it's not a cipher, how could numbers lead us to a place?"

"Alecin, you're a genius!"

"I am?"

"Those numbers *do* lead us to a place. They're latitude and longitude. Hold on." He grabbed his computer. "Let's see where these numbers take us. I could be completely wrong. If they put us in the middle of the Atlantic Ocean, then I'm absolutely wrong."

He worked on his computer for a few minutes. "Well, they don't put us in the Atlantic Ocean . . . but almost. They put us in the middle of the Appalachian Mountains in upstate New York."

"What significant historical location is in upstate New York?" Alecin asked.

"None that I know of. But these numbers put us in the middle of the wilderness. There's no human development for miles from this spot."

"That doesn't make any sense. Everything until now has been . . . well, not in the middle of the wilderness. There was a national park, the Bell, the water, a building . . . actually," Alecin reconsidered, "maybe it does make sense. All of the clues have led us to places and things that are vastly different from each other."

"But there was always the commonality in that, in every case, the retrieval involved something of historical significance to the founding of this country. There's nothing of historical significance in the middle of the New York wilderness."

"Maybe there *is*. I didn't know there was anything of historical significance in Kings Mountain National Park until I did research and walked the park. Did you?"

"No, I didn't."

"Should we try to do research on this place?" Alecin said. "See if we can find something of historical significance there, and if not, cross coordinates off our list of possible answers?"

"But," George pointed out, "with Kings Mountain, we could do a search about a specific place. We can't search coordinates. And we can't just search the Appalachian Mountains. I wouldn't even know where to begin."

"Maybe we should just go to these coordinates. See what's there. We can't know what's there until we get there."

"Well, my momma always said life was like going on a quest for parts of an alien calling device; you never know what you're gonna get. Let's go see what we can see."

The next day, Alecin and George had trail guides and maps spread over the table in their New York hotel room, and they had been poring over them for hours. Finally, Alecin sat back. "Houston, we have a problem. There's just no way to get to this spot"—she put her finger on the "X" on the map that corresponded to the coordinates they had been given—"on foot. Or by bike."

George leaned against the wall, a cup of coffee in his hand, watching her.

"Maybe we could try ATVs?" Alecin suggested. "But that will take a minimum of three days, maybe more, depending on the terrain. That's three days in, three days out. That's a lot of supplies we will need to take. And a lot of time in the wilderness. And this time of year, there will be black bears. But it may be the least bad of all bad options."

George was silent. "Well, what do you think?" Alecin demanded.

"I think another problem with ATVs is that that's a national park. ATVs are prohibited. We'd have a hard time getting them anywhere near a decent starting point. And even if we did, if we were spotted at any point during that week—which I think is a very optimistic time estimate—by a park ranger, we'd get arrested. I'd really like to try to avoid committing another felony."

Alecin let out another long breath. "Me too."

They were silent for a few minutes.

"Well?" Alecin asked at last.

"Well, what?"

"You've got that George look. You have an idea. What is it?"

George hesitated. "How would you feel about rappelling from a helicopter?" he proposed.

"Surely you can't be serious."

"I *am* serious. And please don't call me Shirley."

Alecin laughed in spite of herself. That joke just never got old. "Do you even know how to rappel from a helicopter?"

"I've done it before. As long as you have a pilot that knows what he's doing, it's not difficult, from an intellectual perspective."

"How close could that get us?"

"These numbers give us latitude and longitude to the minute. That's about a two-square-mile area that we need to search. The helicopter could put us right down in the middle of our search area."

"Where are we going to get a helicopter, a pilot that knows what he's doing, and rappelling out of a helicopter equipment?"

George smiled. "I know a guy."

"Of course you do."

CHAPTER 24

Despite her apprehension, Alecin couldn't see any other way to get where they needed to go. *Anyway, she had decided, how often does one get the opportunity to rappel out of a helicopter?* It sounded terrifying but also amazingly fun. And so, two days later, she found herself flying in a helicopter over the Appalachian Mountains while George went over—yet again—what she needed to do.

They each had a backpack but not their usual ones. These were designed to hold everything a human being would need to survive in the wilderness for a couple of days. The backpacks had their boxes, of course, but also 48 hours of supplies—their best guess for how long they would be in the wilderness. Each also had a satellite phone, so they could contact help if needed and also so they could call the helicopter when they were ready to get picked up. And bear spray, just in case. Alecin had insisted.

George had a GPS unit in his hand and was watching it closely. "We're almost to the drop zone. Are you ready?"

Alecin nodded slowly. The ground seemed a lot farther away

than she had imagined. "Will he get closer to the ground than this?"

"Some. But we'll still need to rappel down a ways. Are you okay?"

I don't know, Alecin thought. *Is having your stomach in your throat okay?* But she just nodded again. "I'm terrified beyond the capacity for rational thought," she told him, falling back on her usual coping mechanism.

George chuckled. He took her hand and squeezed it. "You'll be fine. Just focus on the ropes. Don't look down. And if someone asks you if you're a God, you say yes."

Alecin laughed nervously. But joking around had helped calm her nerves.

George thought again of telling Alecin to stay in the helicopter and go back to the hotel; he would do this without her. But he knew she would never agree. This kind of rappelling wasn't difficult from an intellectual perspective, but mentally, it could be very challenging. It could be terrifying, and people made mistakes when they were scared, and he could tell Alecin was scared. But she also seemed incredibly excited. *She can do this,* he reminded himself.

Alecin thought again of just telling the helicopter to turn around; they'd find another way. But this really *was* the least bad of all the bad options. *Besides,* she told herself, *it's too late to back out now. You can do this.*

"Okay," George announced, "this is our stop. Nice and easy, okay? Just take your time. We aren't in a hurry."

And then, before she knew it, Alecin was rappelling out of a freaking helicopter! She did as George had told her, repeatedly. She focused on the ropes, and then suddenly, she was on the ground. George looked over at Alecin and breathed a sigh of relief. She hadn't fallen or done any of the other horrible things he had imagined. But still, as soon as he unhooked his rope, George ran over to her just to be sure. "Are you okay?" he asked anxiously.

Alecin threw her arms around him. "I just rappelled out of a helicopter!" she screamed. "Whoo-hoo! That was so much fun! What an adrenaline rush! We *have* got to do that again! Did you see the view as we were going down? A-maze-ing!"

"That's my girl," George said, smiling, but he wasn't sure she heard him over all her screaming. George was ready to have her curse him for even coming up with such a ridiculously danger-ous idea. He wasn't quite prepared for *this* reaction. Every day, he thought, she continued to surprise him. He just laughed. He'd felt the same way his first time rappelling out of a helicopter.

"Okay, Okay," Alecin said, taking a few deep breaths. "I'm calm." She looked around for the first time since she had land-ed. "What a wonderfully beautiful place," she said, proceeding to take in a peaceful breath.

George looked around too. She was right. The helicopter had put them down in a clearing at the top of a hill. It was gor-geous. Just wilderness blanketing rolling mountain after rolling mountain as far as the eye could see, in every direction. There was no sign of another human being at all. It was exhilarating.

"So, how close did we get?" Alecin asked, walking over to look over George's shoulder at the GPS.

"We're pretty much right in the middle of our search area. Do you see anything with the glasses?" Alecin took them out and put them on. She turned a 360. "Nothing." She handed the glasses to George. "Can you see anything?"

George imitated her 360. "No. So, I guess we just need to pick a direction and start walking." George continued looking around. "I can see why the Kalecians picked this place. There's no flat land capable of cultivation. The ground is rocky, no reli-able water source. Very unlikely this area would ever be devel-oped by humans."

"True, but we aren't looking for development opportunities. We're looking for a direction to go. Maybe we should just walk in circles, you know, concentric circles." She made circles with her finger.

"That would be a good way to search, except human beings are almost incapable of walking in an actual circle. Even with GPS. We're better with straight lines."

"Well, that way"—Alecin pointed to her right—"is forest, and that way"—she pointed to her left—"is mountains. Should we flip a coin? Wait." She put her hand up, indicating she needed a minute to think.

"What is it?"

"I have a niggly."

"About which direction we should go in?"

"Yes. Now shush." Alecin began to pace, her usual thinking mode. George waited.

"I remember," she said at last, "I saw a sign when we were exploring that warned about forest fires. You know, one of those Smoky the Bear only-you-can-prevent-forest-fires signs." George nodded. "Forests catch on fire. Repeatedly and quite commonly. It's the natural way a forest cleans out old growth to make room for new growth. That's why they do those controlled fires—"

"Time and place, my love. Time and place," George interrupted.

"Right. Not the time for a forest management discussion. Anyway, the Appello part can't be in a tree that may get burnt down or in the ground, which would most likely get covered in flames at some point, which would change the entire topography so that it may be washed away or buried too deep to find, or—"

"I got you," George interrupted again. "No ground. No tree. So that only leaves—"

"Caves," they said together.

"These mountains are littered with caves," Alecin said. "If they put it deep enough in a cave, it could stay there for hundreds of years, and fire would never touch it. Likely no human would ever touch it either."

"Well then," George picked up his backpack, "let's head up to the mountains."

"Wait a minute," Alecin grabbed George's arm. "I just realized something. Bears live in caves. We go around exploring caves, we may walk into some bear's home, and he'll probably be pissed."

"I'm not worried."

"Why not?"

" 'Cause I don't have to be faster than a bear, I just have to be faster than you, dear," he said, kissing her cheek.

She slapped him playfully. "I'm serious."

"Before we go in any cave, we'll get our bear spray out. And if that doesn't work," George pulled a shotgun from his bag.

"So, who gets the bear spray, and who gets the shotgun?"

"Arm wrestle for it?" he suggested. Alecin just gave him that look. "Okay, how about rock, paper, scissors?"

"Best two out of three. Go."

Several hours later, Alecin was glad she had lost at Rochambeau. She had grumbled at the time, but the bear spray was much lighter than the shotgun. And she was glad she hadn't had to carry a shotgun around for hours.

"A few more hours," George commented, looking at the sky, "and we'll need to pick one of these caves to set up camp in."

"How much of our search area have we searched?"

George checked the GPS. "About half."

"Do you think we could be in the wrong place?" Alecin wondered. "We haven't found anything."

"We said we would search the whole area, and if we didn't find anything, we'd check this interpretation of the clue off the list and move on. But we knew we may be wrong when we came."

"You're right, you're right. Sorry. I'm just not a patient person."

"No, really?" George asked in mock surprise. "You hide it so well."

"Shut up."

"Just one of the many reasons I love you, babe."

"Nice save. Let's just check that cave up there,"—Alecin pointed—"and then we'll move on to the next mountain."

"What cave?"

"*That* cave." Alecin pointed impatiently.

"I don't see a cave."

"It's right there!" She pointed even more impatiently.

"Babe, I'm telling you, there's no cave there."

They exchanged glances. Alecin took off the Kalecian glasses, and the cave disappeared. She handed the glasses to George. He put them on and looked where she had pointed.

"Oh, *that* cave," he said.

"Those clever Kalecians," Alecin said with admiration as they hiked to the cave, "not only did they hide it in the cave, but they also hid the cave. How do you think they did that?"

"My guess would be a hologram of some sort."

"Like on *Star Trek*?"

"That's my guess. But it's a hologram that the glasses can see through."

Alecin stopped about ten minutes later.

"What's wrong? Why did you stop?" George asked.

"We're at the cave entrance."

"Really? I had expected that the illusion would, I don't know, break down as we got closer. But all I see is mountain."

Alecin handed him the glasses again, and he saw that they were indeed at a cave entrance.

"If we can't see it without glasses," asked Alecin, "do you think bears can't see it either? And maybe not walk, or crawl, I guess, into it either. Maybe it's another one of those things that sense Guardian DNA."

"Or the glasses. Maybe you have to be wearing the glasses to enter the cave?" George wondered. "Like in Boston, where you had to be wearing the glasses to find the clue."

"Hand me the glasses. I'll walk through wearing them," Alecin instructed, "and then I can hand you the glasses."

"Or," George took her hand, "we walk through it together." And he pulled her into the cave with him.

"Wow, that was weird," Alecin observed. "It was like walking through a field of electricity. Not painful but just tingly."

"Absolutely awesome," George said with appreciation, looking back at the cave entrance.

As caves go, it seems pretty unremarkable, Alecin thought as she looked around. It was deep. She couldn't see the end. The top was high enough that she and George could remain upright, at least until they got to the very back of what she could see. *And*, Alecin thought gratefully, *bats don't seem to be able to get through the "hologram" either, so there is none of that pungent and oh-so-disgusting bat guano smell.* The cave was also dry. Whatever water had made the cave was long gone.

"Do you think air can get through the hologram?" Alecin asked.

George didn't answer. He was staring silently at one of the cave walls.

"What? What is it?"

George handed her the glasses. On one wall was written:

ASSEMBLE THE APPELLO

Beneath the wording, there was a natural shelf on which sat a metal bar. The final piece of the Appello.

Alecin looked at George. "This is it? We did it?"

He smiled. "This is it. We did it."

Alecin grabbed George. He picked her up, swung her around, and kissed her. "My love, I think we've got a call to make," he declared.

"Who you gonna call?" Alecin asked. And they both burst out laughing. And then they both just stood, staring at the cave wall.

"This is it," Alecin said quietly. "I can't believe we did it."

"Why do you sound so surprised?"

"I never thought we'd be able to do it," Alecin continued in the same hushed tone.

"You didn't?"

"No. I mean, yes. I thought we would. But a part of me, I guess a part of me still believes this is all a dream—a fantasy. But here it is." Alecin looked at George and smiled. "We did it. We actually did it!"

"Babe?" George asked.

"Yeah."

"What do we do now?"

Alecin looked around, as if the answer was somewhere in the cave. "I guess . . . now we just put it together."

"Here?" George asked, looking around.

"Why not? Here seems a good place to do it. It's hidden. No one knows about it. So, it's safe here."

"That's a good point. Okay." George slapped his hands together. "Let's make ourselves an Appello. Just one question. How do we do that?"

"No idea. Dammit, George, I'm a lawyer, not a . . . whatever a person is who would know how to put an alien calling device together."

"Well, Bones, I think I left my 'putting together alien calling devices' manual at home."

"Ya, me too."

"Think there's a YouTube video?"

"Probably, but we'd have to watch a bunch of commercials first."

"We are only dealing with the fate of humanity. Totally not worth watching the commercials."

"Definitely not. So how do people figure out how to do stuff when the answer is not on the internet?"

"Maybe there are some instructions here in this cave, but we missed them because we stopped looking once we saw the message. Let's look around."

Alecin looked around the cave. Why were things always hidden in caves anyway? Or ancient ruins? Or ancient ruins in caves? *Focus, Alecin*, she chided herself. Painstakingly, George and Alecin shined their flashlights over every inch of the cave, taking turns with the glasses, but they didn't find anything. Frustrated, they both sat on rocks and were quiet, lost in their own thoughts.

"What if they *already* told you?" George asked, jumping up suddenly.

"What do you mean? We've looked over this entire cave. There's nothing here."

"Not in the cave. They said everything you would need would be in the clues, right? That's what the initial instructions said. The Chosen One would find all they needed to complete their quest. What if the instructions to put this thing together were in one of the clues, and we just didn't notice?"

Alecin ran through each clue in her mind. "Wait, wasn't there a clue—the one telling us to go to Boston Harbor—that had a part that we didn't understand because it was completely unnecessary?"

"Yes, I remember that!" George pointed at Alecin.

Alecin quickly pulled out her box. She began looking through all the clues. "Here it is. Here's that part we didn't understand. 'E. pluribus unum,' " she read.

"Out of many, one," they both said together.

"It's the motto of the United States," Alecin said. "How does that help us?"

"But what if it's more? What if it means literally, out of many . . . one?"

"Out of many, one," Alecin repeated. "I get it. We have many pieces, and somehow, they need to become one. So, we just have to put the pieces together somehow, and that's enough."

"I think so. Let's try it."

Alecin carefully removed each Appello part they had so painstakingly collected from her box. Thinking the Appello might be some sort of antenna, they laid them out, end to end, like dominoes. Then stood back. Nothing happened.

"Is something supposed to happen?" George asked.

"I think something is supposed to happen," Alecin responded.

They each sat on a rock, staring at the parts. She was sure "out of many, one" had been the instructions. So, why wasn't it working? She almost felt like the parts were mocking her. *Lying there, doing nothing*, she thought, looking at the parts accusingly. *If only Grandpa were here*, she thought. He *would know what to do*. She thought of her grandfather and tried to remember everything he had said about the Kalecians. Maybe the answer lay in there—somewhere.

Then, it was her turn for an epiphany. "Holy crap on a cracker!" she exclaimed. "Three!"

"Three what?"

"Not three what. The number three. It's significant to the Kalecians. Well, really, it's significant to the whole universe technically, I mean—"

"Time and place, my love. Time and place."

"Right. Sorry. So, my grandfather thought the number three was significant to the Kalecians. There were three Kalecians that came to help. They chose three humans. The original three chose another three. Three, three, three."

"I got you, so we need to arrange them in three stacks?"

"I think so."

They arranged the pieces in three stacks. And waited. Nothing happened.

"Dammit, I really thought that would work," Alecin said in frustration.

George stared at the parts. "Hold on. There's more than one way to skin this cat."

"Ew. Gross. Why would you want to skin a cat?"

"I have no idea. It just means there's more than one way to do things. Instead of three stacks, let's do two stacks of three."

They quickly rearranged the pieces. And stared at them.

"Wait," Alecin said, thrilled and terrified, "do you hear that?"

A faint humming was coming from the parts.

"I hear it," George agreed, the same mix of thrill and terror in his voice.

Then, the parts began to change. They seemed to melt and move into one another. "It worked!" George exclaimed. He grabbed Alecin. "It worked! I was so worried."

"So was I. But we did it; we figured it out."

"Hell yeah, we did," said George, grinning.

"Hell yeah, we did." Alecin suddenly pulled away. "Look," she said, pointing. In their excitement, they had all but forgotten about the Appello. The parts had begun to form a shape. Standing with their arms around each other, Alecin and George watched the Appello take form.

"How hilarious would it be," George asked, "if the parts turned into this huge old-fashioned telephone, you know, with the cord and the rotary dial?"

"Time and place, babe. Time and place."

"Right. Big historical moment. Fate of humanity at stake."

The pieces began to meld into a kind of pyramid shape thing with six sides.

"It's turning into a hexagonal pyramid. Six sides," George commented. "There's your three again."

Once it had formed a perfect hexagonal pyramid, the Appello stopped moving. And it began to glow.

"So, is it like, calling them?" George asked.

"I sure hope it doesn't go to voicemail," Alecin deadpanned.

"Time and place, babe. Time and place."

"Right. Big historical moment. Fate of humanity at stake."

After about ten minutes, the Appello stopped glowing. It stopped humming. It stopped doing anything.

"Well, are they going to answer us?" Alecin said after a minute.

"Rocket scientist here. And I can tell you that signals take a really long time to travel through space. I mean, the Kalecians probably figured out how to make them go pretty fast, but it's still going to take some time."

"How much time?"

"I have no idea."

"I guess we just wait."

"Babe," George said excitedly, "do you realize what we've just done? We're the first people, ever, to have sent a message across space, outside our galaxy, intended to be received by another sentient being. That is so amazing! I wish I could tell everyone at SpaceX about this. They would be so stoked. Especially Elon."

"I thought you said you didn't know him."

"No. I said he wasn't my immediate boss. I didn't say I didn't know him." George paused. "Wow! I am just so thrilled right now. This is so surreal."

"But what are we supposed to *do* now?"

"Like you said, we wait."

"How long do we wait?"

"Until they answer, I guess. We're certainly not going to just walk away and leave the Appello here. Not after everything we went through to put it together."

"Indeed, we're not. Okay." Alecin pulled a blanket out of her backpack. She spread the blanket on the ground so they could sit on it with their backs against the cave wall. "Let's sit and wait." They sat and waited.

An hour passed.

"Still keep waiting?" asked Alecin.

"Yep."

"Okay."

Another hour passed.

Alecin pulled a couple of protein bars out of her backpack. "Chocolate or strawberry?"

"Chocolate. You realize this is just a big Kit Kat bar, right?" George asked after taking a bite.

"Cause of the crispy wafers?"

"Yeah."

"Those are what make it tasty. But they have protein, too. It says so right on the label."

George looked at the label. "Well, what do you know? There it is. Fifteen grams of protein."

Another hour passed.

"You know," George said, "the sun's going to go down soon. It will get cold."

"Why don't you go grab some wood, and we'll make a fire. I'll watch the Appello."

When George got back from gathering wood, he built a small fire. Alecin and George cuddled in front of it.

Four hours had now passed since the Appello had done anything.

"Have you ever noticed," George said, "that this whole being a Guardian thing is a lot of boring, boring, boring, holy shit!?"

"I know. I wish they would have boosted our genes for patience. I hate waiting."

"Me too."

Another hour passed.

"We should probably start setting camp up," George began. "I don't think we will . . . ." He trailed off and looked at the Appello. "Do you hear that?"

They both jumped up.

"It's humming again!" Alecin exclaimed.

They both watched the Appello. It didn't glow this time. It just kept humming. Then, it stopped humming. And a small slot seemed to open up, and what appeared to be a very thin piece of metal popped out. Alecin didn't move.

"I think you're supposed to get that," George said, gently pushing Alecin toward the Appello.

"Yeah, okay." Alecin started toward the Appello, then stopped. "I'm nervous. What if we did something wrong?"

"We didn't," George assured her. "Now take the flat metal thingy."

"Metal thingy? Is that the rocket scientist's name for it?"

"Best I got."

"Okay." Alecin took a deep breath. She reached out and grabbed the 'metal thingy,' as George had so scientifically called it. She half expected it to stick to the Appello. But it slid right out. As soon as she removed it, the Appello made a deafening piercing hum, like a firework going off. She jumped back.

"What the hell?!" George yelled.

"What is it doing?!" Alecin yelled.

Then, the Appello that they had worked so hard and sacrificed so much to be sure would happen, simply disappeared.

"I guess it was done," George stated. And thought it was the most understated thing he had ever said in his life.

Alecin looked at the piece of metal in her hand. "Babe," she said quietly, staring at it, "there's writing on it."

"What does it say?"

She handed it to him. He read it. Then looked at her. They exchanged looks of fear and awe.

It had two words written on it:

MESSAGE   RECEIVED

www.ingramcontent.com/pod-product-compliance
Lightning Source LLC
Chambersburg PA
CBHW051143030726
47504CB00004B/1016